ACKNOWLEDGMENTS

The editors wish to thank the following individuals for their contributions to this book:

Jasmine Sailing, editor-publisher of Cyber-Psychos AOD

Brian Hodge, contributing author

Don Webb, contributing author

Bruce Boston, poet and contributing author

Peter H. Gilmore, High Priest of the Church of Satan and contributing author

Peggy Nadramia, High Priestess of the Church of Satan and contributing author

David L. Tamarin, contributing author

David G. Barnett, editor-publisher of Necro Publications

Thomas Ligotti, author and living legend

Prophet of the Perverse himself: t. Winter-Damon

FORBIDDEN GOSPELS:

THE DEVIL'S CUT

t. Winter-Damon

Randy Chandler

Red Room Press

WWW.REDROOMPRESS.COM

First Red Room Press Trade Paperback Edition, March 2016

ISBN 13: 978-1-936964-60-4

Visit Red Room Press on the web at: redroompress.com
facebook.com/redroompress
twitter.com/redroombooks

RED ROOM PRESS

CONTENTS

INTRODUCTION

by Randy Chandler

Duet for the Devil was published October 1, 2000, by Necro Publications.

Before that, bits and pieces of the unruly opus were published in various small-press magazines and indie journals, often in somewhat different forms.

By the time the novel made it between hard covers, its length had been considerably shortened. Some significant characters were lost altogether as their scenes got the ax.

Subsequently, much of the "lost" segments from *Duet for the Devil* were published by Jasmine Sailing as *The Forbidden Gospels of Man-Cruel Volumes I & II*. These modest little chapbooks also contained several scenes as they appeared before they were edited or reworked for the novel.

Forbidden Gospels: The Devil's Cut presents Volumes I & II as they originally appeared in chapbook form, including the introductions by Brian Hodge and Don Webb. Also included is an all new addition to the Gospels: "The Devil's Cut-Up."

Then comes the **Prophet of the Perverse** section—a tribute, of sorts, to the late t. Winter-Damon. It also includes Damon's long and rambling preface to *Duet for the Devil*, which until now has only appeared in the Advanced Uncorrected Proof and on the Necro Publications website.

Award-winning poet Bruce Boston's moving memorial poem "Forever Tracking" is included here, as are several poems Bruce and Damon wrote together, plus select poems from Damon's *The Hour of Hallucinations*.

Here too you will find remembrances of Damon by some of those whose lives were touched by him and by his works, plus miscellaneous bonus content.

Like the narrator of his poem "from prometheus a treasure stolen" Damon held stars and sand grains in his palm, "galaxies of swirling radiance" that "even gods must fear." And he liked nothing better than to show you those galaxies in his grains of sand—his gritty linguistic fireworks.

RC

THE

FORBIDDEN
GOSPELS OF
MAN-CRUEL

VOLUME I

DEDICATION

To The Zodiac Killer

"By FiRE, By GUN, By KNiFE, By
ROPE"

```
          P
          A
          R
    S L A V E S
          D
          i
          C
          E
```

Hail the High Lord Executioner!

"I'm Afraid Your Condition Is Terminal," And Other Punchlines

by Brian Hodge

If I were motivated to be exactingly precise, I'd go back and look for it, but Lord Bran knows which box it's in, and I'm not anal retentive enough to mount the required excavation. We've just moved, you see, a process that would've gone far more quickly if we illiterates, because one pound of every two belong to a book. Most of which are staying right where they are because we will be moving again in a few months, hopefully to someplace that has lots and *lots* of shelves.

One particular book comes to mind now, and one particular blurb on its back cover: the second edition of *Apocalypse Culture,* from the ever-dependable Feral House. Lovely book, really, full of corrosive rainbows and fluffy dead bunnies. A pity it's not coffee table size, although it does fit nicely atop a toilet tank lid where captive and unsuspecting company can't help but pick it up and see what the rest of us deviant malcontents take for granted about the systolic and diastolic of the subhuman condition.

"These are the terminal documents of our time," says that back-cover blurb. Or close enough. Can't swear to it, but I think it might've been attributed to William Burroughs—oddly synchronicitious, because as I write this it's only been within the past five minutes or so that he's cooled off to ground temperature.

So the subject is terminal documents, because *Apocalypse Culture* has a bit of company. Here are some more, held in your contaminated hands.

I may be doing msrs. Chandler and Winter-Damon a disservice, but I'm about to blow their cover right out of the pond. They'd have you believe they wrote *The Forbidden Gospels of Man-Cruel*. Every word. And technically they did, I suppose, since this English version is indeed their own.

They have their reasons, I'm sure, for having kept mum about the dire authenticity of the documents, but to that I say bugger all. Claiming authorship of these texts may be their idea of a tittering joke, but it's not vey dramatic.

Gospels, testaments, apocrypha, puseudepigrapha . . . these things aren't merely written. They must be uncovered. Rediscovered. Brushed clear of dust and batshit, and reopened with tremulous fingers. Yes. Wastelands, mystery, and drama, by god!

The Nag Hammadi library of Gnostic scriptures? Found in December 1945 by a couple of brothers in a hideous blood feud who parked their camels and unearthed a jar while digging around the base of a fallen boulder.

The Dead Seas Scrolls? Found in February 1947 when a Bedouin shepherd chucked a stone into a cave trying to flush out renegade sheep, whereupon he heard the brittle shattering of a clay pot.

A nice even fifty years later and here we are, with another batch of texts that put the boot to a few cherished complacencies. I wish I could say that *The Forbidden Gospels of Man-Cruel* have the same multimillennial pedigree as the others, but I wouldn't want to lie to you. You deserve better than that.

The originals date to Paris, circa 1866, and are said to have come from the pen of one Lucien Dumay, a contemporary of Charles Baudelaire—who financially assisted the young Dumay until Baudelaire's death in 1867. Virtually unknown in their day (like their author) *The Forbidden Gospels* aren't so much decadent prose-poetry as visions of the future, allegedly revealed to Dumay in his room at the Hotel Lauzun on the Ile-Saint-Louis during a series of indulgences in hashish and absinthe.

It is generally accepted that Dumay participated in necromantic attempts to involve the debouched spirit of his personally revered countryman Donatien Francois Alphonse de Sade. Whether or not he was ever successful is a matter of individual belief. Of much greater controversy is the theory that Dumay and Isidore Ducasse were one and the same . . . Ducasse being better known by his pen name of Comte de Lautréamont, author of Les Chants de Maldoror, dead at twenty-four, then later posthumously canonized by the Surrealists as their proud, if unknowing, papa.

What you have in hand are Chandler's and Winter-Damon's translations of the French originals, but they're less of a literal nature than impressionistic—such as their opting to update language and dialect, as well as the occasionally clunky metaphors that Dumay was forced to rely on when dealing with such then-alien concepts as automobiles. That's quite all right—gospels must inevitably become the malleable tools of those who linguistically tote them into the next era.

But, irreverent pranksters that they are, Chandler and Winter-Damon also interjected the texts with current cultural references, inarguably personal observations, and private jokes, such as metastasizing your humble guest-writer into yuppie scum who has some not-very-nice things done to him. Bastards.

Just how Chandler and Winter-Damon came by Dumay's original text is still something of a mystery. But after a near-mythic evening of tequila shooters and spinach rolls, I was at least able to pry out of them a few terse mentions of a rather unwashed reader of Damon's who, knowing his predilection for most of the nineteenth-century personages involved, showed up in Tucson to hand over the whole reprehensible stack of yellowed old pages in person. They then showed me a newspaper clipping. The same pungent lad, it seems, had been found three weeks later in the New Mexico desert, burnt to a crust after being shot through the back of the head. Mere coincidence? What fun is that?

And from there, to the English language, to you.

Utter bollocks, all of this? Sure. Sure it is. I made it up. Every word. And you just keep telling yourself that, if it helps insulate you from the less comforting aspects of the consensus reality going on around you—probably closer than you'd care to admit. The next stranger who cruises slowly past, staring at you as though he knows just what you look like under that snug skin of yours. The next abrupt disappearance of someone you may or may not know, accomplished with the precision of a shadowy team of commandos.

One quick observation on semantics before I turn you over to the hands of Chandler and Winter-Damon, and then you're on your own.

In its most archaic form the word "gospel" has nothing to do with saviors, nor the texts of religions founded in the name of unsuccessful messiahs. No, the word derives from Old English—*god spel,* literally "good tidings." Good news for modern man, and all that.

And it is.

Because even though the patient and the times may be terminal, I for one look forward to seeing what sprouts from the decay. And perhaps even watering it from time to time. Truth? Lies? Exercise your right to judge.

But know this: While there are varying subtle flavors of dark magick in the pages that follow, predominant among them is Chaos whose only Law can be summarized in the words of Hassan I Sabbah:

"Nothing is true, everything is permitted.

Read, then, and believe.

Brian Hodge
    early August 1997
    east of Limbo

& the Sun Became Black as Sackcloth of Hair; & the Moon Became as Blood

In a cave in the Himalaya Mountains there is an order of Tibetan monks who spend their waking hours meditating for *good,* for *peace,* for triumph over evil in the world.

Their cave is located in western Tibet, near the source of *Seng-ge Kha-'bab* ("out of the lion's mouth"), the Indus River, far above, in the heights of the north slope of Mt. Kailas, sacred to both Buddhists & Hindus.

The nine monks—known as *"Gsum-gsum,"* the "three-three"— have lived in the monastic cave for all of their adult lives. Because they have all taken a vow of silence, the only sound they make with their vocal cords is their prayerful chanting. They eat. They sleep. They meditate. & at any given moment there are no less than three monks in a state of meditation. Their food is carried up to them by inhabitants of the nearest mountain village. The monks live a simple life. They want for nothing. Their collective desire is for world peace.

Jang-bu follows the treacherous mountain trail upward to the monks' cave. He is sixteen years of age & he doesn't mind his thrice-weekly treks across icy rocks & snowy footpaths in the lower altitudes, past meadows filled with the swaying stalks of poppies; higher up the slopes are dotted with the light pink blooms of *tsi-tog* & the white, yellow, & maroon bell-shaped flowers of the *shang-dril.* It is a place of beauty & peace, rich with spiritual enlightenment. He loves the wise monks, & dreams of someday joining their holy order.

On Jang-bu's back is a sixty-pound rucksack filled with their supplies: *r-tsam-pa,* the staple barley flour, yak butter & cheese, poppy seeds & oil, vegetables from the lowlands, brick tea & *chang,* the barley beer, & non-edibles such as candles, incense, & matches. His legs & back are strong from his mountain treks, & his body is acclimated to the frigid air. Only a blizzard could keep him from his journey.

The boy arrives at the entrance of the cave just before the noon hour.

He pauses at the mouth of the cave & sniffs the air as an animal would do.

Something has alerted him that things aren't right.

Jang-bu senses danger.

He enters the dark cave, his heart racing more from fear than from the exertion of his mountain climbing. He has never known the cave to be completely dark. Always there have been candles burning in the meditation cavern.

He fumbles in his rucksack for a candle & matches, then strikes an illuminating flame.

The horror leaps out at him & he screams.

The once-peaceful cave has become an abattoir. The butchered bodies of the monks are lying in a pool of their commingled blood. Their throats have all been slit from ear to ear.

Even in his shock, Jang-bu sees that there are only eight bodies.

Where is the ninth monk?

Shrill laughter echoes inside the cave, Jang-bu spins around & is face to face with the last monk.

The boy knows all the monks by their faces only, not by names (as, of course, they have never spoken to him . . .). He recognizes the monk before him as the youngest of the order, probably in his late forties.

But this one's face is *different*. The bearded face is contorted into a demonic mask. Evil madness shines from the monk's eyes.

In his bloodied hand is a Gurkha knife, its thick, curiously angled, dull edge glittering coldly in the flickering candlelight, its curved twelve-inch blade still dripping crimson from its slender base with notched "blood-letter" tapering to the broad, leaf-shaped, forward-heavy section, to the thorn-sharp tip. The Gurkha is a heavy, machete-like knife, used primarily for hacking. & it has done its job. Thoroughly.

"*Buddha!*" shouts Jang-bu. "What have you done?"

The monk laughs again, making the boy's blood run chill.

He at last breaks his long-held vow: "I gave my brothers peace . . ."

"You murdered them!"

"You are but a foolish boy," says the monk. "You know nothing of the spiritual life. I shall teach you. Watch, foolish child. This is the One True Way to Peace"

The monk puts the blade to his own throat, & suddenly rakes it across the flesh.

He smiles even as his throat opens in a leering grin, spraying forth a shower of bright crimson poppy petals, celebrating his rite of passage into the next cycling of karma . . .

Jang-bu drops his candle & runs screaming from the cave.

The candle's flame sputters out, extinguished in the small sea of blood upon the floor.

... & THOU HAST GIVEN THEM BLOOD to DRINK & They are Drunken with the Blood of Saints & with the Blood of Martyrs ...

(A Passion Play for Resurgent Atavists)

"The whole world's going to Hell . . ."

Yeah, how many times a day a week a month, whatever, do you hear *that* phrase? Usually it's just the preamble for one more rote recitation of the motormouth litany of the world's ills. But how many straight-John citizens really BELIEVE it? The true-believer fundamentalists no doubt do. It's their *raison d'etre*, justifying whatever persecutions their current witch hunt, real or metaphorical, is pushing this week. The televangelists sure give it enough lip service—of course, they're lining their pockets off the gullibility of P.T. Barnum's one-born-every-minute rubes. Crusading politicians. But they've got the same bullshit credibility scam . . .

So, sure it's an overused saying.

But.

Believe us.

There *are* other True Believers.

Count on it . . .

Let's talk-out a couple more hackneyed truisms.

The quasi-zen thing about tossing a pebble into still waters & watching the ripples circling outward . . . ?

& that bit about the ostrich hiding his head in the sand . . . ?

Hang tight. We've got a point we're tryin' to hammer home. Before we get down to the meat of it. Before we open our Trickster's

Little Black Bag o' Magick Tricks, ask you to kick back & pop a cold one, derm a fresh hit of Divine Messenger, brain-boot into the Tarahumara Patterns of the Waking Dream, throw back a handful of screamin' black beauties & yellowjackets, & let that ol' neurosystem sing the hightension-wired chainsaw song electric, let Old Pete dream you *reeeeealll* good, pop the holy spike, hang out with Mary J. & those Rainy Day Women, whiff those poppers, listen to the Omen-voice fire-whispering inside your skull, or maybe fire up a pipe of ice, or perhaps you're into the *painfix* thing?—slap on a pair of nipple clamps, give those labial or scrotum rings a brighthot whitehot tug & twist—*heh, just do it*, whatever your jones is . . . down'n'dirty or designer . . . Before we maybe show you a few new steps in the old bone dance *American Bandstand* & *American Graffiti* & *American Gigolo* never showed you . . .

Okay. Are we straight, yet, or what?

Let's take the one about the pebble & the ripples. Not too obtuse. It's about cause & effect. It's the heart-essence of sympathetic or homeopathic magick—the infinite spiderweb-matrix of charm & taboo. An action performed on the microcosmic scale ripples outward to affect & effect within the context of the macrocosm . . . Deep shit, yeah, but bear with us.

Now about the ostrich. They make some nice Tex-Mex-type boots out of 'em, right? Lizard. Snake. Give it a shake & skin that bird . . . But that's *not* what we're rappin' about. We're talking now about consensus reality. The party line & how Mr. & Mrs. John Q. buy it, & what goes on behind our backs, 'cause if you don't BELIEVE in things maybe they just don't exist. Clap your hands & save Tinkerbell's tight little tush from Oblivion City, right? You remember the scam. The Freudian faerietale gig about Priapic Peter & the Great God Pan? Not the way *you* recall it? Don't sweat you're headed for Alzheimer Land instead of Never Never . . . Or time tripping'n'consciousnessslipping, flashing on Canned Heat doin' "Goin' Up Country" . . . It's called "encoding" & "metaphor" & "sublimation." It cuts both ways, though. People figure if they don't BELIEVE in them nasty thangs, they just don't happen . . .

We'll hit you with a few examples. Cops didn't used to believe in serial killers, so there wasn't no such beast; now the FBI admits there's about 200 running loose, & the glass teat's chuck full of 'em—

total overkill. Court system & the whole Insanity Factory didn't used to believe in physical child abuse as a massive, underlying, concept in god's country, no way, called it "family discipline," kid couldn't take a little discipline & did the runaway, heh, you tacked that "incorrigible" tag on 'em, threw their asses in juvie, gave 'em a poke of the broomhandle, whatever, right?; now everybody *knows* the nature of that twisted beast; everybody's an instant expert. Society didn't used to believe in child sexual abuse & incest & shorteyed Scoutmasters & pervert priests & the kiddie porn network; now it's a daily talkshow topic, lawsuits estimated to hit the Holy Roman Catholic alone for maybe four bil in damages, you know the score. Stranger child abductions didn't happen, not here in the good ol' applepie'n'mom U.S. of A., no way; since the sixties kids've just been running away by the thousands, sure, seven- & eight-year-olds & the whole enchilada, & nobody believed in the snuff underground either. Straight-8 J. Edgar didn't believe in the Mafia & he hated queers & commies; now we know how they had him by the short'n'curlies, while he was worrying about whether his boyfriend or he was gonna be on top this time . . . & the fucker was maybe THE BIGGEST blackmailer in North-Am polit history . . .

Let us tell you this little fable about this gimpy-eyed Montgomery County, Virginia, boy, a convicted serial slayer named Henry Lee. Copped to something like 1,000 kills, though nobody ever believed more than maybe 360 or so of 'em. He was the Texas Rangers' main man. Same song with the FBI, & agents from hundreds of nationwide jurisdictions were whispering sweet nothings in Henry's ear—trying to coax him into laying down the straight skinny on their own unsolveds. They bought his tales of sex slayings & necrophilia. But a funny thing happened. When he & his partner, Ottis, started spilling their story about cannibalistic orgies & a secret society called "The Hand of Death," & hundreds, even *thousands*, of child abductions this outfit masterminded, & how the two of them had been doing a brisk biz in subterranean cash-per-kiddie snatches & custom orders & border runs . . . well, suddenly the door slammed shut—BANG! Shot their credibility all to Hell. Cops didn't used to believe in cannibals any more than they did the Tooth Fairy. Still don't believe in The Hand of Death. Still don't believe in the major weight in angels moving south for the heavy S/M & snuff markets down May-hee-co way . . .

Now, ol' Henry Lee's recanted all, gone born-again, & admits only his involuntary murder of mom. He wasn't scared when they gave him the death sentence convictions. But there *is* something that scares the holy shit out of this stone killer: THE HAND OF DEATH . . .

Reality check:

Guy named Dahmer, up in Detroit, kinda shoved their collective noses in the cannibal shit . . . Arthur Shawcross, too, up in Gennessee River country—did two kids in a sex'n'snuff/cannibal/necrophilia bit, the moke does *15-fucking years* & he's back on the fucking street, offing hooks by the dozen, doin' the nastybit with the I FUCK THE DEAD NUMBER & doin' the sexual mutilation thing, excising boxes & painting 'em up like ol' Ed Gein, usin' 'em like those rubber jobs in the clipout ads in the sex books, dowhackadoo, doin' the cannibal bit—heh, man, it's *SOCIETY THAT'S CERTIFIABLE*— now *he's* locked up they've got *another one*, & it's like oh well they're only hooks, right, it's not like they're *our* kids, think the kill count's up to twenty-odd & climbing . . .

Oh, & they don't have the half of it—no way, Jose!

One last thing we want to mention, before we get down to it—

You remember David Cronenberg's brilliant cult classic, *Videodrome*, don't you? Sleazoid pirate cable T.V. station owner Max Renn (James Woods) is looking to hook his customers with a little rougher programming, something to give their libidos a jump start. He "accidentally" discovers the S/M straight-snuff VIDEODROME signal, falling down a *very dark* rabbithole, explores a mindfucking Wonderland of edged-out pervs & perps, is seduced into boffing & torturing Debbie Harry (rough, man, rough!) playing mondo-bizarro pop psychologist Nicki Brand, witnesses her murder, begins to hallucinate, flagellate, mutate & transcend the limits of past existence, shedding the old flesh, becoming the new flesh, & suiciding so he can complete his transformation . . . "THE BATTLE FOR THE MIND OF NORTH AMERICA WILL BE FOUGHT IN THE VIDEO ARENA," Professor Brian O'Blivion the Media Prophet confesses: "THE TELEVISION SCREEN IS THE RETINA OF THE MIND'S EYE . . ." "THEREFORE THE TELEVISION SCREEN IS PART OF THE PHYSICAL STRUCTURE OF THE BRAIN. THEREFORE WHATEVER APPEARS ON THE

TELEVISION SCREEN EMERGES AS RAW EXPERIENCE FOR THOSE WHO WATCH IT. THEREFORE TELEVISION IS REALITY & REALITY IS LESS THAN TELEVISION." "IT'S A KIND OF BIO-ELECTRICAL HEROIN. YOUR BRAIN HAS ALREADY BECOME AN ELECTRON GUN. YOUR RETINAE HAVE BECOME VIDEO SCREENS. YOUR REALITY IS ALREADY HALF VIDEO HALLUCINATION." Do the image accumulator—Accumicon—& the VIDEODROME transmissions create a brain tumor or a new sensory organ as the Professor suspects? A convoluted conspiracy-theory flick, weaving a demented web of descent into perversion & paranoia . . .

But the group mind, the collective conscious, the consensus reality does not readily embrace conspiracy theories. It took thirty years to shake our ostrich heads out of the sand & look around & see that the one-gunman J.F.K. assassination theory just didn't wash, that Marilyn was murdered to shut her up, & most *still* haven't gotten wise the Bobby Kennedy snuff was a two-shooter deal *despite* the admissions of ex-FBI agents, bullet-hole-riddled walls that outcount a single magazine-load, & angles-of-trajectory that belie the possibility Sirhan Sirhan acted alone, vanishing evidence, a massive coverup by the same LAPD hierarchy that time's proven ultracorrupt & racist . . .

Back to *Videodrome*.

"REMEMBER: IT'S ONLY A MOVIE!", right?

Yeah. It is an extended metaphor.

But Life *does* imitate Art.

Don't believe us? How about if we admit we've got the inside line. Henry Lee's Hand of Death exists. We *know*. We *belong* to it . . .

Now we can get down to it. The wet stuff you've been waiting for . . .

POV: PAN in TIGHT: REZ up: (x 1):

Interior of cloistered conference room (?). Wide & flat. Shaped like a cigar box's interior. Windowless. Damp-stained with unhealthy yellowed splotches; the low ceiling's erratic patchwork of slightly canted & slowly parting acoustical tiles keys the image of an inverted stack of cards or papers, marked by the ancient spillage of strong tea . . .

Centered, dark wooden lectern standing atop low podium.

Illuminated by a recessed spotlight directly above. The glare deepening the shadowed background into a morass of interwoven Rorschach inkblots, suggesting much but divulging *nothing* of the truly tangible, leaving the perceived to the interpretation of the viewer's own unconscious urgings . . .

Flanking a central aisle, rows of stereotypical folding chairs—metallic mauve paint scraped & wear-worn, battered & dented almost imperceptibly through years of jostled, clattering, contact with their neighbors—are aligned, rank-&-file . . .

A well-dressed throng trickles into the room. Men dressed in three-piece suits & freshly buffed & polished shoes. Women in similarly conservative attire: business suits & suit-dresses & dark, flowing, evening gowns.

Attendees at an alumni meeting (?). Real estate sales' presentation (?). Investment counseling session (?). Religious function (?). Poetry reading (?) . . .

They sit. Assuming seemingly familiar places. They chat quietly among themselves. The air seems unnaturally still. Charged with expectation. The crowd swells to room capacity.

Precise in the number of their attendance. No more. No less. As if answering the needs of some intricately complex equation . . .

The moderator steps from the background shadows. Takes his place behind the lectern. He is a tall man, dressed all in black. An *imposing* man. At his appearance, the room hushes itself to total silence. His presence is a looming shadow among shadows.

The tall man gestures a silent greeting to the crowd.

His motions are fluid. Graceful.

POV: CLOSEUP OF MODERATOR'S FACE: (x 5):

His skin is rich, dark, olive-bronzed in the harsh glare of the spotlight's focus. His hair is jet black, glistening like freshly-oiled tarmac or the lacquered finish of an antique coffin, silvered at the temples, backswept from his high forehead, accenting his pronounced widow's peak. His neatly trimmed mustache & beard are studiedly sinister in their effect. Save for the eerie mask of cobalt-blue mirrorshades that he wears, he could be a far darker vision of Vincent Price. But he is decidedly some blend of Latin & Asiatic:

Filipino, to be precise.

& the poetry he will invoke is a Hell-black tapestry of swirling evil . . .

POV: STEADY at CENTERSTAGE: (x l):

The lights begin to slowly dim. Only the bulb above him now spills forth its harsh radiance.

& the yellow-white glare phases gradually cold & deathly blue . . .

The crowd is a gathered silence. Ominous.

One hundred feet above this room, traffic surges through the night streets of Manila, a neon cesspool, steaming with every conceivable form of vice that this lust-petty, insectile, swarm of slithering underbelly humanity can dream . . .

The Soldiers of Golgotha await whatever miracles this night's Passion Play shall reveal.

All is darkness save for that single bulb above the stage.

POV: CLOSE UP OF MODERATOR'S FACE: (x 5):

With his left hand, he strips off the black-framed convexities of his mirrored lenses in slow, graceful, pantomime . . .

POV: CLOSE UP OF MODERATOR'S FACE: (x 25):

. . . exposing the hollowed pits of eye sockets gouged blank apparently *unseeing* . . .

(*but even the most obvious of appearances can prove dangerously misleading*)

The Hellpits of his punctuated stare strip bare the Inner Dream divining the secret World of Correspondences beyond.

(those blank hollows of finger-gouged eye sockets are the self-altered gateway into far *deeper* visions, a ritual act of self-mutilation that transcends the limitations of pale existence anchored in the meat . . .)

POV: CLOSE UP OF MODERATOR'S FACE: (x 25):

The hollow pits of his eye sockets fix the waiting, expectant, crowd with their blank stare that seems to bore into the blackness of their sold souls with the deathly certainty of a .44 Magnum "Dirty Harry Special":

POV: DILATE FIELD: TRACK TO ROOM CENTER: (x 5):

The dark pit of Rorschach inkblot shadows dissolves into a slowly growing flickering of blue . . .

In the extreme background, upright against the rear wall of the subterranean chamber, stand the pitted wooden beams of a cross. The stations of the cross are dark with aged, deep-soaked, stains.

"Bring forth the Lamb!" the moderator orders.

Two hulking figures step forward from the shadows as if willing themselves into existence from the substance of stealth & nightmares. They wear black leather vests; unfastened to expose their thickly corded chests & midriffs, shaved & oiled to slick glistening sheen of rippled flesh. Tattoos of dragons or coiled serpents swirl across their forearms & biceps. Skintight leather pants of the same butter-supple black satin lustre as their vests encase thick, muscular, thighs.

Their faces are both masked with bug-eye lenses of iridescent cobalt blue.

Black motorcycle boots with scuffed brass rings thonged to the ankles' outer curve clump & clatter on the surface of the wooden podium as they drag the struggling body of a young boy centerstage.

Their hands clench the boy's wrists like iron manacles, half-tugging, half-carrying him, obviously against his will . . .

The room echoes with his shrill screams of terror.

He is, no doubt, some vagrant urchin of the streets. Snatched as he ferreted among the city's stinking refuse for something to fill his belly. Or, perhaps, he had sidled up to a stranger, offering to turn a homo trick, to sell his streetwise mouth or ass to buy a place to sleep & maybe the promise of a hot meal . . .

He is *young*. But there are far younger children of the streets willing to play bumboy for even less remuneration. Boys. & girls willing to sell their only assets. Flesh. Homeless waifs. The losers in civil strife, where the lucky, like their parents, are mercifully *dead*.

He is thirteen (?). fourteen (?). & his shrieks of terror climb in a crescendo of torment as the two men hammer rusted spikes of iron into his wrists & ankles . . .

+   +   +

POV: PAN in CLOSE: TIGHTEN FIELD: MAGNIFICATION (x 25):

Young boy's face, contorted into an exaggerated mask of agony. Each strand in the cords of straining musculature is engraved in relief beneath the thin, taut-stretched, surface layer of still childish yet hunger-wasted flesh & exposure-weathered, olive-bronzed, skin. Like one of those portraits-in-copper, whose features are hammered into the blank sheet of metal from *within*.

The lids of his eyes are crinkled tightly shut with the extremes of his suffering as if, by blocking out the light, some inner darkness might help to soothe away what cannot, in reason, possibly be borne . . .

The saltbrine of his anguished tears brings no hint of pity from the intent crowd of onlookers. Only a thrall of silent fascination.

The tiny pores of his face are dilated pits, flooding with the ice-chill sweat of excruciating pain, flooding with the pheromones of bowel-twisting, feral, FEAR.

The caked layer of dust that had grimed his street-urchin/tainted-angel face is etched into a jagged terrain of terror by the acid rivulets of trickling sweat . . .

His mouth shrieks open in a gargoyle-scream that threatens to rip the whitened flesh of his tender young lips, at the narrow juncture where *upper* meets *lower.*

But his raw larynx now betrays the gut-clenching primal scream that seeks escape from some incredibly deep pit far far beneath the bottom of his human soul. The only sound that he is capable of making is a mewling gurgle that can voice neither words nor gestalt of his anguish.

A drying rind of snot half-clogs the opening of his left nostril.

POV: DILATE FIELD: MAGNIFICATION (x 10):

His slender body convulses. again. & again. Wracking shudders of grand mal intensity, *induced* through the dark magicks of his *transformation*—

His *becoming*—a living sculpture of hideous beauty, transcending the limits of mere flesh & bone & . . .

The blood of his stigmata flows black in the deathly wash of ultramarine blue light spilling from the ceiling lamps above him.

"Witness the sacrificial Lamb—" the moderator says.

& the crowd claps in perfect unison. & they cry out in perfect unison a dark invocation: "So *be it* to *all* Men!"

"Now," he whispers, "this *Passion Play* begins in *earnest*—"

From the hidden doorway in shadows a tall, voluptuous, woman with long, black, flowing hair sways out onto the stage—

the spikes of her impossibly high heels click like sharpened prongs of bone or thick thorns of bloody red, stained purple-black as livid bruises in the Death-blue light of deepsea caverns washing the stage

the garment that she wears is skintight leather, a slashed webwork of taunting deceits & exposes of bared flesh & hidden promises of seductive evil—the shaved, bulging, furrow of her vulva, the dark dimple of her navel, the lust-swollen nipples of her jutting breasts, the perfect, jiggling, globes of her buttock cheeks, provoking lurid fantasies of necrophilic longing

the leather, bloodred transmuted to bruise-purple in the Death-blue light of subterranean Hells

She carries a purple velvet robe & wreath of glittering barbed wire.

"I *am* the WHORE E*ter*nal!—" she cries out to the gathered crowd.

"So *be it* to *all* Men!—" they respond.

She bends, slowly, provocatively, & lays the robe of purple at the base of the cross, beneath the twitching, palsied, feet of the crucified boy.

The leatherclad Whore straddles the crumpled robe, squatting obscenely, & looses a gushing, splattering, stream of urine onto the velvet fabric, drenching it with dark, soaking, stains.

"So *be it* to *all* Men!—" the crowd again responds.

"Say OHM, O ye outlaws & outlanders, OHM to that onomatopoetic ontology of orgasmic onus, OMNIVOROUS PUSSY, say OHM to that Olympus of electric orgies, amen. O Man. Omen. ye Sons & Daughters of this Neon Babylon. O ye fornicating filth. ye muthafuckers & babyrapers—" the voice of the moderator is a babbling wail of near-incoherent invections, invocations, & obscenities.

The Whore crushes her own full, tempting, lips to that silently screaming cavern of the crucified boy, kissing him long & passionately, flickering the soft tip of her tongue into his open mouth . . .

"So *be it* to *all* Men!—" the crowd responds.

The Whore withdraws her lips from the boy's mouth. She dips the cupped fingers of her left hand into the naked swell of her groin, wetting her fingers with her own urine, then lifts them slowly; dragging them across the young boy's dry-parched, pain-contorted, lips.

"I anoint *his* lips with *vinegar*—" she taunts.

The Whore impales the wicked, shining, crown of barbed wire into the flesh of the boy's forehead, until the spikes strike solidly on bone . . .

"& the fifth angel sounded, & I saw a star fall from heaven unto earth: & to him was given the key of the bottomless pit." The moderator recites.

"So *be it* to *all* Men!—"

"& he opened the bottomless pit; & there arose a smoke out of the pit, as the smoke of a great furnace & the sun & the air were darkened by reason of the smoke of the pit."

"So *be it* to *all* Men!—"

"& there came out of the smoke locusts upon the earth: & unto them was given power, as the scorpions of the earth have power."

"So *be it* to *all* Men!—"

"& in those days shall men seek death, & shall not find it; shall desire to die, & death shall flee from them."

"So *be it* to *all* Men!—"

"& they had tails like unto scorpions, & there were stings in their tails: & their power *was* to hurt men five months."

"& they had a king over them, *which is* the angel of the bottomless pit, whose name in the Hebrew tongue is Abaddon, but in the Greek tongue hath *his* name Apollyon."

"So *be it* . . ."

"For their power is in their mouth, & in their tails; for their tails were like unto serpents, & had heads, & with them they do hurt."

"So *be it* . . ."

"& the rest of the men which were not killed by these plagues yet repented not of the words of their hands, that they SHOULD WORSHIP DEVILS, & idols of gold, & silver, & brass, & stone, & of wood: which neither can see, nor hear, nor walk:

Neither repented they of their murders, nor their sorceries, nor of their fornication—"

"So *be it* to *all* Men!—" the crowd screams.

+   +   +

POV: DILATE FIELD: TRACK to ROOM CENTER (x 5):

The crowd of precisely twenty-four gives the moderator a standing ovation.

But his litany is far from finished:

"& I looked, & beheld a pale horse: & his name that sat on him was Death, & Hell followed with him. & power was given to them over the fourth part of the earth, to kill with sword, & with hunger, & with death, & with the beasts of the earth."

"So *be it* to *all* Men!—"

"& there appeared another wonder in heaven; & behold a great red dragon having seven heads and ten horns, & seven crowns upon his heads."

"So *be it* to *all* Men!—"

"& there was a war in heaven: Michael & his angels fought against the dragon; & the dragon fought him & his angels."

"So *be it* to *all* Men!—"

"& the great dragon was cast out, that old serpent, called the Devil, & Satan, & Lucifer the Bringer of the Light, & Baal Zebub the Lord of the Flies, Our Lord & Master, who bringeth Truth unto the world: he was cast out into the earth, & his angels were cast out with him."

"Cur*sed* are *those* Days!" screams the crowd.

The moderator unzips his trousers & draws forth a huge, bobbing, penis like a grotesque, blind, one-eyed serpent, & the image is fixed by the tattoo in varied shades of blue, coiling & writhing down his abdomen, & the serpent has a head—

& the Whore bows to him & kneels in supplication.

"& the serpent cast out of his mouth water as a flood after the woman, that he might cause her to be carried away of the flood."

The moderator grasps his penis in his hand & guides a hissing, splattering, stream of hot, brine-salty, urine into the Whore's eagerly opened mouth.

"& the earth helped the woman, & the earth opened her mouth, swallowed up the flood which the dragon cast out of his mouth."

"So *be it* . . ." roars the crowd.

"& I stood upon the sand of the sea, & saw a beast rise up out of the sea, having seven heads & ten horns, & upon his horns ten crowns, & upon his heads the name of blasphemy."

One of the two hulking, leatherclad, men who had crucified the boy struts out into the blue flood of the spotlight.

"So *be it* . . ."

"& they worshipped the dragon which gave power unto the beast: & they worshipped the beast, saying, Who *is* like unto the beast? who is able to make war with him?"

The second of the two leatherclad tormentors struts forward, also.

"So *be it* . . ."

"& I beheld another beast coming up out of the earth; & he had two horns like a lamb, & he spake as a dragon"

A third joins them on centerstage, along with the moderator & the kneeling Whore.

"So *be it* . . ."

"& he excerciseth all the power of the first beast before him; causeth the earth & them which dwell therein to worship the first beast, whose deadly wound was healed."

The three huge, husky, brutes strip naked.

"So *be it* . . ."

"& he had power to give life unto the image of the beast, that the image of the beast should both speak & cause that as many as would not worship the image of the beast should be killed."

The first man lies back upon the podium, his thick, tattooed, serpent of a penis rearing. & the Whore straddles his hips & squats with her legs widespread, splayed to offer her bare pubis for the public joining of their flesh. & she lowers herself, impaling her shaved vulva on his upthrust member.

"So *be it* . . ."

"& he causeth all, both small & great, rich & poor, free & bond, to receive a mark in their right hand, or in their foreheads:

& that no man might buy or sell, save he had that mark, or the name of the beast, or the number of his name."

The second man takes out a razorsharp stiletto, & slits the taut-stretched leather where it spans the sensuous, wriggling, globes of her buttocks. He rips the thin, supple, leather of her outfit with his powerful, pawl-like, hands. & he mounts her from the rear, in the fashion of those of Sodom.

"So *be it* to *all* Men!—" the crowd echoes.

"Here is the wisdom. Let him that hath understanding count the number of the beast: for it is the number of a man; & his number *is* Six hundred threescore *and* six."

& the third man climbs upon the back of the Sodomite, & mounts him as a pederastic priest might rape some pretty young altarboy.

"So *be it* . . ."

"& I beheld, & lo, in the midst of the throne & of the four beasts, & in the midst of the elders stood a Lamb as it had been slain—"

"Notwithstanding I have a few things against thee, because thou sufferest that woman Jezebel, which calleth herself a prophetess, to teach & to seduce my servants to commit fornication & to eat things sacrificed unto idols."

"So *be it* to *all* Men!—"

The moderator takes the stiletto from the outstretched hand of the first Sodomite. He holds its gleaming blade up to catch the blue light in cold, deathly, sparks on razor-honed metal.

Then he plunges it into the young boy's side, as he spasms, nailed upon the pitted wooden cross.

He twists the blade, thrusting it *upwards*, to puncture the throbbing, spurting, heart . . .

The savaged Lamb gives up his ghost, the deathrattle gurgling in bloody foam from between his slackening lips.

The blue light seems to strobe & flicker . . .

The moderator slits the boy from groin to breastbone. He tears out the still-beating heart with his bare hands, then slices off a bit & swallows it . . .

"& when they shall have finished their testimony, the beast that ascendeth out of the bottomless pit shall make war against them *that stand against the Lord of the Flies*, & shall overcome them, & kill them."

The moderator slices another piece of heartflesh, & hands it to the first of the crowd to file up to him to receive the benediction of the beast—the wine & wafer of the slaughtered Lamb.

"So *be it* to *all* Men!" whispers the crowd.

"& their dead bodies *shall lie* in the street of the great city, which spiritually is called Sodom & Egypt, where also our Lord was crucified . . . & in Manila & Hong Kong & Port-au-Prince & London & Amsterdam & Chicago & San Francisco . . .

"So *be it* to *all* Men!" the crowd roars.

"All shall kneel before *The Soldiers of Golgotha*!"

+   +   +

POV: ZOOM in on CENTERSTAGE: AMP-up OLFACTORY & TACTILE LINK TRANSMISSIONS (x 50): MAGNIFICATION

BOOST in RAPID JUMPCUT

(x 5— x 100— x 5):

(x 5):

Shadows boil & part for an eternal instant.

Three brute-clones drag three teenage girls on-stage. Nude. Oriental. Struggling. & screaming. Brothel inmates (?) street whores (?) or kidnap victims (?) . . . their past is now but dream their present nightmare their future nonexistent—

(x 10):

The Whore in Scarlet & Purple enters. Taunting deceits & exposes of slashed leather webwork bare jutting breasts & stiffened nipples, jiggling globes of too-perfect bottom cheeks, dimpled navel, & the razor-bald furrow of tapering mons veneris . . .

(x 15):

The supple rose branch descends. Thorn-barbs rake naked flesh. More screams. High & shrill. Pinpricks & bloody zigzags speak the unspeakable upon the vellum of their pain . . .

(x 25):

Each curved leaf of living flesh quivering in rise-&-fall of breath in captive wriggling beneath the scourge . . . each a tome a canvass of suffering transcendent in its passages of beauty . . .

(x 50):

Droplets of blood & tears & perspiration mingle black beneath the blue-lit bulb . . .

(x 75):

Pores dilate. Huge flies of emerald & sapphire crawl lazily across each girl's quaking curve of bared belly, swarming down inside the sweet-damp sweat-damp crater-rims of navels, black wire legs & mandibles forever twitching as they explore the sparse foliage of pubic forests, the ridgeline of Great Divide between each pair of mammoth thighs, then throng within the parted gates of Venus' Temples, disappearing deep into each Womb of Darkness, feeding on the mingled musk & nectar, feeding on the douche of milk-&-honey flooded there before the Passion Play began . . .

(x 100):

Faceted eyes reflect the scene a thousand-times-a-thousandfold . . . reflect the tortured innocents & the Moderator & the Whore in Scarlet & the five brutes & the audience beyond . . .

(x 5):

Three wooden stakes loom like colossal upthrust phalluses upon the blue-lit podium.

Three brutes lift three struggling captives. Raise them above their dragon-coiling skulls. & ram them groundward. Monstrous shafts impaling ravaged anuses . . .

The pole-sodomized girls shriek until it seems their lungs must burst, as their soft, round, heels beat out the Devil's Tattoo of their death throes on the unrelenting oaken shafts or in midair.

& each of their three brute-captors unzips his fly, draws out his own threatening length, grips one victim by her slender hips or rounded globes of pole-split bottom, then thrusts his penis deep into the dying fires in tidal rhythm—joining the flies that crawl within her Holy of Unholies her defiled vestibule & sacristy . . .

The mingled incense-scents of roses & musk & sweat & blood voided human wastes break across the senses with tsunami-wave intensity.

+　+　+

POV: STEADY at CENTERSTAGE: DILATE OPTICAL FIELD: (x 5):

The twin brutes who earlier had flanked the Moderator return from the boiling background shadows dragging two black ewes by silver choke-chains.

"For they have shed the blood of saints & prophets, & *Thou* hast given *Them* blood to drink; for *They* are worthy—" The Moderator says.

"So *be it* to *all* Men!—" the Soldiers of Golgotha cry out in response.

The brutes mount the beasts as would two rams.

"& I saw three spirits—

"(*They that burned with the Fever of Azoth the Leprosy of Perfect Transformation*)

"—like frogs *come* out of the mouth of the Dragon, & out of the mouth of the Beast, & out of the mouth of the *Eyeless* Prophet *Who Speaks the Sacred Truths*—"

"So *be it* to *all* Men!—"

& the brutes join their flesh with the ewes' & draw tight the chains about their necks, causing them to beat their hooves upon the wooden planking of the stage & to struggle & to thrash their bodies in mindless terror—& the sound of their drumming hooves *is THE DEVIL'S* TATTOO . . .

& the Moderator opens wide his mouth & spits out a huge leopard frog & the Moderator is silent but the frog swells its throat & croaks in a deep, rumbling, voice:

"For *They* are the spirits of devils, working miracles, *which* go forth unto the kings of the earth & of the whole world, to gather *Them* to the battle of that great day of *Final Judgment*—"

"So *be it* to *all* Men!—"

& the frog puffs out its throat again & speaks: "& I shall make testament to You of *The* Woeman *Dressed in Purple & Scarlet Which Sat Upon the Beast*—"

"So *be it* to *all* Men!—"

& The Whore strides forth from the boiling shadows to the clicking of spike-thorned heels, & in her right hand she holds the silver chalice & in the other a leash of human skin dyed brilliant cobalt blue, & she leads a great black billy goat.

"& there came one out of the seven angels which had the seven vials, & talked with Me, saying unto Me, Come hither; I will shew unto *Thee* the *Judgment* of the *Great Whore* that sitteth upon many waters—"

The Whore squats down upon the stage & voids Her bladder in a gushing torrent.

"So *be it* to *all* Men!—"

& the Moderator reaches down, then holds aloft in His cupped palms the Exalted Frog who testifies: "With whom the kings of the earth have committed fornication, & the inhabitants of the earth have been made drunk with the wine of her fornication—"

"So *be it* to *all* Men!—"

"So He, *Lord of the Flies,* carried *Me* away in the spirit into the wilderness: & I saw a Woeman sit upon a *Great Black Beast with beard & curving horns, & I knew Him to be the manifestation of Our Most Holy Lord Baphomet*—"

"So *be it* to *all* Men!—"

The Whore kneels upon the stage & Her white flesh glows blue in the ambient light, & Her breasts & Her buttocks are as if carved jewels of sapphire exposed beneath the slashes of Her purple &

scarlet leather, & She whispers to the *Great Black Billy Goat*—the male manifestation of that Beast Lovecraft visioned in his dreams & termed "SHUB NIGGURATH, *The Black Goat with a Thousand Young . . .*"

"& the Woeman was arrayed in purple & scarlet color, & decked with *silver* & precious stones & pearls, having a *silver* cup in Her hand full of abominations & filthiness of her fornication:—"

"So *be it* to *all* Men!—"

The Whore sets the silver chalice before Her, near the stage's edge. One of Golgotha's Soldiers steps forward from the seated crowd. Grasps the chalice. Kneels with his right knee cocked. Touches the glistening curves of metal to his forehead—the Sigil of Baphomet burns blue on the flesh it has caressed.

& the frog bellows: "BLESSED BE!"

"So *be it* to *all* Men!—!"

The Soldier tips the vessel to his lips. Then passes it to the next supplicant, who repeats the ritual & furthers it along . . .

"& upon Her forehead *was* a name written, MYSTERY, BaB-y-LON THE GREAT, THE MOTHER OF HARLOTS & ABOMINATIONS OF THE EARTH—"

"So *be it*—"

& The Whore spreads Herself to the Beast & thrusts Her hips back lewdly in mock coital thrusts, & again She whispers to Him in some sacred, secret, tongue . . .

& the Exalted Frog continues: "& I saw the Woeman drunken with the blood of the saints, & with the blood of the martyrs of *The Epileptic One*; & when I saw Her, I wondered with great admiration."

"So *be it* to *all* Men!—"

& the Great Black Beast mounts The Whore & joins His flesh with Hers.

"The Beast that Thou saweth was, & is not; & shall ascend out of The Bottomless Pit, & go into Perdition: & They that dwell on the earth shall wonder, whose names were not written in the book of life from the foundation of the world, when They behold the Beast that was, & is not, & yet is—"

"So *be it* to *all* Men!—"

& the room burns blue & flickers, & the two black ewes are nuns, their habits drawn up about their hips to expose their blue-white rumps obscenely to ministrations of the bald-shaved-&-tattooed brutes, & The Black Goat sprouts seven heads & He is no longer *black* but *scarlet* . . .

"& I saw a Woeman sit upon a scarlet coloured Beast, full of names of blasphemy, having seven heads & ten horns—"

"So *be it*—"

"& here *is* the mind which hath wisdom. The seven heads are seven mountains, on which the Woeman sitteth—"

"So *be it*—"

"& there were seven kings: five are fallen, & one is, *&* the other *has cum*; & when He *cummeth*, He must continue a short space—"

"So *be it*—"

"& the Beast that was, & is, & is not, even He is the eighth, & is of the seven, & goeth into Perdition—"

"So *be it*—"

"& the ten horns which Thou sawest are ten kings, which have no kingdom as yet; but receive power as kings one hour with the Beast—"

"So *be it*—"

"These have one mind, & shall give their power & strength unto the Beast—"

"So *be it*—"

"& so, You shall learn that all this world's philosophies that do not honor *Him* are but falsehoods, He *was*, & *is not*, & *is* . . . for He *is* Splendor & He *is* Wonder & He *is* Illusion—"

& the frog cupped in the Moderator's palms is once more but a frog, & the ewes that the brutes use are no longer nuns but only sheep, & the *Beast that Sitteth upon The Whore* is once more nothing save a great black billy goat in rut . . .

DISSOLVE to:

A field of blue writhing through a spectrum of unnatural variety: every conceivable hue that the human mind has identified & catalogued & labeled with a name, of shades & tones & resonations that have no name in any spoken language . . .

A FLICKERING BLUE EXTREME . . .

FADE TO BLACK

Yeah. The world *is* going to Hell . . .

We're here to see that it does.

We're True Believers.

Part of the Conspiracy of the Great Night.

Each does what they have to in the furthering of the Cause. Some are just streetlevel mercs & assassins, like us—the Hand of Death. Some are the elite strikeforce, the Media People, the prophets & politicos—the Soldiers of Golgotha.

"Golgotha": cool word. We like the way it rolls off the tongue.

You know about Golgotha, right? Calvary, the place where the Epileptic One was crucified. Its meaning had broadened over the centuries to include any burial place, any place of agony of sacrifice.

But what it *means* is derived from the Hebrew word *gulgoleth*— "A SKULL. THE PLACE OF A SKULL."

Remember what we were saying about that old ostrich with his head shoved in the sand. You get the picture, right?

Remember what we were saying about the pebble thrown into the pool spreading its circling ripples? Oh, yes, *we've* been making a big splash, a silent splash, 'cause nobody's been listening . . .

Ripples of sympathetic magick.

In a way, it answers that tired philosophical paradox about "what if a tree falls in the forest, but there's no-one there to hear it fall . . . ?'

You see their effects, but you're lost as to their cause.

Others have tried before us.

Hitler & his SS & his Werewolves tried.

But his assault was clumsy. Too involved in the material plane for his magicks to succeed.

Ours *will* succeed. Because it relies not upon brute force, but merely harnesses it, wields it, bends it to the Thelemaic Doctrine: DO WHAT THOU WILL . . .

THE WHOLE OF THE LAW. The Law of the Great Night . . .

The New Age *has* come. 1966 marked its advent. The Age of Satan—

The Kennedy assassinations? The death of Monroe? Of Mansfield? Of Martin Luther King? Of John Lennon?

Ripples.

Serial killers: Manson? Zodiac? John Wayne Gacy? The Unabomber? Henry Lee Lucas & Ottis Toole? Berkie, the .44 Killer, the Son of (p)Sa(l)m? Richie Ramirez, the Night Stalker? (You didn't know *he* was an experiment in *programmed* slaughter, did you . . . ?) Jeffrey Dahmer? Artie Shawcross? All the ones you *haven't* caught yet?

Ripples.

Each is a *nexus of power*, focusing & amplifying the ripples into waves . . .

The Khmer Rouge? Lat-Am Death Squads? The Middle-eastern Conflict? The Jonestown Massacre? The dissolution of the balancing power of the U.S.S.R.? The slaughter in Serbia & Bosnia? The reuniting of Germany? The Gulf War? The rising swell of the Fourth Reich?

Storm waves.

The World Trade Tower Bombing? David Koresh & the Branch Davidian bloodbath? The Columbine High School Massacre? & all the shit that lies ahead.

Tsunamis.

The pebble has been cast.

& the world is going to Hell.

Remember how we were talking about Cronenberg's concept of VIDEODROME, & the image accumulator, & the brain tumor?

Trust us, Life *does* imitate Art.

The Great Night found the way to transform the old flesh into the new flesh . . . & the new flesh *is* the *Black Snake* shedding its skin awakening . . . & the new flesh *is* the *Way of the Werewolf* . . .

Take it from two True Believers.

The Soldiers of Golgotha hold the power.

Take it from two True Believers.

Thou hast given Them blood to drink.

& THE WORLD *IS* RUSHING HEADLONG INTO ITS DARK TRANSFORMATION.

THE NEW REVELATIONS

On whatever side one turns, destruction will be given free play everywhere . . .

A single Man has prepared them because men have deserved them.

A single man will direct them. And this man is a Tortured Man . . .

THE TORTURED MAN WAS THOUGHT A MADMAN BY THE WHOLE WORLD

HE APPEARED AS A MADMAN BEFORE THE WHOLE WORLD.

AND THE IMAGE OF THE WORLD'S MADNESS IS INCARNATE IN A TORTURED MAN.

—Antonin Artaud, Prophet of *le theatre de la cruaute*

Long, slender, fingers. Artist's fingers. They poise, outstretched upon the butcher-block tabletop of blonde oak. Feminine fingers, pale and soft and tapered. Long, lacquered, nails, manicured with such elegant precision. The flesh beneath their glazed, translucent, carapaces pink as the conch's inner curves. White crescents grace each tip, echoing the moonlight sifting through the slit of gauzy, peach-hued, drapes that billow in the fragrant breath of late-April breeze.

Among these protracted, pensive, shadows there is a sudden shifting and a low, moaning, sigh of transcendent ecstasy.

The lustrous curves of burnished steel glisten in a blur of downward motion, a rustling of air stirred in its wake, and the claw hammer's head connects with fragile flesh.

The brittle, shivering, *snap* of shattered porcelain. A shrill scream stifled in mid-note. The moaning sigh, sustained, fades into silent *nothingness . . .*

In the narrow window, high above the garden, The Gentle Man stares down upon the broken remnants of the blue-eyed doll.

Beneath the moon (a lone coin for the eyes of the dead, a single piece of Judas' silver) the highway stretches onward to its vanishing point, beyond oblivion. The highway is a river, sometimes Acheron, sometimes Cocytus, sometimes Styx . . .

Claymore dons the leather mask. It is pungent with the musky reek of sweat, the fevered sensuality of tanned hide soft as moist velvet clinging like a second skin, and, *yes*, the sweet perfume of pain whispering around his skull.

The blur of butterflies' wings, the equation of her arched and angled legs so precisely tensed in motion seemingly perpetual. Spinning, spinning, the frothy pastel of her stiffly splayed skirt (*no, no*, not simply a *skirt*—but her *tutu* of *taffeta*, in hues of icy tangerine and soft, subdued, persimmon!), a twirling parasol the dream juggler—the porcelain-faced mime—weaves above the blond boards of oak, polished to the sheen of glass, endlessly reflecting . . . geometries of flexing flesh above the core of bone, like sand dunes shifting, conjured into new configurations in the hot breath of the moaning scirocco—betrayed beneath her leotards of frosty lemon—*Gluteus medius* and *maximus* . . . *Sartorius* and *Gracilis* . . . *Quadriceps* and *Tibialis* . . . *Gastrocnemius* . . . the *Soleus*, and the *Achilles* . . .

Moonbeams trickle through the skylights; stirring shadows like the wake of sombre rhapsodies across bright waters, each ripple capturing the plaintive voice of violins and oboes . . .

A sigh like wind through winter wheat . . .

The cold, chrome, curve the scalpel describes is the hieroglyph of hamstrung pain, too extreme to wake numbed vocal cords as this frail blossom wilts and crumples.

Sinuous gloves of coffin-black leather encase fingers so tender in their lingering caresses.

He alone can see the blue fire rising from within the zippered sheathes of kidskin, fanning out to web his fingertips in flame. Molten slag is transformed and tempered into the hands of the Clockwork Iron Automaton, called forth from the Catacombs of Animus, this Seeker After Stranger Signs, keyed forth by the taste of Omen saturating every cell within his skull . . . His left knee pins this thing of fragile froth upon her belly, these iron hands bend the pelvic bow now beyond the tolerance of stress, there is a hollow, reverberating, *snap* and he intones his desire as the wishbone splits in twain . . .

And he breathes, he breathes the meanings of meaningless, and he inhales these bright sharp shards of agony . . .

Whether the skin of this peach he splits is satin or taffeta is less than no concern to him. He cares only for the bared flesh of her swan-slender neck, her flawless arc of back, her exposed derriere, its taut pillows of temptation . . . The glittering thorn of the sailmaker's needle darts and darts and darts again, *a stitch in time saves nine . . . saves nein*, his laughter echoes through the deepest hollows of the Clockwork Iron Automaton . . .

He laces the ballerina's back with dark, thick, pitchy cords (the kind from which the nets of fishermen are woven . . .) and, once this obscene lacework is complete, he yanks the stitches taut and leaves this cocoon to contemplate its torment in silence . . .

(*Oh, yes, trust that her lips, too, are sealed!*)

In the narrow window, high above the garden, The Gentle Man stares down into the ragged black spiderhole in the porcelain skull of the broken blue-eyed doll.

Beneath the half-drained cup of a thirsting moon, the highway stretches onward, beyond the sagebrush shadows of the wasteland, beyond oblivion. The highway is a river, sometimes Sorrow, sometimes Lamentation, sometimes Utter Darkness . . .

Claymore selects his instruments of subjugation, lays them out, just so, upon the silver tray. The nipple clamps, teeth hungering for puckered buds of flesh. The dozen chrome dildos in graduated lengths and girths. Spiked cockrings carved from ivory and human bone. Manacles of burnished steel. And, O, yes! *the whips! the black leather thongs and bridles!*

The white border of her black cowl is a ribbon of bone as she kneels beyond the empty rows of stiff-backed pews, begging absolution from the chiseled thing of wood and fading paint that looms above the altar.

There is an outrush of tightened, wheezing, breath, like the wind among the moonlit gravestones.

Her head cocks, her stance suddenly grown tense, but she continues, even so, with her Hail Marys . . .

He alone witnesses the tiny wisps of blue flame flickering around his tight-balled fists clenching the stout staff of oak, flickering in tendrils about its shaft—and he thinks of ignis fatuus dancing about a rearing masthead.

The iron-shod head thrusts. Missing her head by perhaps the breadth of a finger only. The whisper of pole-stirred air and the sudden outrush of air between his gritted teeth mingle into a single hiss of warning.

Ahhhhh, he intones, *how the shadows dance in the candles' wavering* . . .

The hooked spike poises in midair for just a moment, then arcs back, snaring the hem of her habit's hood, yanking the black cloth back to expose the blue-veined curves of her bald-shaved skull.

The black leather of his glove lingers for an instant, caressing the smooth pink globe, this stiff and nippleless third breast, before it clasps itself across her mouth, stifling her startled cry.

His right hand wields the pew, now. And within the fluted hollows of the Clockwork Iron Automaton silent laughter echoes like the roar of thunder. No accident his choice of weapon. No. The Word has become His Word. His Wyrd. And he breathes the meanings of meaningless . . . *ashes to ashes and dust to dust . . . and the fisherman's staff shall gather the shorn sheep from its place of supplication* . . . and the staff thrusts once more, and this time, *Ohhhhh Merciful Jesus! This time* . . . the wicked curve-hook strikes as he has longed to strike, the rusted spike impaling itself in her right eye, rupturing the fluid-filled orb, and ripping away the veiling membrane from her ocular socket. Her body spasms in grand mal intensity at the immensity of her violation. There is the harsh brassy rasp of a zipper as he unsheathes his right hand, baring his palm to her one unblinded eye—then cupping the gouting crimson flood, raising it to anoint his lips and baptize his tongue with the wine of the sacred innocent. He presses his bloody palm to her bared forehead, chill and damp with the terror-sweat of shock, and marks her with its print and the raised scar tissue, his unmasked flesh emblazoned with the sigil of *Caper diabolus* . . . And in the quivering stillness brimming with her silent moans, there is the sound of yet another zipper rasping . . . and the serpent rears and the serpent strikes and her skull is like the Apple of Carnal Knowledge tainted with a vile, wriggling, worm that *knows* the white depths of the apple's flesh and divines the secret Seeds of Darkness cradled within its core . . .

In the narrow window, so high above, The Gentle Man stares down into the garden, surveying his dominion. Sometimes the window is set with three small panes of glass, one above the other. Sometimes the drapes are crimson damask. Sometimes they are blue velvet. Yet other times they may be deep, regal, purple satin, intricately brocaded, or mere wisps of violet chiffon or saffron-yellow silk. And sometimes the window is set with three rusted bars of iron, fixed side by side, vertically, into the casement. But, when the moon's belly waxes round and swollen . . . *then the rosebushes' branches weave black bars of thorn across the milky panes of isinglass, and the panes are veiled in sheets of dripping blood* . . .

Beneath the silver chalice of a half-brimmed moon of promise, beneath this grail that spills to earth its gathered drops of wine or blood (or, perhaps, the *succus lunariae*, whispered in the tomes of alchemists . . . ?), the highway flows beyond these endless, whispering, corn rows whose cultivation pays lingering tribute to Our Lord the Flayed One of sacred golden clothes the skins of the slaughtered, *Night Drinker*, for whom blood drips in sympathy for the fertile, spring-sweet, rains . . . The highway is a flood of Universal Menstruum. The *acetum fontis*. That which dissolves all into the solace of Oblivion . . .

Claymore stands in the Room of Mirrors, his gaze fixed upon his image echoed on into infinity. He is a puzzlebox of figures, the ferric flux frozen into semblance of life—forged from the souls of fallen stars, the meteoric iron—one contained within the other: the

Clockwork Iron Automaton and the Iron Maiden with her embracing emptiness that pierces (dual scourges of That Which Dwells in the Inner Darkness: *Excariatus*, those ragged scraps of flesh fluttering in the Winds of Limbo, that which *is* Life because it can *destroy* Life, the paradox that forms THE TORTURED MAN . . .):

Claymore stands in the Room of Mirrors, and the *argentum vivum*—the Silver Planes that conjure forth the reality of the Silver Cord unreeling away into the Inner Darkness—becomes rainbows and swirling smoke above the rippled waters as the mind of the watcher reels in the eye of the gyring falcon in the eye of the cyclone in the I of the Maelstrom, *and gravity unhinges itself* . . . and the Clockwork Iron Automaton stands within the Iron Maiden within the Clockwork Iron Automaton within the Iron Maiden . . . and the planes that once demarked the Eight Prime Directions multiplied by the Four Elementals that once were the Thirty-Two Points and Degrees of the Compass Rose are now transformed to the Zodiac circling above and the Tarot's Major Arcana laid out below

(save for the two that are one that are the legion that stand within the center of the gyre: Sometimes they answer the dictates of numerology and *are* Fifteen and Seventeen, The Devil and The Sun/The Son, and sometimes they are a Trickster's Hand, Sixteen (the Square of the Elementals) and Sixteen, The Moon doubled, and Thirteen, Death, enters the Wheel of the Zodiac and *is* its axis . . .)

and as it is above so it is
below,
and

outside the Room of Mirrors is the Room of Lost Innocents of Innocence Lost . . .

They are the coaxed and cajoled. They are the defamed. They are the things of porcelain (*so very white and pure! so fragile and translucent the moonlight transfixes them, conjuring the chill blue-white fire from deep within!*). They are *the Dolls of Bellmer*, twisted and disfigured, dismantled and reassembled, bizarrely juxtaposed, lying now among beds of rusted spikes and gleaming razors, sometimes wreathed with thorny crowns of barbed wire or pinned like butterflies on little wooden crosses (*sometimes it is the crux immissa, sometimes commissa, sometimes crux decussata or gammata* . . .), beyond the kenning of swarming ants that are The Sane . . . They are the flowers, the dainty roses (vibrant crystals of red and blue, tinctured as the prowl cars' two-phase strobe . . .), *that no longer are* . . .

The ragged black spiderhole in the skull of the broken blue-eyed doll forms a well between the worlds of Life and Death, of Suffering and Ecstasy. *And it speaks the meanings of meaningless as the Four Winds share its whispered secrets* . . . (how Papa was really an evil raven that lived within his hollow guise of flesh—*you can tell by the hard black pebbles of his eyes*! and how Papa told him he was his sweet young darling, His Little Rosebud, and kissed him on his cheeks and mouth and neck . . . *just before the thorny black switch tore ribbons from his bowed back and the flame entered him and seared within* . . . and how Papa embraced the swans and geese and babbled bits of nonsense to them just as he wrung their necks and the elegant economy of motion his hands and blade expressed as he beheaded them, and how they danced to the ancient mindless rhythms as the stumps of their necks gushed fountains of steaming blood, and how Papa bathed him in The Wine of Suffering after he had drunk his fill . . . and how Papa confided what he planted in the dark rich upturned earth that made the flowers bloom with such full round pretty petaled faces and why the brambles grew so wild and savage . . .

In the narrow window, high above the garden, The Gentle Man purses his blood-red rose-red lips and brushes a vagrant strand of coffin-black hair from his noble brow, and he trifles with his ruffled collar and his shirt sleeves trimmed in a froth of lace, and he lifts a hand mirror framed with twining flowers and vines and cherubs all wrought in silver and stares into its depths like the Spring of Narcissus, then smashes it against the windowsill and slashes his palms and fingers with its glittering fragments and licks the rosebuds and poppies of crimson that blossom from his transformed flesh . . . and the remnants of the broken doll lie crumpled in the dewy grass beneath the window and the changing faces of the moon, and a clock strikes somewhere in the darkness and something stirs within the earth, and rusted nails and other ferrous artifacts poke through the soil and clink and clatter as they seek form . . . And Claymore breathes their meaning . . .

& ANSWERETH ME NO MORE, NEITHER by PROPHETS, NOR by DREAMS . . .

(censored chapter from DUET for the DEVIL)

Background:

Truman Gilmore, Bible salesman, en route from his home in Oklahoma to service his scheduled accounts throughout the Midwest, takes a familiar backroad shortcut through northwestern Missouri and is ambushed, crippled by bullet-strikes to both kneecaps, and taken captive by a trio of incredibly vicious serial killers. The trio is comprised of the occult-influenced slayer, Maldoror ("Mal" for short), once known as the San Francisco-based Zodiac killer, his longtime henchman (whom he befriended as a street urchin in 60's era Haight Ashbury), Snuff, and Snuff's thirteen-year-old daughter Juliette ("Julie").

While Truman is held prisoner in the trunk of his own car, the trio pick up an unsuspecting young female hitchhiker, Heather Riley, and take her captive, as well. They stop for the night at a sleazy, rundown, motel in Quincy, Illinois, and Truman and Heather's torment begins in earnest . . .

THE DEATHLY BLUE LIGHT FLOODING FROM THE T.V. SCREEN TWITCHES LIKE A FEVERED PULSE:

Mal listens for the sound of the lock clicking as the door slams closed.

Assured that it has firmly latched, he steps to the dresser, his stiff penis bobbing & jiggling as he moves, his body completely naked save for the pair of black socks he still wears on his feet.

All he needs is one of those black masks that were the trademark signature of that genre of film-making art (?) the boys from the old school once referred to as "BLUE MOVIES," Truman's Demerol-loosened mind free-associates, *but the floozies in them never looked like . . .*

His somewhat unsteady focus keeps flickering back to the naked girl tied spreadeagle to the other bed. His fat face flushes with his guilty & illicit knowledge of her so-seductive jailbait flesh, but his eyes seem *possessed* by some lustful demon. *Blue Movies. Even saw a couple myself. At those "smokers" Bart (?). No. Bradley. Bradley Crawford used to throw down at the V.F.W. hall in the backroom on Thursday nights . . . Never mentioned THOSE to poor, trusting, Bertha! She never . . .*

Truman's helplessly unfaithful eyes spill a hot flood of tears as he flashes on the very real possibility he may never see his wife & the kids & *their* kids the grandkids ever again *in THIS life . . .*

The phrase *"this Veil of Tears"* flickers through his consciousness for a second-long eternity then dissolves into the wavering haze of lachrymose dewdrops & Demerol . . .

& Truman intones the words of the Twenty-Second Psalm from a memory filled with the holy words of *The Word*:

"My God, my God, why hast thou forsaken me? *Why art thou so far from helping me, & from* the words of my roaring? O my God, I cry in the daytime . . ."

"Well, My Dear, I have brought you something *very* special, something just for *you*—" Mal says, holding up the whiskey bottle. "I have gone to a *great deal* of *trouble* on your account—"

"They cried unto thee, & were delivered; they trusted in thee, were not confounded—"

"I had to search through the *dumpster* outside, in the service alley, to find this special little treasure for you—"

"But I *am* a worm, & no man;" Truman's penis gives an unwanted jerk & wriggle at the sight of Mal bending at the bedside, guiding the smudged & cigarette ash dusted bottle between Heather's wide-stretched legs. "a reproach of men, & despised of the people—"

The dregs of the liquor slosh in golden-amber wavelets within the bottle, as Mal gazes into the distortions of its curvature.

". . . they shoot out the lip, they shake the head, saying—"

Mal tilts the bottle downwards, angling it in between her thighs, the golden droplets spilling from the lip to splatter Heather's bald-shaved privates, the alcohol drawing a sudden wince, a shudder of pain, a choking, stifled cry, as it burns her raw & battered labia & vulva . . .

"I am poured out like water—"

"Old Grandad, here, I guess you may not know it, but he's a bit of a gynecologist, really—you never know what he may get into if you're not very very careful—"

"But thou *art* he that took me out of the womb—"

Mal inserts the slender neck of the bottle into the girl's lewdly exposed sex.

". . . & all my bones are out of joint: my heart is like wax, it is melted in the midst of my bowels—"

Heather struggles futilely against this new *invasion.*

". . . the assembly of the wicked have inclosed me—"

". . . they pierced my hands & my feet—"

Mal's face is twisted into a malevolent monster mask, a *t'ao t'ieh,* hovering above the helpless victim of his twisted lusts . . .

"I may tell all my bones; they look *and* stare upon me—"

THE BLUE LIGHT FROM THE TELEVISION WRITHES IN HIS DEVILISH EYES, DEVOID OF ANY HINT OR HOPE OF MERCY, ONLY THE LUST TO DOMINATE TO VIOLATE TO SAVOR THE SUFFERING OF THE LAMBS LED IN CADENCE TO A SYMPHONY OF BLUE TO THE MOMENT THE HOUR THE ETERNITY OF THEIR SLAUGHTER . . .

". . . all they that go down to the dust shall bow before him: & none can keep alive his own soul—"

There is a Generation, Whose Teeth are as Swords, & Their Jaw Teeth as Knives . . .

He who lives by the sword shall die by the sword . . .
& it *is* true. That "VIOLENCE BEGETS VIOLENCE."

(But there sure seem to be a Helluva lot of flies in the collective ointment of the existential lately, ehhh . . . ?)

It's only a short walk down the block & into an open alleyway's mouth between the darkened storefronts of **BILL'S ARMY SURPLUS & SUTTERS AUTO PARTS EXCHANGE,** perhaps sixty or seventy feet down the alley, then 'round the back & into the service walkway into the motel's courtyard for the white-halter-top-&-shortshorts-clad Julie to rendezvous with the once-Zodiac Maldoror & her father, Snuff, & their two captives in Room Fourteen.

But she has to take a detour. To pick up a few things that Mal had said He needed. Down to the end of the block across the street to a late-night drugstore that in its better days had boasted a **REXALL** sign in neon, but now simply has a pair of spots shining on a painted "**RX**" on the wall above the smeared & BB-holed glass of the once-pneumatic swinging doors.

The three-&-a-half-inch heels of Julie's sandals click noisily on the asphalt as she crosses at the stoplight, careful to avoid the temptation of jaywalking the corner . . .

Being a "good little girl" as usual, avoiding possible infraction of wildly varying state laws & city ordinances for a mere citation that might link her legally to *place & time . . .*

&, after all, she *does* look like some teenie-bop slut out hookin' . . .

No reason to attract further *undue* attention . . .

+   +   +

Behind the counter is a grossly fat black woman with a yellow bandanna tied around her head. Her huge hips & buttocks seem to be melting down over the sagging seat of the stool she's perched on in vast flows of blubber & the riotous Bird-of-Paradise-patterned fabric of her size XXXXX *muumuu*. She's reading some story about aliens from Aldebaran & two-headed babies in *The National Enquirer*, & it's pretty obvious that she's one of those "enquiring minds that really want to know . . ."

The only other customer is an elderly, emaciated-looking, man wearing a gray tweed coat that hangs on him at least five sizes too large & a fedora in the same tatty tweed. He looks like a scarecrow with the straw fallen out or an aging horror writer back from a six-month stay at the Dachau Hilton.

His choice in reading matter seems pretty weird, as well. He's got a *Teen Magazine* in his hand & a *Hustler*, a *Penthouse*, & a *Swank* on the counter. Along with a Garfield doll, an enema bag, a jar of Vaseline, & two dozen Trojan rubbers . . .

The pharmacist who's helping him reminds Julie of that wired druggist from the old *Fridays* T.V. show, the one who used to tug at invisible cobwebs on his face & keep shrieking, "I can *handle* IT! . . ."

By comparison, Julie thinks she must come on like a "straight."

She waits until the perv leaves, then steps up to the counter with her own purchases: two plastic drop cloths, a pack of *Gillette Super Blue Blades*, a roll of micropore bandage, & a packet of assorted-sized sewing needles.

"*Fffuckkkkk!*" she curses under her breath, *they were all out of goddamn duct tape* . . . Mal is bound to whoop her ass good for not bringing back everything he'd asked for.

She hands the pharmacist dude a ten-dollar bill, then wriggles the change down deep into the skintight slit of her right front pocket.

Julie struts out onto the neon-jittering street, carrying her odds & ends in a plain brown shopping sack.

She looks over her shoulder for a moment. Thinks she sees a shooting star in the southern sky.

She waits impatiently for the light to change. Then crosses.

Her route back to the motel is already planned, but there's a pink Continental parked right in front of **SUTTERS AUTO PARTS EXCHANGE** & there are two big black bucks in leather jackets trying to drag a struggling peroxide-blonde bimbo in a faux leopard coat into the back seat of the car. The bimbo is drunk or stoned, she's staggering & shouting obscenities at her two assailants (?) companions (?) . . .

Julie decides to cut through the alley in front of her, exactly one block down from her intended access.

She's only about twenty-five feet in when she realizes that she may have made a first-class mistake:

this alley either deadends or turns a corner up ahead, & it's one helluva lot longer than sixty feet. It's like a filth-strewn box canyon of brick & concrete

& there are three black youths entering after her, blocking any hope of *exit* or *escape* in that direction

& she lent Mal her switchblade—

fuckin' goddamn shit on my luck, she berates herself, *was I ever a friggin' asshole for not following plans . . . !*

Julie *knows* she can't risk bringing attention to herself by screaming for help. Her only alternatives seem to be: WALK. Or RUN . . .

She considers running. But she'd have to take off her shoes or she'd trip for sure. & the ground is littered with jagged shards of broken glass, glinting in bright slivers as they catch a stray ray of light from a passing car *outside*.

She'd rip her feet to bloody shreds before she got halfway . . .

She decides to walk.

Faster.

She scans the near-pitchblack darkness of the alley for some makeshift weapon. If she gets *really desperate*, she can slash at them with a spike of glass. But she's not into slicing her own hand to ribbons on it.

FFFucKKK! Another one just stepped into her path from *somewhere*—a doorway . . . ?

FUCK is right! That's EXACTLY what these skells are planning for her, she thinks—*Oooohhhhh SHIT! gangbanged by four hopped-up niggers if I'm* LUCKY . . . *if not . . . then . . .*

Julie's normal cool dissolves into a flood of cold sweat reeking of fear pheromones.

+ + +

"HHHeyyy! Bro—! Feast yo *EYES* on wh'dwego*tus* he-*uh*—"

The four black punks are closing in on her *fast*, sure of themselves, sure that they can *take her down* with only minimal resistance . . .

"Hhhmmmmm—look like sum cracker-*ass* hoochie bitch!"

Julie does another quickscan of the shadow-black alleyway, assessing her chances, weighing her alternatives, sizing up the potential strengths & *weaknesses* of her opposition, trying desperately to gauge what tactical actions *hardcore experience* has taught her may yield the greatest possible odds in favor of *SURVIVAL*—

(this all sequenced in the split-second of an eye-blink— *subconscious, streetwise*, practiced in the ways of swift DEATH)

"Yeah. Yeah. H-HHhheyyy, Shawty! Yo wanna PAR-*ty* . . . ?"

(but *this* time Julie knows the fear of the *hunted*, rather than the blood-thrill of the *hunter*)

Cold sweat trickles down the taut ridge of Julie's spine, trickles down the smoothly rounded dome of her forehead causing the silky, dark fronds of her short bangs to cling to her throbbing temples, trickles down her cheeks & chin & neck, down between the budding mounds of her still-girlish breasts, down the curve of her belly, the droplets gathering in the dimple of her navel, swelling & trickling further down the tapering "V"-shaped outjut of her *mons veneris*, matting the sparsely curling pubic hairs, dripping into the already moist crevice of her sex, the soft, trembling, flesh of inner thighs, mingling with the fear sweat trickling the ripe melon-globes of her so-perfectly-rounded buttocks . . .

But with *fear* can come the numbing paralysis of the wounded prey, & Julie wills *herself* down down down past this *layer* of psychological stunning to trigger the *rush* of adrenaline from the primal, feral darkness within her that is the *lair* of the *hunting BEAST*—

Julie is forced to spend precious seconds fumbling in the paper sack, but she retrieves the objects that her instincts guide her to—

the cardboard-backed blister-pack of razor blades, which she quickly rips open, tossing the remnants of torn packaging as inconspicuously as possible, slipping the plastic slide-casing that sheathes the blades into the tight slit of her pocket—

& the packet of sewing needles, which she fingers carefully, assuring herself of the positioning of the sharp, bristling ends, she chokes off an involuntary *ouch* of pain when her skin is snagged & pricked on one tiny spear, drawing a droplet of blood, but she succeeds in tearing back the thin cardboard flap, exposing the rigid quills of metal . . .

All the while feigning retreat from the larger grouping of her stalkers Julie sidles ever closer to the lone black "gangbanger" who stands spread-legged in the center of the alley, blocking her avenue of possible escape. She keeps the paper sack clutched tightly in her left hand, cupping the vicious surprise she clutches in her right, palm-downward, feigning a loosely outreaching posture of mock-helpless terror.

"Come on, baby, I got yo ass—" the hulking badboy says, waiting for her to come just in reach . . .

But, Julie, far from the fear-numbed victim she has played, dodges lithely as her assailant grabs for her, moving *under* his outstretched arms, then straight up, putting every ounce of her feline strength into one split-second & into the youth's exposed face, & *connects*— ramming the bristling row of bright, glittering metal thorns with that one desperate, perfect, stroke—impaling both his eyeballs head-on, letting the cardboard slide back & away, driving the needles all the way home . . . feeling the *squish* of fluids spurting from his multiply-punctured orbs, like juice spritzing from a pair of very ripe, fork-jabbed, white grapes . . .

The boy rears back, tottering on his feet in the sudden shock of excruciating *blindness*, clutching futilely at his ruined eyes.

"OOOOOOOOOOOOOOOOOOOOOOOOOOOOOOOOOOOOOooooooo oooHHHHHHHHHHHHHhhhhhhhhhh!MMMMMMMMMMM MMMMMMUTHHHHHHHHHHHFFFFFFFFFFFFFFFFFFFF FUUUCKKKKKKKUHHHHHhhhhhhhhhh!" *he screams in total, babbling, terror—*

Short lived.

as the upthrust heel of Julie's palm slashes upward, striking as she has seen Mal & her father do to administer the *executing stroke,* as the impetus of motion is released in *IMPACT*, mashing the shattered upper lateral cartilage & septum that form the bridge of his nose, & the lower lateral & the medial cartilages of the *columella*, ramming the nasal bone through the fragile floor of the brain cavity in a spurt of blood, terminating both olfactory senses & brain function almost instantaneously.

Julie recovers her balance as the youth crumples, falling backwards. Away from her.

This seventeen-year-old would-be rapist is coughing blood as his body jitterbugs, spasming to a silent swelling symphony in *BLUE*, his hands & feet tapping out some reflexive mambojive *gris-gris* rhythms on the pavement as he *kicks it* . . .

Julie scrambles for the looming promise of escape down the now-unguarded alley *eastward*, her high-heeled sandals slipping & sliding on the skitterish, shifting layer of broken glass refuse & assorted chunks of rubble, she teeters, one foot skewing out from beneath her, regains her balance, plunges headlong down the alleyway, gaining perhaps another sixteen (?) seventeen (?) steps toward potential safety when her luck fails her, she trips over a bundle of oil-soaked rags (?) a dead cat (?) the remains of a rotten watermelon (?) . . . & pitches face-forward in the litter, skinning her knees & hands on asphalt, slicing them on brittle glass shards, rolling, saving her face from impact with the hard, pebbly, tarmac, just inches from possible concussion & disfigurement . . .

But the lost seconds have *cost her*.

She hears the rasp of zippers.

The groping touch of greedy hands upon her body, ripping off her halter top & short-shorts, feeling & fondling her with clutching, painful, eagerness, as the three gangbangers *take her down* . . .

"Dis fuckin' cunt's done wasted ou-*uh* bru*dthuh*, man, *d*is cunt's fuckin' snuffed fuckin' Clyde, man, I can't fuckin' beeee-*lieve* dis fuckin' goddamn jive shit, man!"

"Bitch, you gonna *pay* fo *d*at!" a voice growls from somewhere above her. "Yeah, Bitch, you gonna pay in *blood*—"

+   +   +

The alley is black as Hell.

Black fuckin' hell-faced cocksuckin' coons, a voice whispers in some very deep dark corner of Julie's brain. & another whispers, *it's all just meat* . . . & yet another whispers, *this isn't real, only a movie that we're watching, just some hardcore stroke film where some little cunt gets gangjumped by these three hopped-up spades* . . . *only a movie a movie a* . . . *all just meaT meAT mEAT MEAT* . . .

Julie's flesh screams with excruciating pain. She's lost track of who has done what to her & how many times. Can't afford to keep score—

gotta' convince yourself this ain't *you* that this is happenin' to. SOME OTHER BITCH. & you're just watchin' them *do* her like you *always* do. But it *is* YOUR sex that's ripped & bleeding from the fury of their assault. YOUR cunt that redhot iron poker of a prick is hammering. YOUR sex that they're taking turns tearing at & tossing their rocks into. THEIR filthy black cocks that are inside *you*, pistoning & pumping & spurting their sperm like they're pissing into *you*, YOUR scalp thumping against the pavement with each brutal thrust, YOUR back & buttocks that are sliced & shredded & punctured by shards of broken glass, bleeding from dozens yes dozens of minute gashes each an echo of that battered bleeding gash between your wide-pried thighs, YOUR mouth belly breasts legs arms neck face that are slick with their spattered semen . . . YOU are nothing but a PUSSY a CUNT another HOLE for them to FUCK off into . . . YOU are NOTHING to them but a BUCKET FULL OF CUM . . . a WHITE BITCH to make PAY for every slight they've ever suffered . . . & when they tire of using *your* cunt *your* mouth *your* asshole (?) *your* (?) to take their pleasure. THEN WHAT WILL THEY DO TO YOU WITH THEIR KNIVES YOU KNOW THEY HAVE KNIVES & YOU KNOW THAT THEY WILL TAKE AN EYE FOR AN EYE & THEIR BRO CLYDE IS DEAD BUT YOU DON'T WANT TO LET THAT TAKE YOU OVER THE EDGE NOT YET NOT YET NOT YET . . .

+ + +

Snuff traces the path that he & Mal expected Julie would follow—through the alley behind the motel, taking a ninety-degree turn westward, then exiting in the gap between **BILL'S ARMY SURPLUS** & **SUTTERS AUTO PARTS EXCHANGE.**

No sign of his daughter. He walks to the corner across from the **RX**.

Crosses.

Enters the drug store.

Waits until the three giggling, pimple-faced, teenage boys finish deciding on their purchase. A pack of RIBBED TINGLERS in *"A Rainbow of Exotic Passionate Colors."*

"I'm looking for a girl—she's young—"

"Hehhh. Sorry! We don't carry *those*. But. Hehhh. Maybe those *boys* that just left could fix you up with something juicy—" The wired-out pharmacist quips.

"Yeah. Ass*sshole* & I'm a fuckin' plastic surgeon! So, cut the fuckin' crap—she's about *yea* tall. Long black hair. White halter top & short-shorts . . ."

"Oh! *That one*! Sure. She was here but left. Maybe twenty-five. Thirty minutes ago. Bought her stuff & left. Little *young* for you *isn't she*—?" the druggist cocks his right eyebrow suggestively & winks.

Snuff would love to shove this dickhead's brain up his ass like a suppository. But he's got to keep a lid on it. Cool his impulse to blow a hole through the dipshit's head with a nine-mm slug.

He spins on his heel, & strides post haste to the exit.

+ + +

The two gangstas stand on either side of the young white girl lying on the rubbish-strewn tarmac of the alleyway. Watching the shadowy form of their bro' humping her, his naked buttocks pistoning up & down into the hollow of her outstretched thighs & belly.

From his frenzied strokes it's obvious that he's getting ready to shoot his load again.

"C'mon, Man, c'mon, Wylie! Get yo NUT in *d*is bitch! Sink it *TO* her, Man! Shit or git off the pot!"

"Yea-*uh*, bbbllooddd!—Get yo stones off so's we can try us a litt'l *FUDGE-PACKIN'* wid dis pasty-ass bitch! Her pussy be bout used up."

"Yea-*uh*, get *down* 'n' *brown*! Man, I want me some *TIGHT* young *JAIL-TAIL*, yea-*uh*—"

The needle-thin beam of red laser stabs out, sighting on the silhouetted skells, tracking in on the back of one eye-level, dreadlock-dangling, cranium—

ffftt.
ffftt.
ffftt.

The gangboy's skull frags under the dead-center impact of three nine-mm dum-dum slugs.

The other boy just begins to pivot toward the sound . . .

ffftt.
ffftt.

The slugs rip off the side of his face, tearing away fist-sized chunks of temple & cheekbone & jawbone with a sick *sssssmmmmmuussshhhhh* like a rotten melon splattering.

"Yeah. Three fuckin' niggers havin' some fun. Pulped two of them niggers & then there was—"

Snuff stoops, kneeling behind the pistoning youth as he hammers out his climax in Julie's battered little cunt.

"ONE!"

Snuff grabs the boy savagely by the afro'd hair at the nape of his neck, tugging him out of the saddle, sensing him spasm his climax into empty air—

"EEEEEEEEoooowwwwwwhhhhhhhhhhwwwwwwwww!" he shrieks.

Snuff smashes him face-downwards into the asphalt, pulping his nose, ripping the flesh away from his lips.

"You got about six seconds to fuckin' tell me what I wanna know—& I'll let you fuckin' live, niggerboy—"

Nothing.

"Nod yr fuckin' black head or I squeeze it off RIGHT NOW!"

Mr. Badass gangbanger nods—FAST!

The tip of the silencer is shoved into his quivering sphincter, giving him just a hint of what his companions had planned for Snuff's already-ravaged daughter.

"Now. Nigger. What gang're you runnin' with—?"

"De Slik Shivs—"

"& who're you bangin' heads with—?"

"Cold Stones, Man, Cold Stones—jis don' hurt me, Man!"

"Thanks! Jigboy—! Now, pack it where the sun don't shine—"

Snuff squeezes off, giggling hysterically as the nine-mm rips the kid's fuckin' guts out, the muffled *ffftt* of the silenced muzzle burst sounding like a big wet blood-bubbling fart . . .

"So I lied—so fuckin' *sue* me—!"

ffftt ffftt. Two more just for good measure.

Snuff holsters the COBRA.

He helps Julie to her feet.

He retrieves her clothes from where the boys had tossed them. Then helps her pull up her short-shorts, his hands sliding in the blood & semen drooling down her thighs.

He hands his daughter her switchblade.

Snuff searches in a nearby dumpster. Finds a rag. Soaks it in the boys' blood. & scrawls a message in blood-graffiti on the wall of the nearest building:

sLiKsHiVZSuK!
cOLdStOnEzIzkInG!
BLUeBlOodZFuCKAlL!

Julie, meanwhile has recovered sufficiently from her ordeal to slice off the four boys' genitals & stuff them into one another's mouths.

"SUCK DICK YOU BLACK MOTHERFUCKIN' STIFFS!" a staggering Julie snarls at the corpses.

Snuff frisks them. & pockets the .38 Police Special & the stiletto that he finds concealed & no longer needed . . .

Snuff digs into his pants pocket, & tugs out the container of blow.

He sprinkles it across the butchery.

"We'll try to make it look like some kind'a drug ripoff or gangthing—

"Where did you drop the stuff you bought—?"

Julie totters about, scuffing with her feet until she finds the bag. "Here—"

Snuff walks over to where she's standing, & scoops up the bag & his daughter.

He carries her down the dark tunnel to the first southward turn, then heads toward the motel in cover of full darkness . . .

BUT the TENDER MERCIES of the WICKED are CRUEL . . .

The white Buick Regal follows the almost-empty highway 96 just east of the Iowa border, heading south through Lima, Illinois. Mal carefully observes the speed limit, as well as all those minor dictates of Illinois' traffic law.

No errors. Ever.

The air is crisp with the night-chill that intrudes even into this unseasonably-warm autumn, and with that peculiar clarity characteristic of the wee hours just before the breaking dawn.

The red and green and amber of traffic signals seem to wink approval of this stranger, this ghostly presence who bows so courteously to their dictates, never cheating their honor system, even though no enforcers wait with summons books in hand.

It glides by beneath the yellow blur of residential street lamps, beneath the muted pinkish aura of mercury vapors lined along the major traffic arteries.

The man known as "Maldoror" or "Mal" (He who was once called Zodiac, though He has used many names in His travels down *the Road of the Beast* . . .) spots a likely spare set of wheels, an older model black Ford Fairlane.

Snuff hops out of the Buick, walks back a block-and-a-half, and hotwires the battered Fix-Or-Repair-Daily special.

The area appears deserted.

The unsteady *chug chug chug* of the Ford's idling engine transforms itself to a throaty rumbling as Snuff shifts out and the car rolls slowly forward.

Mal and Julie follow in the smoothly purring Buick, hanging back just in case their companion's actions have drawn any unwanted attention.

They head through Marcelline, then Ursa, where they catch 61 East, traveling as if to meet the sunrise.

+ + +

As the trio near Rushville, the black Ford's throaty rumble (only that asshole would boost a junker with a busted muffler, Mal curses silently) assumes an asthmatic wheeze, then begins a fitful jag of coughing, the tailpipe belching forth clouds of dark smoke that swirl and eddy in the Buick's headlamp beams.

"Fly's. in. the. buttermilk. shoo. fly. shoo . . ." The ex-Zodiac intones the words of the familiar folksong as if in some warding litany. Juliette rolls her eyes in the direction of her mentor, far from surprised by this seemingly meaningless burst of mumbo-jumbo jingle; she has long since become accustomed to His eccentric behavior and volatile moodswings. It is merely curiosity that draws her attention. This and the hidden hope to fathom these fleetingly exposed fragments of His power-core of occult wisdom, His seeming ability to manipulate minor rivulets within the ebb-and-flow of the material to the patterns of His desire . . .

The coughing eases, the carburetor's functioning less strangled, the bursts of evacuated smoke dwindling.

Another quarter of a mile passes by beneath their humming tires.

Then the Ford dies.

The engine gives forth one last wheezing cough, the idiot lights of OIL and CHARGE burn like two gleeful demon eyes alive within the dashboard, the white-noise hum of the treadbare fiberglass belteds drops an octave as the gyring of the wheels slows, and Snuff coasts the TKO'd clunker as far as its momentum allows then edges off onto the shoulder pullout.

The car rolls to a stop.

Snuff kills the lights. He gives the glovebox a quick once-over, scavenging for any interesting tidbits. He takes a state map. The rest is useless flotsam: the crumbling yellowed remains of owner's manual and repair logbook, a couple of dusty plastic forks, a crumpled wad of napkins, and a pocket flashlight that merely clicks—tipoff of failed batteries. *Too bad*, he thinks, *no stashed self-protection: no hand-gun, no hunting knife, not even a goddamn canister of MACE . . .*

The sun visor yields a cached ten-spot, which he pockets.

He pulls the registration. Carries it with him as he exits the Fairlane, whips out his lighter, and torches the slip of paper, watching as it chars to ash. He grinds it to dust beneath his sole.

The screwdriver blade of his pocketknife serves to loosen the screws fastening the license plates. These he removes for future use.

Less than a minute lost, before the parked Buick Regal guns away into the darkness, Mal and Co. momentarily rejoined.

+   +   +

Rushville supplies Snuff with another Ford. This one much newer, far more dependable: a silver Taurus. *Mal will get a kick out of the Zodiac reference, as He always does with those and Dodge Ares, as He free-associates with Mercuries . . .*

A few seconds' handiwork, and he's traded plates, foxing identification from potential quick-scans cross-ref'ing make and model with license number of the GTA.

He pulls the plastic-rolled Midnite Auto kit from where it's tucked into the back of his Levi's, nestling against the small of his back.

He slips the thin, hacksaw-like, blade of the latchpick down alongside the pane of the driver's window into the narrow well. With one quick, deft, tug he pops the mechanism to OPEN position.

Forty seconds flat, and the switch-puller has tugged the ignition key-cylinder free. Snuff shorts the wires, and the starter motor kicks over, setting the pistons stroking, the engine idling smooth as silk.

The Taurus slides out from the curb, cruises three blocks down the still-deserted residential street. A few scattered lights glow through closed blinds or curtains, but, for the most part, the neighborhood drowses, languishing in the scant span before alarm clocks rouse the dreamers from the little death of sleep, their insistent buzz or wakeup music or recorded whispers of feminine persuasion intruding upon the bliss of Morpheus.

Snuff hangs a ninety-degree at the next right, and pulls up in the first free stretch of parking space along the sidewalk. Julie steps from the shadows of a hedgerow, carrying their suitcases.

Her father leans over and flips the locked door handle to OPEN. Julie reaches in and pops the rear door latch, tossing the suitcases onto the backseat. She scrambles in, slams the door, and secures the belt-and-harness rig across her waist and chest.

Snuff waits until the white Buick cruises by, then pulls out, trailing Mal by a block's length to avoid any bystanders connecting the two as traveling companions . . .

On a deserted stretch of pavement, Mal eases off onto the pullout. Snuff parks just behind Him, gets out, and trades his spare set of plates with the out-of-states that mark the Regal.

The Nebraskas. Snuff flicks them like sheetmetal Frisbees, far out into the tall grass and weeds and underbrush along the roadside . . .

From Ursa to Rushville, they've been following the backroads. But now, Mal catches the onramp for U.S. Highway 67—heading southeast.

The stars fade out, and the dark horizon transforms to ribboned tints of rose and salmon as Buick and Taurus near the bridge across the Illinois . . .

At the Beardstown exit, where 67 junctions with State Route 125, Mal takes the offramp into town. Snuff lags back, letting the distance between the two cars lengthen as they cruise through the waking streets, the early morning traffic meandering around them, past clumps of cars swelling the parking lots of the doughnut shops and pancake houses.

Mal stops to buy gas at a Texaco. He self-serves. Pays, borrows the key to the GENTLEMEN's where He voids His swollen, aching, bladder.

They catch another backroad east to State 87 North. There they cross the junction and disappear down a winding dirt road into the Panther Creek Conservation Area, quickly hidden by the dense stands of flame-hued foliage.

Mal seeks a secluded glade, where He ditches the Buick. Snuff helps him transfer their suitcases into the Taurus' surprisingly spacious trunk.

"Yank the carpeting from the Buick's trunk, Snuff. Siphon a can of gas, and torch it. Don't bother to do the car. Unnecessary. It's clean. But I want the bloodstains and the-Devilknows-what-fibers that may have caught there charred to ash. Understand? Fuck Forensics. No evidence-trail to link it with the motel room. Strip off the Illinois plates, we'll need them later. No evidence of foulplay. Leave the possibility the owner may simply have skipped . . .

"And, Julie, tuck a 'stray' tube of lipgloss in the crack beside the seat. Not yours. From that purse you snatched in Memory Park in Houston . . ."

+ + +

"Snuff. The goddamn sun is searing my retinas. Push your visor down over that bloody window before I go blind. Or take a headache. and. nobody. shall be happy. If I take a headache."

One wiry hand slaps the visor into place.

Mal may not welcome it but the Sunday morning sun blazing through the canted pane of safety glass burns with a ruddy, hearthlike, incandescence on the flesh of His companion's gaunt cheeks. The unruly strands of spiked beard and shoulder-length mane glow like heated tungsten filaments it passes through their fragile shafts and plays across the tender skin beneath.

Mal keeps the speed at a generic safe-and-sane 25 as they pass through Chandlerville, on the northwest corner of the preserve.

The Taurus is a silver bullet in SloMo, as it glides up State 78, nearing the crossing of the Sangamon River.

They pass over, and, not far beyond, Mal's watchful gaze spots the peak of a lone tent, pitched way back from the road among an almost-concealing stand of pines. There is a glint of sun on well-polished chrome, and a splash of gleaming white glimpsed for a split-second through the intervening screen of needles.

Mal's bootheel taps the brake pedal, pumping gently, slowing the Taurus' forward motion in a fluid glide of ballet-precise deceleration, and hangs a left on the dirt access road some hundred yards farther down the highway.

The Taurus is a silver-sleek feline, stalking. Or a belly dancer, its suspension doing a sinuous bump-and-grind as it rolls along the rocks and ruts of the hip-narrow lane silent and smooth as whispering silk.

"I took a peek through the pines, and sought a victim, as some day it may happen that a victim—" the once-Zodiac pauses for emphasis.

His gloved hands grasping the steering wheel in clockwork-perfect mimicry of the classic "ten-and-two" positioning dictated by driving manuals. Symbolic. Fetishistic. Clockwork, like the Zodiac watch, His Clebar skindiver, underwater chronograph, glinting on his left wrist.

"—must be found. Yes. A victim must be found." His singsong all the stranger for its recital in His eerie monotone. "Twelfth and Thirteenth arias. The Lord High Executioner. Anyone care. For a cup of. Cocoa? . . . Ko-Ko?" His phrasing serves as a parody and paraphrasing of his twelfth Zodiac letter, mentioning His "thirteen slaves," and a postcard addressed to "Paul Averly," deliberately misspelling the *San Francisco Chronicle* reporter's name, and which referred to "victim 12."

Wordplay. Sex. Death. The occult. Inner musings forever His obsessions . . .

+   +   +

The harsh rasping as the tent flap unzips is her sole warning that something is seriously amiss.

But it is too late.

Far too late.

Snuff is on her before she can even voice a scream. Her mind is still half-locked within the shadow world of dreams. Her huge, fawnlike, eyes register disbelief. But this is a waking dream. A dream of horror.

His hand is clasped across her mouth. The razor-honed steel of his switchblade drawing a thin crescent of blood trickling across the tense, white, curve of her throat.

Mal follows. His own twelve-inch butcher knife, His "Count Zaroff"—a dead ringer of that used by the mad hunter of humans in *The Most Dangerous Game*—slithers from its wooden, handmade, scabbard at His waist.

"I want your money and your car keys."

The blade pressed to the young man's jugular stills any hope of active resistance.

Byron Hodges' only hope is that these psychos will be satisfied with the worldly wealth of His request.

This he can live with. The stock demand of a thousand T.V. and movie dramas flashing by in instant rerun. "YOUR MONEY OR YOUR LIFE . . ."

The twenty-eight dollars and change. His Gold Card. And Visa and American Express. And the shiny white Acura Legend coupe with personalized plates and the four-hundred-plus-per-month monkey of showroom-financing hanging for another fifty-five with its teeth sunk gleefully into his back . . . Gone the classic '67 Mustang and its Big Zero payment book—thanks to Erica's insistence . . .

He can deal with it, providing it is *or* . . .

He points to his acid-washed 501s crumpled in a heap next to the inflatable air mattress bolstering the goose-down cocoon of oh-so trendy sleeping bag in which he lies, no longer curled in blissful slumber.

Now it is his straight jacket, restraining him, trapping him within this nylon asylum of suddenly threatening angles and shadows. A slight breeze ruffles the thin fabric of the tent, and the flapping sounds like frantic wings. Byron can hear his own heart pounding bass, filling the cramped quarters with the four-four snarling beat of colossal Kenwood woofers big as all outdoors.

"I want your car to go to Mexico." The stocky man says.

To Mexico . . . ? Hell, anywhere, as long as it's away from here.

Those owl eyes stare down into his, framed by heavy, black-plastic-rimmed, glasses. A sturdy elastic strap secures His Clark-Kent-style specs. They remind him of those X-Ray Specs they used to tout in DC comics, back when he was still a kid. And costumed villains with improbable names just added to the fun . . .

"Still no duct tape, goddamnit. They need gags. We shall have to use whatever comes to hand.

"Drag the girl out of her sleeping bag. See what she has on—"
Dust motes swirl in a blue wash of light and shadows . . .

Snuff needs no further urging. He peels open the canvas bag. The zipper's harsh, metallic, grating echoes in the silence.

He drags the girl, Erica, out of her sack.

She's wearing a pair of flannel PJs with tiny roses printed all over and cute little "footies" and a trapdoor in the back.

The soft material is damp with perspiration. It clings to her curves, while lending her a childlike innocence. As do her eyes.

Her eyes stay.

The PJs come off with a ripping sound like a buzzsaw tearing into pine planks.

She looks even better naked.

She isn't wearing any panties.

Snuff's cock gives an appreciative lurch as his Levi's-clad groin grinds against her bare butt, and the tip of his knife traces circles around her nipples, flickering across her flesh with a butterfly touch that teases but does not break the skin, the cold steel raising gooseflesh, causing her nipples to pucker up and stiffen into jutting nubs of fear.

Her hair is chestnut-brown. Shoulder-length. And permed into tiny ringlets.

"Nice titties. Nice ass. Looks like you've got a choice little fuck, there, Daddy Dear—" Julie is peeping in at the doorway, "—a bit *old* for Uncle Mal's tastes, but He can always *do me* if He wants to . . .

"I'm gettin' *hot* already . . ."

"Uuuummmfff Ccchhrrrissst nnnnnohhhhh," Byron mumbles through the leather of Mal's glove.

Julie steps inside the tent, stooping as she enters through the flap. *The shadowy interior ripples deep ultramarine . . .*

She is wearing a navy blue skirt and blouse, with little appliqués of stars and stripes in red and white, a sailor suit, with wide lapels and brass buttons. All sugar and spice and . . .

Her small, slender, hand dips between the captive girl's thighs. The thin membrane of micropore glove sheaths her fingers, as she pushes through the mossy strands of pubic bush sprouting at the lower taper of the brunette's belly, inserting them into the slit of her sex, feeling the petal-like folds part as she thrusts savagely up into her searing heat and wetness . . .

"Ooooohhhh. Erica's all *wet*! She *must* have been having NAUGHTY DREAMS! Or, maybe, Daddy's big cock rubbin' up against your ass-crack has just got you all horny and ready for a nice fuck in there . . . *already* . . . ?"

Julie stoops, picks up the severed pajama bottoms and rips a strip of the flannel off. She uses it to gag her father's shapely captive. She tosses the rest of the rag to Mal. He gags Byron.

Julie kneels between Erica's struggling thighs.

"Uuuhhh Ohhhhh. Naughty! Naughty! She's already *been*

fucked—I can taste the *cum* still up there in her . . .

"And it tastes *nice*. I *want some* . . ."

Julie stands. Steps over to where Mal pins Byron within his sleeping bag.

"YOU BEEN FUCKIN', HUH? YOU TWO BEEN FUCKIN' . . . ?" Snuff rhetorically queries the gagged girl. "AIN'T NICE T' FUCK 'N' NOT GIVE ME NONE—" He forces her shoulders back, cruelly, arching her pelvis forward in an unnatural, pained, posture. One hand claws and pinches at her bare breast while the other rifles the furred mound of her lewdly exposed genitals.

Julie's senses are heightened in the adrenaline rush triggered by the violent promise of the confrontation, by the sight of Erica's helplessly bared flesh, and by her sexual contact with the girl. She tugs down the zipper, goose pimples puckering her flesh at the acuteness of the echoed ripping sound.

Mal approves of what he senses the young girl has in mind.

So does her father. The stiffness tenting the front of his denims jerks lewdly, swelling to even greater length and thickness, and he grinds it up into the simmering, sweat-damp, cleft between his victim's lushly rounded bottom cheeks.

"Hold him for me, Uncle Mal, I wanna suck him," Julie pleads, even as she unsnaps his fly and pulls his dangling penis into view. *The light quivers cobalt, dark as oceanic depths* . . .

"He's hung nice, huh, Erica? No wonder you like having him stick it up you. He ain't as big as *Daddy*," at this she rolls her eyes and winks knowingly, "but I bet he can give you a good fuck, hhhhmnmm?" She toys with the man's limp flesh, and, despite himself, the sensations the young girl's hand arouses as it circles his penis cause the shaft to stiffen slightly. She begins to stroke it, tugging the thick foreskin back-and-forth back-and-forth.

He is half-erect.

But he struggles to free himself from her violation of his privates. He is shocked by the sexual aggressiveness of this *child*, terrified by the taboos it represents . . .

Erica stares, unable to believe the obscene spectacle enfolding before her, trembling with frustrated rage, as the little whore seeks to seduce her as-yet unwilling husband.

Julie begins to fellate him.

He is still caught in the borderline between wakefulness and dream-state. This is all just too *unreal*. Her hot, puckered, lips ovaled around his penis and suckling on his tender flesh prove too excruciatingly pleasurable for his hormones to ignore. His manhood swells within her eager mouth.

His wife is shocked when she sees him start to undulate his hips in mock coital motions, driving his stiff shaft deeper and deeper into Julie's receptive oral orifice and down into her slender throat.

While his daughter fondles and fellates the captive husband, Snuff binds Erica's wrists behind her back with a short hank of clothesline, yanking the knot painfully tight, the cord biting into the sensitive flesh—chafing with her slightest motion.

Mal binds Byron likewise while Julie gives him head.

When she has Byron nice and hard from sucking, Julie stands up and lifts the hem of her skirt up around her waist.

She wears no panties: her father and Mal forbid it.

"Heh, Sailor, you hot for young pussy? You get off on tight young teenage cunt?" she asks him, winking suggestively, then puckering her lips in a feigned pouting kiss.

She fondles herself while she stands above him.

Her legs straddle his face, and she lowers herself, squatting until her privates are squashed against his nose and mouth, nearly suffocating him in her twin, steamy, musk-scented furrows of vulva and anus. And she ruts herself on him like some young bitch in heat.

Snuff has closed his switchblade, and is using the handle as a surrogate dildo to violate Erica's slick and slithery vagina.

But the short shaft barely penetrates her heated vault, and Snuff scans the confines of the tent for some more suitable appliance . . .

"Holy Shit, Mal! *This* ain't big *enough*—I *do* think she wants sumthin' b*igger* up there in 'er!" Snuff chuckles lewdly.

He spots one of those chrome flashlights, the kind with the long, narrow, handle that holds four "D" batteries.

"Heh, Julie, get that thing there for me, willya," he asks, pointing to the object lying on the crinkled plastic flooring.

She picks it up, dutifully, and hands it to her father.

"It ain't no damn VIBRATOR, but it should do . . ."

She watches, pupils lust-dilated, as he forces Erica down into an obscene squatting posture—similar to her own, but infinitely more uncomfortable as her hands are still cinched behind her back. He rams the cold, unyielding, chromed handle up into her squishy, heated, depths . . .

The girl groans in pain and humiliation, struggling to free herself, but he is far too strong and too determined for her to escape its brutal penetration.

"FUCK HER WITH IT, DADDY! FUCK HER WITH IT! FUCK HER UP REAL GOOD!" Julie moans.

She raises the hem of her skirt and points to her own widespread slit, parting the soft, pink, folds slightly to expose the entrance to the dark, coral-corrugated, sex-tunnel to Byron's captive gaze.

"You wanna stick THIS—" she reaches down with her free hand, yanks on his penis and squeezes it for emphasis, "—in HERE . . . ?"

She doesn't expect an answer from the gagged man.

"Well, PISS ON YOU, you dirty fucker!"

And she does. All over his upturned face. Drowning him in a hissing, steamy, stream of urine.

Mal and Snuff both laugh in appreciation of her sick humor.

Snuff has already tired of his current game, and throws the bound girl face-downwards on the sleeping bag. He tugs her up onto her hands and knees, kneeling like a slave-submissive, with her plump, curvaceous, buttocks thrust lewdly, temptingly, into the air.

Snuff rams the ridged metal barrel up Erica's vagina from the rear, raping her with it doggie-style.

Julie unzips her father's pants, and pulls them down around his ankles. She begins massaging his huge erection with her left hand, while she continues masturbating the humiliated Byron with her outstretched right.

The posture Erica has been forced to assume is most suggestive. It doesn't fail to fill Julie's wicked little mind with wild ideas.

"You always *do her straight*? Or do you ever *fuck her in the ass* . . . ? Huh?" She queries, teasing the embarrassed husband's unwillingly inflamed libido. "Oooohhh. You *want* to, huh, but she won't *let* you? Is *that* it . . . ?

"I like it *that way*. So I *know* she would . . . Daddy likes to fuck me that way. So does Uncle Mal. Says I feel like I'm even younger, when he *does it to me that way*. He says it's a whole lot tighter, doin' a girl like that, up the ass . . . and Mal likes 'em *young . . . real young*.

He likes to make 'em hurt. He likes to make 'em *bleed . . .*"

The man's face flushes beet red.

"Nnnnmmmpppphhhhhh." he mumbles.

"Well, *now's your chance . . .*" she whispers.

He doesn't budge. He only glares.

"Go ahead and *do it to her in the ass.*" Julie commands, savoring his fear and obvious revulsion at the unnatural act she now suggests.

"I heard you receive an invitation," Mal says. "It is not at all. Polite. To refuse. A young. Lady's request." He slices a quarter-inch deep crescent into Byron's throat. "Do it. Now."

He drags the bound man over to where his wife kneels, the wiry, bearded, sadist still gleefully engaged in violating her vagina with the flashlight's cold, chrome, shaft.

"Get that thing out of her, Snuff. What this hot little bitch needs is a stiff cock."

Snuff complies, and Mal, knife at the man's throat, forces Byron to mount his wife dog-fashion.

Julie is eager to help. She reaches down between them and, clenching the man's penis in her hand, inserts the tip of its flared knob into Erica's tiny, puckered, rectum.

Mal shoves the man forward, impaling his hard cock in his wife's lewdly exposed, and obviously *virgin*, behind.

Erica writhes in pain, struggling futilely.

Mal grasps the husband by the hips, and begins rocking him back-and-forth back-and-forth in forced coital thrusts.

The man tenses, seeming as though he is nearing orgasm.

Julie whispers in her father's ear. He hands her his switchblade. She flicks the button, and the blade whips open with a resounding *click.*

She grasps Byron's penis by the base, her hand tickled by his wiry thatch of hair. The knife *swishes* through the air and severs the stiffened shaft, its head still lodged in his wife's backside, while blood jets from the stump instead of semen . . .

Byron collapses on the rumpled sleeping bag, writhing in agony. He is screaming. But his screams are almost silent. The gag stifles them.

Mal is masturbating Himself as He watches. So is Snuff. Snuff grasps Erica by her hair, tugging brutally, forcing her head back so

When she comes to, Snuff is still hunched over her back, shagging the plump swell of her buttocks, pumping fiercely into her wide-stretched sphincter, her nether tunnel shrieking with the flamethrower agony of her sadistic impalement.

Julie is lying back on the sleeping bags, her legs thrown wide, her knees crooked and resting on her shoulders, she rocks back with her hips slightly raised, anally masturbating with the fleshy dildo of Byron's severed penis. She is moaning obscenities, and babbling: "A new cock for my collection! Oohhhhh, Uncle Mal'll fix it up for me! Oooooohhhhh, yessss! Save it for me in a jar! Cast a mold from it—make me another latex prick! I'll let you watch me whenever I use it—you and Daddy can use it on me anytime you want!"

The ex-Zodiac clambers over, straddling the young girl's face, and flops his now-flaccid, blood-and shit-stained, penis into the "O" of her eagerly opened mouth. She coaxes it back to erection with her well-practiced lips and tongue; then, fully hard, He plunges forward, driving the blue-veined shaft deep down her receptive throat . . .

An eternal instant of torment passes in Erica's suffering, and then the wiry, bearded, man shudders; he lets out a bestial, keening, howl and his semen erupts into Erica's backside.

Then, still lust-inflamed and juttingly erect, he sprawls back on the tent-floor, pulling Erica astride his loins, forcing her into a squatting posture, his huge penis now probing against the furry V of her soft, tapered, belly, now nuzzling between the hairy lips of her vulva, rubbing against her clitoris, now entering her vagina, still lubricated with her husband's semen. She reels drunkenly as he grasps her hips, bounces her on his lap, and moves the moaning woman up and down on his shaft, puppetlike, helplessly compliant to his Hellish whims.

The sight of Erica's innocently wriggling buttocks as she squats astride His henchman's bucking thighs and upward-pummeling groin spurs Maldoror to contemplate what further indignities He may inflict upon the captive wife—her naked, mutilated, husband writhing in agony nearby, a gagged and bound witness to her rape and degradation, unable to help either her or himself . . .

Meanwhile, Julie has pulled Byron's severed sex organ out of her behind and has carefully wrapped it in a scrap torn from Erica's pajamas.

. . . Mal crouches behind the father-daughter coupling, grasping her conelike titties in his huge, brutal, hands, savagely mauling them, and slapping at her asscheeks . . . Julie orgasms again and again, insane with the shrieking pain-pleasure of her unnatural, incestuous, impalement, fingering her hot little cunt and rubbing her clit as her father buggers her . . . And then Snuff is groaning, shuddering, as he pumps the volcanic rush of pentup sperm into his thirteen-year-old daughter's ass . . . as he has done to her, with varying degrees of penetration, since she was only eight . . .

And Mal has done since she was six . . .

+   +   +

Julie straddles Byron once more, squatting.

"FUCK YOU, SHITHEAD!" she snarls. Her voice sounds strained. *and with good reason—*

She evacuates her bowels onto his face and chest.

Then she takes Mal's knife and plunges it up under his breastbone, into his wildly pumping heart . . .

Julie simply can't resist the final putdown: "EAT SHIT and DIE, YOU STUPID YUPPIE BASTARD!"

+   +   +

The collapsible trenching shovel from Snuff's suitcase quickly excavates a foot-and-a-half-deep grave in the soft, loam-rich, deep-black earth. He piles the uprooted topsoil onto the outspread nylon of the severed and dismantled tent, so as not to disturb the surrounding forest mulch.

Mal hacks off Byron's head, and Julie chops off his fingers, laying the grisly remnants on another section of the tent.

The two men toss Byron's mutilated body into the shallow pit, along with the aluminum tent poles and other assorted refuse. Then cover the remains with the shroud of slashed air mattresses. Just enough topsoil is shoveled back into the hole, smoothing it to ground level. They scatter pine needles and surface mulch across the backfilled grave, blending it with the landscape.

The balance of uprooted earth they dump into a nearby gully. Several hundred feet away, another hole is dug, this time, deep and narrow. Byron's head and fingers are dropped to the bottom, covered with the shredded tent, then buried. The excess soil is scattered inconspicuously nearby.

"Those goosedown sleeping bags are too messy to slash and trash what with all those feathers, and they are too bulky to bury. Dump them in the trunk, along with the girl," Mal orders.

"Tight fit," Snuff says, "but so is she . . ."

+   +   +

The Taurus and the Acura pull out of the deserted campsite, following the endless highway north, crossing and crisscrossing the geography of America, haunting the isolated backroads of rural Heartland, scouting the National and State Parks for prey, painting the small towns and the big cities red in the wake of their odyssey of sex and slaughter . . .

THE

FORBIDDEN
GOSPELS OF
MAN-CRUEL

VOLUME II

LET IT ROT

by Don Webb

"So much for his encore," Boner says, unsmiling.

Jasmine Sailing asked me to write the introduction to this book—the book which answers the question, "What was Mr. Hyde's evil twin like?" Now it's not generally known but Robert Louis Stevenson wrote a brief short story on his deathbed that suggested Mr. Hyde mainlined Dr. Jekyll's blue serum and became for one night an even worse creature, who stood to Hyde as Hyde stood to Jekyll. That story was consigned to the flames by Stevenson's heirs, only to manifest in this little book. I don't know how to write an introduction, because I only write fiction, so I thought I would tell you about the night Randy Chandler and t. Winter-Damon found out about the color *blue*.

The Octave Doctor sent me to watch the Initiation of t. Winter-Damon and Randy Chandler. It was in a BBQ joint in El Paso, Texas. Right on the border of Texas and New Mexico. You could watch a hill that was in Texas, New Mexico, and Mexico. It had a statue of Jesus on top of it. Mexican bandits liked to rob American tourists who would climb to the top of the hill, as they spiraled around they would leave US jurisdiction, and the bandits would rob them while US marshals looked on. It was their little jest.

You can do special things at Borders, it's one of the cracks that Reality comes in by to this unreal world.

I saw two clean-cut young men having a drink at the bar. Not Damon and Chandler (whom I have never met) I decided, but probably some kind of mirror—some brighter reflection of the two fictioneers.

The one young man said to the other, "I think I've got the symbolism of the American flag figured out. You see the white's for purity and the red is for courage, being all the blood's that's been shed for democracy."

"What's the blue for?" asked the other young man.

"It's for the Holy Ghost."

I wandered through the bar. It had begun to lightning outside. God I love El Paso, all burned-out volcanoes and weathered terrain as though you are on some other planet far, far away and immeasurably *older* than Earth. I spotted my old friend Mary Denning, who used to run the Gift of the Magi bar in Austin. I sat down beside her and watched her knit. I told her why I was here.

"The men you want," she said, "are over there. They are learning a lesson about the Imagination."

I walked over. There were two serious looking guys listening to this cadaverous seedy fellow, whose teeth I noticed (with some disgust) were light blue. He was saying, "I'm the Bachelor of Battles, PhD of Death, & I can show you a fine fucking time if you possess the proper mettle."

I walked back to Mary and asked, "So what are they learning from Professor Punk over there?"

"They're learning the first step in making the Philosopher's Stone. The Stone isn't made of any physical thing, not out of vulgar mercury or cinnabar or sulfur—it's made out of Imagination, and the first step is to close off the Imagination and let it rot. The first step is called *negrido* and when the Imagination has turned into a mass of a million black maggots fucking and eating each other, it is ready to change. To go up, the first place you have to go is down."

I thought about Chandler and how I enjoyed his *Bone Chilling Tales* that used to publish people like Janet Fox and A.R. Morlan and me or his imaginary novel *Horros*, parts of which live in this prose, and I thought about t. Winter-Damon with his Billy Blake prosy and his surreal collages, and I decided I didn't want to know what kind of writings they would produce if they let their imaginations rot. The horror, the darkness, the violent sex of that universe more real than this one, would be a terrible thing, a book not merely of darkness but of anti-light more to be dreaded than the fabled *Necronomicon*. Such a Book would be Forbidden by all authorities, burned by right thinking people, and shunned even by the decadents that over-populate this apocalyptic time.

The imaginary BBQ joint began to shift at this time (I told you I write nothing but fiction. There is no Randy Chandler and no t. Winter-Damon, there is no Jasmine Sailing, there is no Don Webb, no places called Texas or Mexico). Cracks began to appear in the floor, the walls, the tables, the *people*, and thousands of roaches came scurrying through, over everything, eating everything until Darkness alone remained, and in the Darkness was a single star of anti-light that began to form these pages . . .

Don Webb
    early August 1997
    (east of Limbo)

HITCHER'S JUDGEMENT

Bobbie Wainwright couldn't believe his luck. He'd only been standing by the roadside on busy 22nd Street for maybe ten minutes with his thumb stuck out, and bang, there was this car nosing off the blacktop and onto the dirt shoulder, kicking on its brakes, raising a small cloud of dust and skittering gravel.

Waytogo.

A man's broad hand and hairy arm beckoned briskly to him out the passenger-side window. The body language was self-evident—hurry up, kid, don't dawdle, catch this falling star and put it in your pocket. Pronto. We haven't got all day to waste on stragglers . . .

Bobbie wasn't about to blow a chance like this. No way, dude. Not with storm clouds rolling in and the late-autumn air far too crisp for his t-shirt and denim-jacketed chest. He could already feel phantom twinges of pleurisy needling deep within his lungs and back. He wasn't born yesterday. He had enough sense to know when a hard rain was gonna fall. Damn straight. Fuckin' A! He beelined it for the promised shelter of the road-battered and carwashchallenged hulk of the waiting, aged Chevy sedan.

He grabbed the passenger-rear handle, swung open the heavy door, groaning in a tortured protest of metal on metal, hopped inside, and slammed it shut.

The close confines of the car reeked with the overwhelming stink of stale sweat and cigarettes and beer.

The car rocketed into the traffic flow with a shriek of squealing tires and a coarse growl of crunching gravel. Bobbie's nose caught the acrid pungency of burning rubber. His eyes bugged as the car slamdanced its way between moving cars and trucks, veering viciously from one lane to another like an angry, ravenous pitbull chasing down a fleeing litter of panicked kittens. The burly driver was hunched over the wheel, ramming it first this way, then that, as he muttered incoherent obscenities.

The man in the passenger seat chuckled like a merry maniac, slapping his thighs, whooping and guffawing at some secret jest.

Bobbie's eyes drifted down to the top of the nearby doorframe, something striking him as vaguely amiss but not quite filtering through at first glimpse, then noted the total lack of either a door-latch button or even the protruding stalk of bare, threaded shaft. His eyes drifted lower and found the door handle was also absent. He shot a glance at the righthand door panel and noted with a sudden sinking feeling in the pit of his stomach that it, too, was devoid of either handle or latch-button.

Bobbie began a rapid reassessment of his current situation, and realized this ride may not have been an act of providence, after all.

The passenger turned around, staring at Bobbie over his shoulder. He chortled drunkenly, his soured, beery breath gushing out like a slap right in the boy's face, making his gut clench up, in pre-puke mode. The man was grizzled, unshaven, bleary-eyed. He pointed at he driver. "He don't know howta use the goddamn brake. He jus' knows howta use the friggin' *accelerator!*" He brayed and cackled insanely, spraying droplets of foul spittle with every new outburst.

"I uhhh . . . I think I want out, here . . ." mumbled a now terrified Bobbie. He figured they must be going seventy-five in what was an often a risky fifty-per limit, considering the congested driving conditions. "I uhhh . . . want . . . OUT! P-please!" he stammered.

But the men totally ignored him. The driver veering wildly through the traffic. His companion laughing and repeating over and over and over—"He don't know howta use the goddamn brake . . ." like some madhouse mantra.

When Bobbie began to pound at the door and started yelling for help, the brawny passenger hauled off and gave him a skull-reeling backhand slap that felt like a sledgehammer blow to the cranium. Despite Bobbie's many past street-scuffles, he'd never been hit with a haymaker punch that came close to packing the wallop of this man's almost-casual slap.

It knocked him unconscious for several minutes.

He came to, shaking his head and spitting blood from his nowsplit lip.

Bobbie sputtered rudely awake with something warm and wet splashing his face. He lay in the dust by the side of the car, parked on a desolate dirt road in the desert. He blinked and stared up groggily. Both men loomed over him, their pants unzipped, their huge, filthy horse-like penises spurting streams of stinking beery piss in his face. His own Levis and undershorts were tugged down around his ankles, hobbling him. They'd stripped off his jacket and t-shirt, leaving him bare from the waist up, as well.

An open toolbox rested on the ground beside him.

One man held a pair of tinsnips, the other clutched a hammer and chisel.

"Don't worry none, Boytail, we ain't no queers 'r nuthin'," the once-silent driver growled with a dirty chuckle. "Equal opportunity, Punkie . . . We gonna fix you up real good. Cut you a nice lil' slit down there so's we can do ya *all three ways*, jus' like we do them sweet young *girlies* we play our special games with . . ."

& BEHOLD,
THE GREAT BEAST, LOTAN . . .

(a passion play for resurgent atavists)

POV: Pan IN TIGHT: SHARPEN FOCUS (x 1):

Interior of office suite. Luxurious appointments. Motifs in eclectic mix of Sino-Nipponese. Hand scrolls of sparse brush strokes. Writhing forms of soapstone carvings & polished curves of porcelain sprout everywhere. Translucent window/wall of outward-mirrored glass, overlooking kinetic anthill expanse of Hong Kong harbor . . .

COLOR OUT OF SYNC:

No red. No gold. No black. Window's tinted inner surface bleeding a wash of fluid ultramarine, shifting subtly, suggesting systolic rhythmings of veins or deepsea grotto's tidal pulse. All within peripherals bone white or blue—phasing from midnight shade to palest shimmerings of sky . . .

POV: TIGHTEN FIELD: SCAN INTERIOR ON MAGNIFICATION (x 15):

Details of figurals a riot of Tao-gone-madhouse . . . Yin & Yang bizarreries inverting/subverting/perverting spiritflow into demonic twists of torment . . . beasts both mythical & representative coupling dementedly with intertwining humans running the gamut of age & physique & sex . . . *suckling babes/sumos/& toothless hags* . . . ritual sacrifice gone *snuff* . . .

POV: DILATE FIELD: TRACK TO ROOM CENTER: ROTATE OPTICAL FULL AXIS (x 5):

Lone man sits at desk, staring at (unseen) object on desktop . . . Tall, fragile, almost-skeletal in stature . . . Whites of eyes, yellowed, scrimshawed with webwork of bloody veins . . . Irises seemingly dissolved in black pools of pupil . . . Oriental . . . Characteristic epicanthic folds facial structure . . . Old. Wrinkled as a salted prune . . . Perhaps even *ancient* . . . ? Forked beard & trailing mustache, midriff-length, wispish as a catfish's whiskers, white as winter snow on rushes . . .

Man (he is known as *"Lotan"* to his followers . . .) sucks occasionally on long slender pipe, scrimshawed intricately as his eyeballs, frenzied danse macabre swirls across its surface . . . thin, pallid, lips like waterlogged wounds suckle at its stem . . . smoke drifts in phantom arabesques, coiling & writhing, serpentlike . . .

Desk pedestal of ivory (?) bone (?) intricately carved as a five-clawed *fu-ts'-ang lung wang* (imperial sigil dragon guard of vast wealth hidden in waters' depths). Desktop of cobalt blue glass.

Scythe-like nails tip bony fingers, cradle polished human skull resting on table's surface . . . an *artifact* of incalculable rarity value . . . of *inhuman evil*: rumored cranium of the notorious Gilles de Rais, 15th century baron, Marshall of France, & child-murderer extraordinaire . . .

POV: TIGHTEN FIELD: CLOSE-UP: MAGNIFICATION (x 25):

The hollow sockets of the eyeholes taunt the jaded libido as might a peepshow screen . . . a hologram-like image fills the deathshead with pseudolife:

A battlefield at the edge of the world where a bloodmoon looms over the chaotic clash of opposing armies & the screams of fallen soldiers are hymns to the merciless gods of war—This is the place where Hell invades Earth, marked by human spillage exploding entrails sacrificial cannonfodder smoldering gore headless torsos . . .

The sky above them boils with storm . . .

& the line wavers, ever so slightly, yet indeed noticeable to those observers who witness in eternal vigil, standing their appointed watches with a devotion that transcends that which is commonly termed "religious"—bearing witness to those revelations *that transpire within the grander scheme of life & & . . .*

The plain *of (Ragnarok) Vidrigr (?) (Armageddon) Megiddo (?) Neon Babylon (?) . . .*

The plain *of* nahui-ollin's *catastrophe (?), when the fifth sun is swallowed by the rift of shifting earth, when the great dark releases the* tzitzimime *from the white house of the west . . . the Lords of the*

Night *slaying all of humankind . . . to begin the world's next cycle . . .*

    & the line wavers, ever so slightly . . .

The armies *of Surtr & Muspell's Sons & Loki & the Sons of Hel & Hrymr with Frost Giant Legions & Fenris Wolf press forward . . .*

    & *the line wavers, ever so slightly . . .*

The armies *of the Antichrist press forward . . .*

    & the line wavers . . .

The armies *of tzitzimime, the skeleton monsters, the undead press forward . . .*

The time *of Nidhoggr (?) . . . of the beast that rises from the sea, with seven heads & ten horns, & upon his horns ten crowns, & upon his heads the name of blasphemy (?) . . . of Leviathan (?) . . . of Tiamat (?) . . . of Quetzalcoatl (?) . . .*

    & the line wavers . . .

POV: DILATE FIELD (x 5):

    & the scythe-like nails & the bony fingers of Lotan tremble with excitement . . .

DISSOLVE to:

POV: PAN IN TIGHT: SHARPEN FOCUS (x 1):

Interior of office suite. Lotan's sanctum sanctorum. The old man's red-webworked eyes still stare into the hollow eye sockets of the skull . . .

An area of wall at his extreme left swings outward. Silently. The brush-stroke painting of "Four Maidens Ravished by Bull & Dogs" is a sick masterpiece of twisted Taoist erotica . . . & a cleverly concealed doorway into an adjacent room

(or perhaps into some twilight-blue zone of interface with the opened gates of a very special Hell . . .)

A man enters through the doorway. If he is a man at all (?) He is a brawny giant with huge, corded, muscular arms, & a belly like a wine barrel of blubbery flesh overspilling the top of his white loin clout, & great pendulous slabs of breasts that wobble as he moves— the gold rings that pierce their nipples jiggling, catching flashes of the ultramarine blue ambient light on the tight, polished, curve of metal. Glinting. Sparkling. With a an eerie, deathcold fire . . .

If he was once truly human the resemblance has long since been *transformed* into the horribly mutilated mask of a leering demon. A BLUE DEMON: his skin is deathly cyanic blue. Gold rings pierce his lips, his nostrils, his cheeks, his eyelids, & even his tongue. & his face is a slashed ruin of tattered meat that would shame a Hun's scarred features as the angelic features of a choirboy . . .

"The boy*th* are rea*th*y for you, Ma*th*ter." The giant announces, bowing steeply in reverence as he does so. The rings pierced through his tongue & lips jingle as he speaks.

The old man draws himself up like a preying mantis on his spindly, almost-insectile, legs. The illusion is further suggested by the way that he holds his hands folded before his chest, his fingers lethal claws despite their seeming fragility . . .

"I shall do you honor, O Venerable Head of Bone—" Lotan speaks whisperingly to the skull upon the table as he rises.

He tips his head & torso ever so slightly, bowing to it with undisguised reverence . . .

"This time, Hsuan Chieh, with *delicate* strokes, create a masterpiece of subtle & lingering beauty—make their exquisite songs of torment & death an infinity for my enlightenment . . ."

He shuffles toward the opened threshold with mincing, crippled-insect steps.

He enters the door.

DISSOLVE to:

POV: PAN in TIGHT: SHARPEN FOCUS (x 1):
Interior of room. No doors. No windows. That the eye can discern. All four walls & floor & ceiling padded. Fitted with the finest acoustics that technology can supply & *money* can obtain. Sound *whispers* here, as if in reverence or terror, sucked greedily into the unremitting expanse of dead-white muffling surface. The air is cool & sterile & hermetic, tinged with the apprehensive scent of alcohol & antiseptic, keying memories of doctors' offices & surgeons' operating rooms. Ceiling-recessed lamps spill a flood of ultramarine illumination down upon its occupants. & the fittings of a secret abattoir:
POV: TIGHTEN FIELD: SCAN INTERIOR on MAGNIFICATION (x 5):

A throne of bonewhite marble overlooks the remainder of the room. Its gracefully towering structure is alive with the sculptured forms of naked, writhing, shrieking cherubim.

A long, narrow, table of tubular stainless steel & cobalt blue glass stands just before the throne—parallel, & spanning halfway across the room's width. Its dark blue surface glitters with a profusion of scalpels & bone-saws & tongs & exploratory probes, all of lovingly polished surgical steel. Glistening strands of barbed wire. & there are whips & flails of every conceivable configuration—thonged & handled all of glossy midnight black.

At either extreme of the table are situated dentists' chairs, perpendicular to the throne & bristling with the spiderleg array of drills & bits & curved mirrors bright with the promise of potential pain. Echoed in the soft, supple, leather of their upholstering . . .

But the center of the room. *Ooohhh! Merciful Jesus! If there were divine mercy in this world, surely, no such abomination could exist!* But there is no mercy here, in the center of this Hell on Earth. There is only pain & blasphemy & terror. There is only *the* Palette of the Perverse: a vaguely heart-shaped trough with a raised lip some several inches deep; its diameter perhaps eighteen feet at the broadest spot, wide enough to accommodate the cluster of meat-hooks & gaffs & chain-&-pulley rigs sprouting from the ceiling above . . .

. . . & a large drain hole in the trough's bottom, near center of the right "lobe" of the "heart"—just where the artist's thumb would be inserted, were this the mundane, far smaller, palette of convention . . .

But this is the palette of the savaged flesh & senses, not some mere board from which the simple pigments are selected!

Lotan admires the raw stock from which his servant, Hsuan Chieh, will strive to create his masterpiece of "subtle & lingering beauty":

Two small boys, naked & chained spread-eagle by the manacles of surgical steel clamped around their wrists & ankles.

"Noti*th* the delightful contra*tht* of *th*kin tone*th*, Ma*th*ter—" Hsuan Chieh comments, pointing to the helpless children.

"The very fine*tht* that the black market ha*th* to offer—*th*ee the cream white of the Cauca*th*ian boy'*th* pale fi*th*-belly fle*th*, *th*ee the tawny yellow ochre of the Chine*the* boy'*th* *th*kin, both *th*aded, altered *th*o beautifully with the cold blue light *th*pilling acro*th* them . . ."

& in the background, against the farthest wall, rise tier-upon-tier of glass shelves lined with hundreds (?) of small, fragile, carefully cleaned-&-polished skulls—

nameless memories of Lotan's slaughtered innocents . . .

DISSOLVE to:

POV: PAN IN TIGHT: SHARPEN FOCUS: SLOW SCAN: (x 1):
Interior of room.

No doors. No windows. All padded in dead white.

The air is cool & sterile & hermetic. Pervading scent of alcohol antiseptic &—

BLOOD.

Fresh & saline & coppery in the nostrils; keying images of desolate beaches & dead things washed up along the strands of shore, corrupted flesh & bare-picked bones & tiny, insectile, life that feeds . . .

Sound *whispers* here, as if in reverence or terror. Or some soul-sick, sad, sadistic mingling of both—

Sound *clings* here, speaking its secrets to those who would long to *listen*, far after the last echoes have been sucked into the thirsty silence of acoustics . . .

Yes. There are those here for whom the silence of the slaughtered still eagerly speaks. Those who feed on PAIN. Those who thirst for the shriek the whine the whimper of savaged torment. The Sweet Wine of Suffering.

Lotan & his servant, Hsuan Chieh.

They savor the last fading *frissons* of their masterpiece of subtle & lingering beauty. A mad feast of fleeting *sensations* to delight the most *demanding* of depraved dilettantes. Baudelaire. Lautréamont. de Sade. de Rais. Surely tears of jealous joy would have welled from their merciless eyes at the indignity of such perfection—the exquisite songs of torment & death, coaxed from once-human flesh with strokes of such *delicacy* & *gentleness* that even the most hideous of their crimes is *transmuted* into a symphony of sensuous, crystal chords, an evanescent psychic sculpture of such vibrant line & substance so as to sicken the stomach with a haunting quiver of purest fright & empathic suffering & set the mind aflame with the fierce, frenzied, fires of Hell . . .

A SYMPHONY BEYOND THE BLUE EXTREME . . .

Hsuan Chieh's cyanic flesh trembles with the echoes of his ecstasy.

The tattered ruin of his face betrays the leering grins of countless scars, each a tiny mouth that gapes & gasps with the intensity of his demented pleasure.

His face & hands are stained black with the blue-lit blood of slain innocents.

The bright cold metal of the rings that pierce his nipples, his scrotum, his lips, eyelids, & tongue jingle & clink & chime their melodious tribute to torment as he lifts the glittering blue-lit blade of the filleting knife to his mouth & licks it slowly, tauntingly, tasting the smeared droplets of still-warm blood upon its razor-edged steel . . .

The Palette of the Perverse is ankle-deep in the crimson pigment of opened arteries & severed veins, all transformed *black* in the pure BLUE light of Hell flickering throughout the chamber of the abattoir . . .

Above, the cluster of meat-hooks & gaffs & chain-&-pulley rigs glisten steely blue . . .

& two new trophies will be added to Lotan's crowded shelves . . .

DISSOLVE to:

POV: TRACK to ROOM CENTER: PAN in TIGHT: ACTIVATE OLFACTORY LINK-UP with SENSORS: SHARPEN FOCUS: (x 15):

Pungent smoke swirls from the pipe hand-carved from the thigh-bone of a human infant, white tendrils caressing Lotan's expressionless face & clinging to his trailing, catfish-like, whiskers as he blinks his burning eyes & watches the blue-black storm clouds boiling in from the South China Sea. A sickly smile contorts his face . . .

. . . *Even with their orbiting weather satellites & their*

sophisticated computer tracking system, the world's meteorologists will not be able to explain the origin of this monstrous typhoon & will label it a "freak storm".

Lotan alone knows the dark origins of this fury . . .

He tenderly touches his fingers to the polished skull on the desktop of cobalt-blue glass. "It comes, O Venerable Head of Bone," he whispers in a rasping, insectile, voice. "It comes with the storm & nothing upon this *plane of battle* can stop it . . ."

His trembling left hand moves toward the far periphery of the camera's watchful eye . . .

POV: TRACK with LOTAN'S HAND: (x 15):

His fingertips caress a single set-piece selected from among the rank-&-file of thirty-two . . . *(is it not strange that their traditional number corresponds to the configuration of human teeth . . . ?)* . . . the effigy of a hideous & grotesque water-demon . . . from among its fellow figures . . . a chess set intricately carved from the bones of Lotan's slaughtered innocents (as is the board) . . . yet another perverse masterpiece created to his exacting specifications—hand-carved by the same secret cult of adepts who birthed his pipes & numerous fetishes of power from the raw stock of their components . . . adepts dually trained as shamans in the ancient Tibetan way of Bon & as Tantric sorcerers of the Vamacara path—the most dangerous path to enlightenment—. . . each of the thirty-two figures representing the *Kar-ma Sgar-bris* images of angry deities & the pantheon of demons . . . the former half the pale yellow-white of polished bone, the latter fired in a brilliant blue glaze of magickal synthesis

(sea-sand gathered from near the mouths of the Yangtze & the Huang Ho, perhaps drifted down from their tributaries—the Tibetan 'Bri Chu & Rma Chu; river sand "out of the peacock's mouth," from the Rma-bya Kha-'bab; graveyard clay mixed to slip with water from the brackish lakes of the Byang-thang plateau, remnants of vanished Tethys Sea; peacock-eye malachite ground to dust; & powdered lapis, sacred of the Babylonians, bestowing invulnerability upon the weapons of the ancient kings of Ur, in the East, symbol of heaven, with oil, the pigment ultramarine . . .),

as are the alternating tiles that the form *the plain* of his cosmic playing board . . .

In the choppy waters ten miles out from Hong Kong harbour a huge mako shark shoots through black water, striking what its senses say is small prey, but the shark's primitive guidance system has made a fatal error: what it takes for small prey is but a small appendage of a great beast rising from the uncharted depths of the sea, the likes of which the shark has never before encountered. Temporarily blinded by its own wide-open jaws, the shark doesn't see the gigantic maw of the beast as it hurtles upward & swallows the head of the shark & tears it off with six rows of jagged teeth.

The explosion of blood draws two more makos, their deep blue backs & glistening white bellies slicing through churning waters . . .

The ancient sea god sounds. Breaking its fast of nearly two-thousand solar cyclings, it settles its leviathan's girth on the oozing ocean floor to digest its appetizer & to await further communion with its namesake upon the shore—from the one who summoned it from the collective millennial slumbers of all its seven heads . . .

The storm lashes Hong Kong, driving the human ants deeper into their neon anthills & deeper into their nightmares. At the end of a dangerous alley between the towering ferro-concrete walls of two skyscrapers an iron door appears out of the darkness, & slowly swings open with a deep-throated groan. A rectangular slice of flickering blue light at the end of the tunnel of rainy darkness.

The screaming can be heard above the din of the storm . . .

DISSOLVE to:

POV: HOLD at ROOM CENTER: DILATE FIELD of FOCUS: (x 5):

Lotan's laughter is the sound of a thousand insects scrabbling up his dry throat. A curl of smoke lingers in the hollow of the baby-bone pipe. The sacred skull of the child-murdering necrophile & martyr-turned-monster Gilles de Rais grins at its own reflection in the plane of cobalt-blue glass . . .

DISSOLVE to:

The ancient one at the bottom of the sea receives the screaming . . .

. . . & the laughter—

feeding on both & shaking off the last lingering effects of its eon-spanning aestivation in the long afternoon that has been the Christian epoch . . .

& the beast shudders with the pleasure of the approaching twilight of the Crucified One for he *is* Lotan the Primeval Serpent, the Crooked Serpent, the Close-coiling One of Seven Heads whose awaking shall signal the twilight of the Pale Gods & Guardians of Order . . .

DISSOLVE to:

POV: SLOW SCAN: DILATE OPTICAL FIELD: SHARPEN FOCUS: (x 1):

Interior of room. No doors. No windows. That the eye can discern. All four walls & floor & ceiling padded . . .

Sound sighs & *whispers* here, as if in reverence or terror . . .

The air is cool & sterile & hermetic, tinged with the apprehensive scent of alcohol & antiseptic . . .

POV: TIGHTEN FIELD: TRACK to FAR END of ROOM on MAGNIFICATION (x 10):

Light dances blue upon the silver rings that pierce his flesh. The air seems razor-edged & swollen with a clinking & jingling like tiny bells. The ragged 'lips' of his uncounted scars open & close open & close as if in the silent laughter of a gathered host of miniature demon-mouths.

The filleting knife's blade twitches with flickering blue luminescence as he peels away the pallid-yellow, thin, rind of translucent skin from the muscle & tendon & all that lay beneath . . .

The young boy, a lad of Chinese ancestry, a boy bought or bartered or stolen from the swarming, human ants, the san-pan folk of Hong Kong's harbor, shrieks as Hsuan Chieh strips the parchment from the warm, bloody, still-thrashing meat. Tears of blood trickle down the taut-stretched cheeks outstretched, drip drip dripping into the shallow Well of the *Palette of the Perverse*. A frail puppet of pain among the clustered meat-hooks & gaffs & chain-&-pulley rigs sprouting from above.

Wisps of smoke swirl in the slow drafts of the room's ventilation system, & Lotan's long, bony, fingers tremble as he cradles the slender pipestem & draws deep the Smoke of Dreams conjured forth from the tiny, carven, bowl.

His laughter is not silent. It is brittle. & without a hint of human mirth.

It is the mirth of demons—chill & fragile & sharp as thorns of ice . . .

& his aged loins his withered loins his loins like the wrinkled flesh of salted plums tremble the shivering of birch leaves in an ancient haunted forest, & the seedpearls the Pearls of the Philosopher patter as the hint of winter's rain into the swirling waters black with blood . . . the ultimate yang-essence conjured (*for what unutterable purpose* . . . ?) in rituals beyond the comprehension of the sane . . .

DISSOLVE to:

He pulls deep. Savors the Smoke of Dreams. Inhales. Exhales. His thin lips part, relinquishing the stem of his baby-bone pipe for a moment or an eternity of contemplation . . .

His long, forked, beard & trailing whiskers tremble with the dry, reedy, whisper of his chill laughter . . . His laughter is the wind stirring the snow-tipped rushes above rippled waters deep & dark & unfathomable; an ancient river fed by subterranean springs whose bed neither human mind nor human hand can ever touch, though human skulls stare upward, hollow-eyed, & untold human bones poke through its muck & silt like strands of straw through a well-worn sleeping mat, & within this timeless River of Desolation lie treasures & wealth beyond imagination, & above the distorted mirror of its surface huge dragonflies of glistening cobalt swirl on iridescent sapphire wings, & the sky is an azure so intense it sears the retinas & sears the soul . . .

Wisps of the Smoke of Dreams coil & flutter, stirred by the draft of his exhaled breath . . .

The skull of the Gilles de Rais (the true Bluebeard?) stands on the table of cobalt glass & the dragon carved of foam-white bone . . .

Its hollow eyes see many things, many wonders great & small

. . . things trapped in Time & things that are not of the true-blue substance of its web . . . things of *this* world & things from dark worlds beyond the grave . . .

Wisps of the Smoke of Dreams coil & flutter, forming dragonwraiths that coil & writhe & hiss . . .

Or is it only the chill gusts of Lotan's laughter, that animate them, that stir their forms to life . . . ?

Four cobalt-blue dragonflies soar above the skull, gyring in the writhing wraiths of smoke . . .

Another balances on the tip of the scythe-like nail of one tapered, bony, finger . . .

Once more, he sucks upon his carved pipestem . . .

Whites of eyes, yellowed, scrimshawed with webwork of bloody veins . . . Irises seemingly dissolved in black pools of pupil . . .

Inhale.

Exhale.

They muse the magick of hidden correspondences . . .

His laugh fills the blue-lit room with the dark joy of timeless wisdom & the perfection of his perfidy . . .

Inhale.

Exhale.

Dragonwraithes of Dreamsmoke coil & writhe & hiss . . .

DISSOLVE to SWIRLING MISTS of BLUE

& To Him was Given The Key of The Bottomless Pit . . .

IN THE WAR ROOM . . . THIS NEW WAR ROOM CONJURED IN THE WAKE THOSE FIRST TSUNAMI WAVES OF FUTURE SHOCK . . . the techno wizards of the notorious *Esoteric Order of the Severed Ones of the Black Lotus of Mara & the Asuras* keep watch upon the Watchers & the watched . . .

(Their order is a syncretic union of the extremists & "dark" followers of various Buddhist & Taoist sects: the exiled Tibetan Dhali "Great Ocean" Lama, the practitioners of the Tibetan *Gcod* "cut off" rite—the night-conjuring of demons in cemeteries & in places where the dead lie exposed—& various perverted Tantric sorcerers & the worshipers of devils & of demons . . .)

This is the Order of the Black Lotus.

This is a world transcending time. A world transcending distance. This world is a ghost world a world of shadows within shadows. A DOOR beyond the world of commonplace existence & the perceived domain of Super Powers. A DOOR between The Third World & The Spirit World, *the underworld of Yomi: the Land of the Dead* . . .

The walls of the sprawling War Room complex are lined with countless monitors, huge rear-projection screens, & banks of CRT terminals & touchpads linked into the braincore of the prototype *Ichiko* AI. The *Ichiko* is the SOTA spawn of the Susanowo think tank, the "black" enclave of expatriate Wang R&D systems savants who disappeared from public scrutiny to continue their controversial experiments into the production of the first true artificial intelligence. In a pique of sardonic wordplay, "Susanowo" took its collective name from that of the wild & arrogant Japanese trickster god who was assigned the role of governing the sea, but, growing tired of his appointed station, sought for himself to share the rule of heaven—

(one of those archetypical ribald anticreators common to the gamut of myth systems, who often, through their wicked schemes & machinations, serve to bring forth a countercreation . . .)

& the enclave's creation was this sentient beast (or godhead?), *Ichiko*, conceived as a medium or oracle through whose inhuman "mouth" the spirits of the living & the dead might speak, sharing the uneasy secrets of the grave & *beyond* . . .

Down the center of the room are mounted the hologram grids, their massive, rectangular, housings of matte-black plexiglas sprouting from the floor & ceiling. Within these housings over a billion kilometers of fiber optic serve to transmit the *visions of Ichiko*, translating them into the seeming substance of three-dimensional imagery, & the evoked illusions of tactile sensation & sound & scent:

A battlefield at the edge of the world where a bloodmoon looms over the chaotic clash of opposing armies & the screams of fallen soldiers are hymns to the merciless gods of war—

The sky above them boils with storm . . .

& the line wavers, ever so slightly . . .

The armies *of Surtr & Muspell's Sons & Loki & the Sons of Hel & Hrymr press forward* . . .

the line wavers ever so slightly . . .

The armies *of the Antichrist press forward* . . .

& the line wavers . . .

The plane *of* nahui-ollin's *catastrophe when The Fifth Sun is swallowed by the rift of shifting earth, when the great dark releases the* tzitzimime *from the white house of the west . . . slaying all of humankind . . . to begin the world's next cycle* . . .

& the sub-micro circuitry of the video cameras the eyes of *Ichiko* monitor & transmit—pirate signals tightbeamed off corporate satellites circling ever circling this globe of earth—on closed & scrambled frequency the watchings of the Watchers the watched:

A room washed in ultramarine-blue light . . .

Lone man sits at desk. Lone man sucks occasionally on long slender pipe, scrimshawed intricately as his eyes with their webwork of bloody veins. Forked beard & trailing mustache, midriff-length, wispish as a catfish's whiskers, white as winter snow on rushes. Scythe-like nails on bony fingers cradle a polished human skull—

cranium of the infamous Gilles de Rais . . .

Second man enters room. A man (?) or a BLUE DEMON (?). A brawny giant with huge, corded, arms, & a belly like a wine barrel, & great pendulous slabs of breasts, & his face is a slashed ruin of tattered meat, his lips & nostrils & cheeks & eyelids & tongue all pierced with gold rings . . .

His tattered face trembles, countless scars each a tiny mouth that gapes & gasps with the intensity of his perverse pleasure . . .

& the hollow pits of the skull's eye sockets reflect & fix the eyes of the exultant crowd, & the two hulking figures in black leather step forward from the shadows & hammer the spikes into the young boy's wrists, & the woman who is The Whore performs her rituals & the three human beasts copulate in a daisy chain of deviations, & the moderator slays the boy, & the crowd consumes the slaughtered lamb . . .

The countless monitors that line the walls of the sprawling War Room complex are crowded with these images & many more. & the probes of *Ichiko* thrust through the info-space of Matrix & feed on the electromagnetic energies released in pain & torment & death, & they conjure the visions of the *slayers* & the *slain* . . .

OPEN THINE EYES,
& BEHOLD OUR DESOLATION

(or, BEYOND the BLUE EXTREME)

Rupert, the house dick, clad in his customary plaid pants & suitcoat & blood-spattered tie, leads the rube, this cracked-out Heavy Metal wacko in his badboy black leathers, down into the subterranean pleasure pit of Mermaid's Inn.

"I've gotta attend to a recent *checkout*—" Rupert tells this high-wired hearse-heaping handjob artist.

Rupert is an anachronism, albeit a most deadly one. A self-perpetuating holdover from the bygone days of fascist Amerika, a Chicago Vice-veteran corrupt in the finest tradition of Bible-thumping, Old Glory-waving politics, payoffs, & poontang-tradeoffs spawned in the Windy City. A once-Pinkerton railroad bull, headbasher & tongue-twister of homeless misfits & drifters all along the hobos' highway of hummin' rails. He still speaks the hardboiled lingo of those Chandleresque detective tales from that quaint age of flagging innocence . . .

He motions to the brute with the shaved head & mascara purple eyeshadow who just flowed out of nowhere. "Hey, BellaDonald, show our own Mr. Death here to THE CHRIS WILDER ROOM, okay—?"

Mr. Death's eyes light up at the mention of the infamous serial killer's name. "Man, that's pretty fuckin' tacky, Dude, y' know, like I can dig this shit! y' knowwhatImean . . . ?" so-eloquently articulates this self-styled theatric Mr. Death. Death Burns. Satanic Rocker of the chart-bustin' thrice-gold-record'ed WICKED KING WICKER, lead singer & composer of such family (Manson, maybe—?) favorites as "Cum-On BA-B Lite My Pyre" & "Na-Palm Nannied" & "Burnt Orphans O-vr & E-Z."

(a classic PUNK, straight out of *The Undertaker & His Pals*)

"Yeah. *tacky*. that's *choice*. real *choice*." the brutish BellaDonald giggles in a glass-shattering falsetto, "P-unnn-yyyyy' I like *that* almost as much as the one Rupert always tells me: 'Is it LIVE? or is it MAMMARY-WREX . . . ?' He just *can't* go in the JERRY BRUDOS ROOM without wisecracking about it—"

"Don't tell me, Dude—that's where y' do all yr *tit-jobs*, ain't it—? Brudos wz th fucker that cut bitches's tits off to make paperweights. Right? Like I'm not fuckin' *stupid*, I mean I'm inta this shit. I *read* about it . . ."

BellaDonald leads the crack-snapped punk six doors down the corridor, & opens an iron door on the left. They seem to wade through oceanic depths in the slow-pulsing flicker of cobalt blue light.

"There she is, *the girl of your dreams*—" the brute says, pointing to the skinny little Cuban cooze dressed in a white cheerleader's outfit. The sweatshirt is emblazoned: **"BLUE DEVILS."** The pleated skirt is *the* shortest the fastlane-jaded Mr. Death has ever seen—the flared hemline doesn't even come close to covering her barely hair-fringed pubes. Her wrists & ankles are manacled. She's chained with her limbs forming a crude "X" suspended from floor to ceiling.

"Hey, Bitch, you *always* hang out like that—?" Mr. Death is quite elated at his sudden flair for double entendre.

"SsssEEEeeittt! Dude! Where th fuck you get'cher extras—Fidel Castro Junior High—? I *know* that little twat sure ain't gettin' paid *scale*! & she goddamnwell as fuck ain't no Tom Savini F/X special!"

"May we recommend—" says BellaDonald, & gestures like some brain-burned maitre D' to the small table just to the side of the spread-eagled youngster. The circular top is made of translucent blue glass. & the pedestal is a slender & seductive mermaid, sculpted from a single chunk of polished bone. There is a silver tray on the table, with an even half-dozen tubes of SUPER GLUE.

"Go ahead, Kid—get yr *fingers sticky*" BellaDonald tells the Rocker.

"OOOoohhhhhhhh! Holy fuckin' SHIT, Dude! I've *always* wanted to *do* some little prick-teasin' groupie . . . JUST LIKE *THAT*—"

His tongue flicks out like Gene Simmons' The Demon. He doesn't need the Kiss facepaint to look demonic.

"No fuckin' wonder you fuckin' charge six big bills for this!" Death says, lifting the girl's sweatshirt up around her out-splayed shoulders, exposing her small, budding, breasts with their large, dark, fear-swollen nipples.

"Some guys start with their lil' sweetheart's mouth or eyelids," Rupert comments. (He's just entered the room unnoticed in all of the excitement.)

He pauses for emphasis: "Other guys like to start by gluing her cunt lips shut."

"Now, *there's* some glue sniffin' I could really get into!" says badass Mr. Death.

"Had one guy with a real knack for it—managed to seal & peel some sixteen-year-old runaway I think it was forty-six or forty-seven times, him & a coupla buddies slidin' it to her in between . . ."

"That's what y' call 'RAW SEX' by friggin' Jee-Zusss n' Mary!" BellaDonald quips to the hard-rockin' rube.

"Hhheeeee. Hheeeee. HHhhheeEEEEE!" Death Burns is comin' apart at the seams, the eggshell of his sanity cracked as a stoned Humpty Dumpty. He's got his hand down deep in his leathers, playin' pocket pool with that jutting cue stick.

"Yeah, 'RAW SEX' . . ." the brute echoes, giving Mr. Looneytoons in Leather another deliberate *push* off that narrow brick wall of SANITY . . .

Rupert continues, ". . . before she finally kicked from the shock & trauma! Fuckin' amazing shit happens around here'"

The girl screams. An Ella FitzGerald imitation. Very convincing. Authentic although purely accidental. So piercing that the blue glass top of the table shatters . . .

"I'd start with her mouth," BellaDonald advises sagely.

THE ROOM FLICKERS, A CHUCKLE OF SAVAGE SHIMMERING *BLUE* . . .

BEHOLD, I WILL MAKE THEM of the SYNAGOGUE of SATAN . . . / I HAVE POWER OVER WATERS to TURN THEM to BLOOD . . .

"This is the House of the Devil."

"Here—the one they call the Devil. I offer Him to you, as I offer you to Him. You know why they are so eager for you to eschew Him. Of course you know. It is because they don't want . . . (you) . . . to have power. Be smart. Come this way. I can arrange it . . ."

—Adolfo De Jesus Constanzo, *brujo*, *mayombero*, ritual cannibal.

The-Man-He-Once-Was searches the night-alleys for a phantom legend. The whisper of the sea is close at hand. The alleys twist & disappear. These are the blackest shadows of a city/town/village soul-sick & evil-rumored, cankered with the traffickings of grossest blasphemy & vice. He has searched through many alleys, through many towns, through many lands. In this particular cesspool of rat warrens & wharves, of taverns & tattoo parlors & slut-mills & shooting galleries & gambling dens, he searches for the ultimate, elusive, place of tainted forbidden pleasures—a place where torture & death are bought & sold . . .

It may be Jamaica, 1716, the pirate stronghold of Port Royal

It may be Marseilles, the waterfront in 1857

It may be London, 1865, in the slums that infect the quays & banks of the Thames, where the Beggars' Banquet meets

It may be Algiers or Tunis, where the flesh is bartered on the block, where ru' asa' rule & nurture pain-as-art, circa 1649

It may be Shanghai or San Francisco, 1856, (fourteen-hundred murders in three years . . .), the smoke of opium coils in the breeze

It may be Canton, white slaves & yellow, city of sampans & secretly-sold children, the year: 1905

It may be Havana, 1948, haven of the decadent, its trade in gambling & blue films & whores

It may be New Orleans, the funk of Blues whispers of sin & sex & Mary Jane & needles, 1927

It may be Saigon or Copenhagen, 1970, child-sex & S/M

A single thread connects all these, a certain rumored *visitation* . . .

Of an evil that transcends the boundaries of Space & Time, weaving a haunted spell of perversity & pain, then *disappearing* . . .

The-Man-He-Once-Was searches the night-alleys for a phantom legend. The ultimate snuff-parlor, the place known always (although in the lingo of a hundred tongues translated . . .) as "THE MERMAID'S INN."

+   +   +

He remembers moving through the tinted smoke as though walking underwater, buoyed by something unseen in the thick atmosphere, for he is as yet unburdened by the weight of history (*his* story or someone else's?).

He remembers detouring around the dock workers' game of poison darts & approaching the bar which resembles the prow of a miniature ship.

He remembers the cadaverous barkeep staring at him with dead eyes, & saying, "What's your pleasure, mate?"

He remembers giving the question deep consideration. The moment hits him in a holo-vivid rush of flashback . . .

 . . . as he formulates his answer but doesn't dare speak the unspeakable—not yet, not while he still walks on sea legs. Instead, he orders a glass of ale & pays for it with one of the gold coins he took from the damp pocket of the rotting corpse he stumbled over in that fog-choked alley an hour ago.

The barkeep sniffs the coin, then bites it.

"Dead man's gold," he mutters as he moves stiffly to the other end of the bar to refill the mug of a big man with a hairless head of assorted tattoos . . .

An amplified voice echoes above the din of THE MERMAID'S INN . . . the lights begin to dim . . . but that moment is lost, in a sudden, brainsearing, blaze of blue light, the words a blurred incantation beckoning him down down allthewaydown into the very heart of Hell . . .

& beyond.

"Fucking impossible," he remembers saying, banging his mug of ale on the bar—the bitter liquid sloshing a flood of foam across his quivering hand. The room filled with a din of demented hoots & catcalls . . .

"Nothing's impossible here," says the barkeep, looking more & more like a holocaust victim.

+   +   +

"There's always room at the Inn," he remembers the words of the emaciated man quite clearly, the flash of those cobalt quicksilver shades

(*just a moment ago, his dead eyes stared nakedly exposed—or was it an illusion . . . ?*)

The emaciated innkeep leans against the brick wall.

No. He is chained to the brick wall.

The front of his pants are tented slightly. By an erection of obviously pitiful proportions.

Bizarre.

But then again, this whole fucking *place* is fucking bizarre.

"You the innkeeper?" the snuff seeker asks, impatiently rubbing the stubble on his chin.

"They call me 'Professor,'" the emaciated man says with a snarl-like twist of thin, bloodless, lips. "'Professor Punk.'

"The Inn needs no keeper. It keeps itself. I keep tabs on the comings & goings of mindless mortals. Scum like you make your pitiful marks on the world, & I mark it down in the Devil's history book. I'm Bachelor of Battles. Ph.D. of Death, & I can show you a fine fucking time if you possess the proper mettle."

"You know what I'm after?"

"Fucking A, Jack. You're all after the same sad shit."

The man reaches down for his boot knife & thrusts the blade against the Professor's throat. "How's this for the proper metal? Now, you listen to me, Doctor of Death. They call me 'Slice'. I'm sure you can guess why. Now, where's the *real* action in this joint?"

Professor smiles, showing stained teeth, & then everything wipes away again in an explosion of blue flame flickering within his skull, his every vein & pore, causing the room to throb & strobe . . .

+ + +

He remembers.

But whose memories are they?

His own, or someone else's?

Or shared memories, in the waves of a sea that washes away all sense of self & joins all things in one long, lingering, moment of death . . .

IN THE WAR ROOM . . . he sits Buddha-like & naked on the stone floor, the steel blade of the ceremonial sword bridging his loins & raising a crop of goosebumps where steel teases flesh—His frosty eyes fall upon a Civil War battlescene wherein Walt Whitman contemplates a bloody pile of amputated limbs & human debris, then the eyes fall out of focus & the amputee-ghosts roam within the confines of the deadly silent room—The candleflames flicker in the ghost-stirred air & shadows lick the brick walls & awaken the soldier-spirits sleeping in other oil paintings—Uttering the ungodly incantation, he awaits the succubus; his ritual erection rising to kiss the blood-hungry blade of the sword, swelling in blood-engorged anticipation of her arrival & of the carnal pleasure/pain to follow—One of the nine candles loses its flame as it is snuffed out by wet invisible fingers & the succubus appears as a snaking tendril of white smoke, billowing, expanding, languidly forming itself into the shape of a lithe woman, her fingers swimming toward his thighs as smoke becomes supple flesh—Wordsmoke whispers from her perfect lips, a solitary puff: "*Zzzhhhzzz . . .*" (She whispers the word so low its sound is not a name, but only echoes of the wind & sea . . .) & she touches his thighs with a delicate spiderkiss—He trembles as she lifts the sword from his loins—He whispers as she carves shallow designs in the flesh of his hairless thighs—He moans in tortured ecstasy as she

111

laps blood from the precise etchings—"Come, *zzzhhhzzz* . . ." (She whispers the word so low its sound is not a name, but the buzzing of insects.) Then louder, more brazen, "Come, Lover . . ."

She straddles his bloodslick loins & draws him into her snug center & he is transported to a battlefield at the edge of the world where a bloodmoon looms over the chaotic clash of opposing armies & the screams of fallen soldiers are hymns to the merciless gods of the place where Hell invades earth, marked by human spillage exploding entrails sacrificial cannonfodder smoldering gore headless torsos . . . glory of war &

He explodes in a deathless profusion of semen & blood & the succubus sucks him dry, his soul shriveling geometrically with each thick spurt & beat of pulse—

+   +   +

Slipping his blood-whetted knife back into his boot, Slice opens the heavy wooden door & descends groove-worn stone steps in darkness. The air is damp, stained with the slaughterhouse scent of bloody death—this not lost on his twisting, tumescent, member, nor is it lost in that cavernous pit of carnal hunger, dark & inexplicable, that squirming serpentine nest of overpowering lust for painpleasure & death-the-mystical-doorway to some godless eternity—

+   +   +

He remembers.

His memories are a tide, flowing & foaming & crashing against his perceptions—then ebbing into echoes of a distant sea . . .

&, now, he howls with the frenzy of remembrance . . . FEAR, FURY, FERVOR, as he senses the New Flesh of his transformed existence . . .

Until he prays to the deaf/dumb/blind god of his forefathers, to *Baal* (He whom the ignorant, pious sheep call upon when they mindlessly invoke "Our Lord," seeking the supplication of Yahweh/ Jehovah, unknowing whom it is they serve whose name *is* "Lord" . . .), He Who Has One Name That Is Many, The Lord of One Face & Many Masks—*Baal-Berith*; *Baal-Phegor*, Lord of Dogs; *Baal-Zebub*, Lord of Flies; *Baal-Zebul*, Lord of Dung; *Baal-Zephon*, Lord of the Sky—to Lord Azazel, Scapegoat of the Wilds (whom

Lovecraft's conceit renamed, "Shub Niggurath, The Black Goat with a Thousand Young"), to the Lords of Chaos, to the four compass-points of Black Ritual—Hail Satan, Lord of the South! Hail Lucifer, Lord of the East! Hail Belial, Lord of the North! Hall Leviathan, Lord of the West!—to Lord Baphomet, the Goat of Mendes, to the Mermaid, the Female Principle Embodied, Creator/Womb & All-Devouring Destroyer; to the Devil, aaahhhhhh, yes, Blue Devil . . . & he realizes he *is* The Word Made Flesh . . . he *is* the New God of the Apocalypse . . .

He prays to Himself, Deified Man Incarnate, The Will to Power, for FORGETFULNESS, the Waters of the River Lethe not the bitter brine of these seas of savage sensation he long craved . . .

For the pleasure/pain is so great it threatens to splinter him into a thousand jagged, cobalt-blue, shards, a thousand selves, each living out their personal version of Hell on Earth . . .

He remembers.

Two brutes seize him, one on each arm, & throw him against the wall & clasp manacles on his wrists. Slice tries to fight them off but his arms are now chained to the wall & the brute with the shaved head & mascara & purple eyeshadow punches him in the gut.

"Hold him still," commands Rupert, the house dick. He is holding a needle & syringe glowing with blue light. "Time for a jolt of Blue Devil." Slice tries to voice a protest but there is a partial vacuum in his lungs from the gut punch. The needle slips into a vein in his left arm & blue light is injected into his bloodstream. The world suddenly tilts on an axis of madness, the house dick's voice seems a faraway place & has the crackling, thrashing, sound of a tree falling in a lonely forest, "Ever killed anybody, pal?"

Slice attempts to answer but his mouth won't work.

"No matter. You're cocked & loaded now. A fine dose of death hunger."

Light-headed & queasy, Slice notices a blue luminescence—then realizes he is its source; his skin is glowing with blue light.

The dick releases Slice's wrists from the manacles.

+   +   +

He remembers, oh, yes, he remembers, the Tide of Remembrance rushing in to overwhelm him—his very first kill with the wired awareness of Blue Devil Serum pulsing through his corded veins . . .

His eyes eerie & glowing with blue light, Slice clasps his powerful hands around a teenaged girl's slender throat, rushing on the feel of soft, fear-sweating, flesh, the windpipe crumpling like a discarded milk carton (*imagine*: the graphics in red, "HAVE YOU SEEN THIS CHILD?," imprinted on its waxy surface . . .) in his viselike choke-hold. The necklace of purple bruises glowing like amethysts, imaged through the wired vision of Blue Devil. His head is a skull of cobalt crystal resonating to her vibes of terror, a symphony in blue, scintillating the essence of all blue, an extreme beyond blue, fireworks rainbow of blue exploding through his every cell, shattering his perceptions into a million jagged fragments, each a holographic prism-chord of DEATH IN BLUE . . .

He senses her vertebrae snapping like fragile wishbones, & he keys off the childhood memory of strangling a clucking, wildly thrashing, hen (his younger sister's pet) while he brutally violates the stupid creature . . .

The scent of death glows in every molecule of air; the pheromones of fear thick in the intermingling of sweat & evacuated body wastes, the final flood of impurities exiting en masse from every pore & orifice, the purging ritual of death . . .

The deathrattle gurgles from her crushed esophagus . . .

+   +   +

As the man called Slice—his lapis lazuli brain languishing in the bluesy afterglow of his inspired work on the killing floor—leaves Mermaid's Inn, Professor takes the private elevator to the small "lab" over the snuff parlor.

He sits at the compact computer keyboard, turns on the juice, keys in the four-digit command code: "7734". The video monitor flashes through each color of the programmed spectrum, finally locking on an intense sapphire blue. Then he inserts the sterile needle into the last good vein in his left arm & sets the IV drip of glowing blue liquid at ten drops per minute . . .

Feeling the first-stage euphoria of blue rush, he plugs the tiny jack on the end of a matte black cable into the dermal patch on the back of his neck.

Twenty drips later he has created a new psychic profile:

codename "Slice".

He punches the "Homing" code, hits "**ENTER**" & leans back in his chair like a kid getting set for a roller-coaster ride.

The monitor's screen suddenly displays a kaleidoscopic dance of every conceivable shade of blue. His brain begins humming an electronic symphony of bluenotes, his penis pops out of his pants, thick veins pulsing with blue hunger, & his mind is catapulted

(stage two) into the computermind, running the circuitry in milliseconds & shooting off into blue ether . . . searching . . . homing . . .

(stage three) **MINDLINK:**

Waterfront. Salt-spray wind. Bootheels beating blue funk tattoos on the misty street. Dark alley deathrattle from dying drunk. DUI. Dying Under the Influence. Beyond the yellow glow of streetlamps darkness breaks into a mosaic of soft blue. Yellow dented taxi turns corner & noses along waterfront. Hail the taxi with your stiff dick, look at the driver with murder in your eyes, silencing him before his lips have a chance to move, slide into the backseat & give him the address that came to you from nowhere (?) & check to see that your bootknife is still in place—snuggled coldly against your ankle like a steel kiss tempered with deathhunger & ready for action. Taxi stinks of dried puke, stale tobacco smoke, aged-on-upholstery booze, cheap cologne & pungent body odor filtered through dirty clothing. The Hispanic driver is rapping about baseball, basketball, & pussy, watching you in the rearview mirror. Though he tries to hide it, you smell his fear. He is going on about John Dillinger's dick when the taxi arrives at the address you gave him.

"Pull into that alley," you tell him.

After a long moment's hesitation, he drives into the dark alley formed by the tenement building & a liquor store. He starts babbling in Spanish, *something about money*, you think, & your hand drops to the handle of your bootknife. With a whisper of steel on leather the knife comes out & with your left hand you grab a handful of his curly, greased, hair, yank his head back, & bring the blade around swiftly & core his Adam's apple. He makes a wheezing, gagging, sound as you force the blade deeper & rake it across his throat. Warm liquid sprays your hand & wrist. His head comes further back over the driver's seatback & you feel the blade make contact with vertebrae in his neck. His entire body shudders. You cream in your jeans & withdraw the knife. Leaning back in your seat & closing your eyes to the blue haze, you savor the bloodsmell.

The scent of copper.

"A penny for your thoughts . . ." you quip to the corpse, giggling in stoned elation at your free-associating, gallows', humor . . .

You get out of the car, open the driver's door, expose the dead man's blood-wet chest, & carve "7734" into the flesh of his abdomen.

You reach down into the jingling depths of your pants pocket, draw out two pennies in spare change, & lay the twin discs of grimed & battered coinage meticulously across the whites of his gaping, deathblind, eyes . . .

"Buy yourself a ride with *the Boatman*, chump," you say to the cabbie, his internal meter reading: **"PERMANENTLY EXPIRED. "**

"Come to think of it, you can still get your two-cents worth in with the coppers—*right* . . . ?"

Professor fumbles over the keyboard, finds the **ESCAPE** key & punches it. The monitor's screen goes blank. He disconnects himself from the electronic apparatus, removes the IV needle from his arm, & gets up to change his pants.

On the elevator trip down everything starts to go wrong, so wrong that he curses science for its insidious & demonic tendency toward chaos, the unpredictable fly in the fucking ointment, the fly in the hard-won formula, the aftereffects of his techno-chemo experiment in sweet horror, his empirical thrusts into the psyche of a killer primed for slaughter by Blue Devil (Li Di 9) . . .

"This should not be fucking happening . . ." his words sound muffled in the elevator—the low-high vibration of the elevator's cable is a hypnotic hum, insinuating snakes of unwanted stimulation— muffled & wrong, like the way the ceiling-recessed lights in this descending box (a coffin lowered into the earthen trench) are now burning blue, when a few seconds ago they were yellow, or the visionary flashes to that other brain, that other over-stimulated bundle of nerves & flesh & blood & muscle, tense & coiled & ready for a kill, another place . . . Another kill, you feel it coming as the elevator drops in terminal slowness, going lower than it should, descending into chaos . . .

"Fucking scientific shit!"

. . . & you sink to the floor, your eyes rolling up toward your brain, & blue-tinged visions unfold, take physical form, but the words on your lips never quite take shape ("Fuck physics") . . .

. . . Climbing a stairway steep & dimly lit by a naked 60 watt bulb, you run your fingertips along the wall of peeling paint, spray-painted graffiti, & knife-carved runes . . . You are unstoppable, invincible, & you can almost see through the fucking walls to the other side where human hearts are beating lust-tightened skins, jungle drum drum boogie down dirty hot jam yeah baby that's what I like There right there uuuuhh yeah OK uuuooh Oh Oh mmmmmmmm Don't stop don't stopdontstopdontstopstopstopstop . . .

. . . you *know* the door is unlocked before you touch the knob & you are moving with blue stealth across the stained cat-shit-smelling carpet, to the bedroom where the lovers are going at it for all they're worth (which, at this moment, ain't a Hell of a lot) amid crimson shadows thrown by the red party bulb in the Mickey Mouse lamp on the bedside table—You already have the knife in your hand & an erection in your pants—You/Professor/Slice are about to merge minds with your victims for orgasm-in-death, true multiple personalities, true Blue you old Devil . . .

The woman is on top, straddling the guy's loins, wild in the saddle, taking the saddle horn deep, moaning & tossing her long hair. You creep up behind her, knife ready, & you hook your left arm around her neck as you spring onto the bed. Holding the breathless woman in a choke-hold, you raise the blade high then plunge it into the guy's chest. His eyes swell like balloons & you know he is shooting his last hot wad. Your cheek is against the woman's sex-tangled hair & you savor the scent of perfume & lust. The down of soft, silky, hairs glistens an almost-subliminal blue-lit haze across the curve of her shoulders & upper back. Tiny beads of perspiration trickle the fear-taughtened ridgeline of spine. Tiny beads of cobalt blue. & you realize that glow is the cold blue fire emanating from beneath the translucent parchment mask of flesh you know as "face . . ." She tries to scream, but your hand covers her mouth. Your erection probes the crevice of her supple rear. Leaving the knife in the dead man's heart, you unzip your pants & pull out your bluish prick. You jerk the corpse's cooling cock out of her & replace it with your own loggerhead. Keeping her back arched against your belly, you pump her & it comes to you that what you shoot inside her will be blue—glowing. When you can wait no longer, you yank the knife out of the man's chest & stab the woman's abdomen. She screams through your fingers. You twist & jerk the blade inside her, & your mind merges with hers in that brief, beautiful, moment of death (like stabbing yourself in a hari-kari-like ceremony of sex & snuff), & blue light explodes into her & across the ceiling, flickering blue stars showering the bed, the dying woman, everything.

+   +   +

Rupert, the house dick, finds Professor on the floor of the elevator, his wang hanging out of his fly.

"Crazy sonofabitch," he mumbles. "For a fucking genius, you sure pull some dumbass shit."

+   +   +

He remembers.

IN THE WAR ROOM . . . he sits Buddha-like & naked on the stone floor, the steel blade of the ceremonial sword bridging his loins & raising a crop of goosebumps where steel teases flesh—

. . . his ritual erection again rising to kiss the blood- hungry blade of the sword, swelling in blood-engorged anticipation of her arrival & of the carnal pleasure/pain to follow— One of the nine candles loses its flame as it is snuffed out by wet invisible fingers & the succubus appears as always as a snaking tendril of white smoke . . . forming itself into the shape of the same lithe woman, her familiar fingers feathering his thighs as smoke as so many times before becomes supple flesh—Wordsmoke whispers from her perfect lips, that same solitary puff: "*Zzzzhhhzzz* . . ." (whispery echoes of wind & sea . . .) . . . He trembles . . . she lifts the sword from his loins—whispers as she carves shallow designs in the flesh of his boyish thighs—moans in tortured ecstasy as she laps blood from the precise etchings—"Come, *zzzhhhzzz* . . ."

Then louder, more brazen, "Come, Lover . . ."

She straddles his bloodslick loins & draws him into her pulsating center

. . . & he explodes in a deathless profusion of semen & blood & the succubus sucks him dry once again, his soul shriveling geometrically with each thick spurt & beat of pulse—

How many times, how many times . . . ?

+   +   +

He remembers.

Before he became something more than human, he liked to hang out in punk joints & coffee houses like Nouveau Expresso & 90 Night—funky little clubs where young radicals & anarchists & Post-Beat post-hip poets & punk musicians gather for mutual ego massage or to have their philosophies styled in the latest fashion. In that previous life, Slice was an angry young poet known as "The Bard of Bones" because he always wore his hand-tooled leather-&-bones outfit when he read his mad poetry in public. T-bones, chicken bones, porkchop bones, dog bones, cat bones (painted black), squirrel skulls, a human femur, all rattling musically as he moved about like a demented witch doctor, mouthing his bone-chilling poems & death hymns. His outfit was topped off with a spooky hoodoo headdress made of a cow's skull & hung with chicken feet & bird feathers. He strutted his killer stuff & the tight little pussies in the audience (those with the kinkier libidos that flamed darkly to the spark of his Hellcoals-&-gris-gris-laden rap) would get wet & squirmy, aching for that big bone bulging beneath his loincloth. The Bard of Bones got a lot of pussy in those days.

Then came his Bloodbone Poems & his subsequent arrest on obscenity charges.

(The arresting stormtroopers were pretty riled about his stacks of photo albums filled with their lurid headline clippings screaming an obsession with sordid sex, urban bloodbath, & mega-violence. Neither did they appreciate his state-of-the-art collection of S/M, fetishist, & bondage zines. Their bootheels & balled-fists-in-the-gut made that rather clear . . .)

He was convicted, placed on probation & ordered to undergo psychiatric counseling. He enjoyed the cat-&-mouse mindgames he played with the shrink, entertaining private fantasies of extremely creative carnage. The drawback was that he lost interest in writing poetry. But he convinced Dr. Howard (who looked too much like Moe of The Three Stooges) that he had no desire to perform in public again. The baggyeyed quack never scratched the surface of his mind's core—that dark chamber of id horrors inhabited by a psyche blown wild by storms of evil. The stupid shrink never even caught a glimpse of the blood-lust boiling behind those hooded eyes. His Freudian flimflam was a total flop. The Bard of Bones became "Slice" right under Herr Doktor's big nose . . . about the same time he started cross-ref'ing microdots & Crowley . . . Before he delved into darker ever darker wells of heavy occult & S/M. Before he found references to the place called "The Mermaid's Inn." Before he shipped out as a merchant seaman, searching for the elusive place of pleasure/pain . . .

& now he is someone else—*something* else. Something more than human. A nocturnal predator attuned to the poetry of the blooded flesh. He sees the universe in bones laid bare by his blade. Slice, become the hunter of the blue nocturne.

+   +   +

Like past life experience intruding on present time frame, but these are many lives, shared lives, past, present, future, Time is not a forward-flowing river but a sea that washes many shores . . .

+   +   +

The mirror returns his reflection as if it wants to get rid of it as soon as possible, spitting the distasteful image back to its outlandish source. The latex on his face has been applied unevenly, giving his face a freakish facade, certain to draw unwanted attention. But then, Slice is no makeup or special effects artist.

GOTTA DO BETTER THAN THIS, SCUMBAG, says the voice in his left ear. What the fuck?! Who is that? He looks behind himself, then glances all around the room. The woman's naked, mutilated, body is on the blood-soaked mattress, just as it should be. *No way SHE said anything. She's got a mouthful of fucking intestine. Who said that?*

YOU LOOK LIKE A FUCKING REJECT FROM NIGHT OF THE FUCKED UP DEAD. LIKE A RETREAD GETTING READY TO BLOW OUT BIG TIME . . .

Who are you?

WHO DO YOU THINK I AM, YOU ANUS? GET THAT SHIT OFF YOUR FACE & START OVER. WE'VE GOT PLACES TO GO. PEOPLE TO DO . . .

It ain't that bad. You can't see the New Flesh, that's the main thing. & it's dark out. Who's gonna see?

IT'S GONNA GET A LOT FUCKING DARKER BEFORE WE'RE FINISHED, MR. HYDE.

Slice begins peeling the latex mask from his face. Blue pebbled flesh is revealed as each piece of latex comes off. Beautiful, isn't it?

WORDS CAN'T BEGIN TO DESCRIBE IT, ZIT SUCKER. DO IT RIGHT THIS TIME. THAT FUCKING WHORE YOU DID IS STARTING TO STINK. & WE'VE GOT MILES TO GO BEFORE WE SLEEP.

I know who you are.

OF COURSE YOU DO, SHIT STICK. YOU'VE ALWAYS KNOWN ME.

But I was never sure . . .

WELL, YOU CAN BANK ON IT NOW, HEMORRHOID.

You shouldn't talk to me like that. I'm the New Flesh . . .

I'LL TALK TO YOU ANY WAY I WANT TO, SCOURGE OF THE EARTH. WHO DO YOU THINK MADE YOU WHAT YOU ARE?

Blue Devil made me what I am. Not you.

THE MOON IS BLUE, BUTTFACE. WHERE DO YOU THINK THE FORMULA FOR BLUE DEVIL CAME FROM?

The one called "Professor".

BULLSHIT, ASS-LICK. BLUE DEVIL IS MY FERTILE SEED. & YOU ARE MY FUCKING OFFSPRING. NOW SHUT THE FUCK UP & FIX YOUR FACE.

With encouragement from his unseen companion—the voice in his left ear—Slice re-applies the latex skin.

A fly lands on the nose of the corpse on the mattress & crawls into the black, blood-crusted, cavern of her nostril, looking for a good place to lay her eggs. It scuttles down the back of her throat, stopping just inside the ragged piece of intestine lodged against her uvula. The fly lays her eggs there.

+ + +

Needle slips into blue vein. No pain. Not even the tiniest prick. Odd thumb depresses the plastic plunger & the blue liquid in the syringe is forced into the bloodstream. When the syringe is empty, Slice removes the hypodermic from his vein & tosses it into the ocean. The waves rolling under the dock catch his attention & hold it, the ebb/flow/ebb associations setting off liquid visions in his mind.

COME ON, SHIT STICK, YOU'VE GOT WORK TO DO.

"Where do we start?" Slice asks of his invisible companion.

YOU KNOW.

"Washington?" His memory is hazy, his mind reeling & rolling like shore-pounding breakers as the Li-Di-9 surges through his system.

BINGO, BOZO.

"Pynchon's hit list?"

WORK YOUR WAY TO THE TOP OF THE CHARTS.

"Then New York. The Mafia motherfuckers."

JACKPOT, CROTCHROT.

"What about my face? My flesh?" Slice asks, his forefinger & thumb clamping down on a particularly vicious- & viscous-looking boil on his left cheek, festering blue filth exploding in a splatter-pattern on the dock's rough-hewn planking that keys a depraved parody of fusion Jackson Pollock—Theosophic/Jungian/Surrealist periods & Abstract Expressionist/Action Painting . . .

He chortles at his imaged gallery hanging.

NO PROBLEM. OTHERS DON'T SEE THE NEW FLESH. NOT YET.

"You mean it's all in my head? Like hallucinations?"

SOMETHING LIKE THAT.

"Then why the makeup?"

USE YOUR BRAIN, POND SCUM. YOU DON'T WANT TO BE RECOGNIZED AS YOU'RE BRINGING DOWN AN EMPIRE. THESE BIG BOYS ARE PROS & THEY WILL SWAT BACK IF THEY SEE THE FLY THAT BITES THEM. WE CAN'T GIVE THEM A TARGET. FROM HERE OUT, IT'S HIT & RUN. YOU'RE ABOUT TO BECOME THE ULTIMATE URBAN GUERRILLA.

Slice's face cracks into a leering grin, causing the latex makeup on his face to form odd wrinkles & lumps so that he looks like a man who has been stung by a hundred wasps. "I can remember now. All of it. The whole program." What he remembers is the late Pynchon's knowledge of the international power structure, the interconnected underground factions, the vast networks of the Shadow Bosses who run the world, the political gangsters living-dead corporate corpses who hide the whole humming machine from Mr./Ms. John/Jane Q. Citizen with media mirrors & smoke. Slice knows his destiny lies in throwing a monkeywrench into the hulking machine by making precise hits, from the White House to the palaces of the Colombian drug Kingpins. He *is* the hard-cyber sabbat-eur . . .

He will conjure forth the Snakepit of Chaos & loose it upon the multinational machine till it runs amok, triggering economic & political havoc all over this fucking anthill-world of existence. Then he & his companion will sit back & watch the power structure devour itself, like the WorldSnake locked in perpetual rectal-cranial inversion. After Armageddon, Slice will reveal the New Flesh & he will be the Dark Savior to the New World of Unleashed Serpents.

A sudden thought intrudes. A key perhaps unburied. Longforgotten delvings into Jungian metaphysics bob surfaceward (no doubt some bullshit hype implanted by that assfuck Dr. Howard, that baggy-eyed quack, that retard reject Moe-of-Three-Stooges-clone, who played all those verbal cat-&-mouse dick-&-puss mindgames that only scratched the surface of my mind's seething Black Hole core, right? RIGHT . . . ?). In a tidal gush like pure-crystal rush, Slice asks: "Who the FUCK *are* you *anyhow*? The Unknown Man, my Shadow-Self? Or maybe some diesel-dyke deviant of *Anima*, the Dark Side of Primal Womb Personified, *yeah*, the Lilith, the Female Death Demon, the One Who Follows After the Shadow . . . ?"

GETTING IN A BIT DEEP, NOW, AREN'T WE, DR. HECKLE-&-JEKYLL FAUSTUS..? OR IS IT MR. HYDE-THE-WEENIE . . . ? GONNA START THAT PSYCHO-LOGIC-AL FLIMFLAM, NOW, OKAY, YOU THINK . . . ?—

I'LL FUCK YOUR MIND TILL IT BLEEDS, YOU PATHETIC POETICK PERVERT! I'LL POP THE FUCKING CHERRY OF YOUR MIND'S CORE, YOU FAGGOT-DANCIN' PANTIE-PRANCIN' NIHILISTIC NANCY BOY—I'LL EFFACE THAT TIGHT LITTLE ERASER SPACE INSIDE YOUR BRAIN CASE, & I'LL MAKE YOU BEG FOR IT . . . *HARDER . . . DEEPER . . . FASTER . . .*

WANNA PLAY SOME GUESSIN' GAMES, WANNA DIDDLE OUT SOME LITTLE RIDDLES, MR. EX XXX BARD OF BONERS . . . ?

"AB EO, QUOD NIGRAM CAUDAN HABET ABSTINE, TERRESTRIUM ENIM DEORUM EST . . ."

NEED A TRANSLATOR FOR THAT, MUCKJUMP . . . ? OKAY:

"KEEP YOUR HANDS FROM THAT WHICH HAS A BLACK TAIL, FOR IT BELONGS TO THE GODS OF THE EARTH . . ."

SO, LET THAT BE A WARNING TO YOU, EHHH . . . ? YOU BEEN TRUCKIN' 'ROUND WID DAT BLACK TAIL AGAIN, AIN'T YA, BRO . . . ?

YEAH? HOW 'BOUT *THIS* ONE . . . ?:

"FILI, EXTRAHE A RADIO SUAN UMBRAM: ACCIPE ERGO QUARTAM PARTEM SUI, HOC EST, UNAM PARTEM DE FERMENTO ET TRES PARTES DE CORPORE IMPERFECTO . . ."

DIG THE GIG, PIGSHIT?:

OKAY. OKAY. "SON, EXTRACT FROM THE RAY ITS SHADOW: THEN TAKE A FOURTH PART OF IT, I.E., ONE PART OF THE FERMENT & THREE PARTS OF THE BODY . . ."

& I *AM* WHAT I *AM*, OLIVE OYL, & I *AM* THE FIRST PART & I *AM* THE FOURTH PART & ALL THAT TRIPE HYPE . . .

FOLLOWIN' ME SO FAR?:

"FUNDAMENTUM ARTIS EST SOL ET EIUS UMBRA . . ."

CAPISHE, YOU COCKY LITTLE COCKSUCK . . . ?

"THE BASIS OF THE ART IS THE SUN & ITS SHADOW . . ."

PERFECTLY CLEAR, *QUEER* . . . ?

OR LIKE MY OLD PAL RAYMUNDUS (SASSY LITTLE NOM D' ARTS NOIR, HUH . . . ?) USED TO RAP: "TAKE OF THE BODY THAT IS MOST SIMPLE & ROUND, DO NOT TAKE OF THE TRIANGLE OR QUADRANGLE BUT OF THE ROUND, FOR THE ROUND IS NEARER TO SIMPLICITY THAN THE TRIANGLE. HENCE IT IS TO BE NOTED THAT A SIMPLE BODY HAS NO CORNERS, FOR IT IS THE FIRST & THE LAST AMONG THE PLANETS, LIKE THE SUN AMONG THE STARS . . ."

YOU KNOW, DIPSTICK, LIKE "ROUND ROUND GETTAROUND I GETTA ROUND," & ALL THAT PSEUDO-BEACHBOY BULLSHIT, RIGHT?

ALL JUST CRYSTAL CLEAR, NOW, RIGHT, MR. REDRUM RECTUM . . . ? JUST SIMPLE HOKE-US POKE-US LUST-T'-CROAK-US ROSE-OF-THE-WORLD STUFF, HUH, MR.

WIZARD O' THE LIZARD . . . ?

DIG IT, CRAPTRAP?

"'TIS RUST ALONE THAT GIVES THE COIN ITS WORTH!": THALES . . .

DEEP SIX SICK SIX STUFF, POWDERPUFF . . . ?

OR LET'S TAKE THE *ROSARIUM*: "OUR GOLD IS NOT THE COMMON GOLD. BUT THOU HAST INQUIRED CONCERNING THE GREENNESS (THE *VIRIDITAS*, THE *AZOTH*. . .), DEEMING THE BRONZE TO BE THE LEPROUS BODY ON ACCOUNT OF THE GREENNESS IT HATH UPON IT. THEREFORE I SAY UNTO THEE THAT WHATEVER IS PERFECT IN THE BRONZE IS THE GREEN ONLY, BUT THAT GREENNESS IS STRAIGHTAWAY CHANGED BY OUR MAGISTERY INTO OUR MOST TRUE GOLD . . ." ONLY THE *GREEN* IS *BLUE*, RIGHT, MR. 2-B-OR-NOT-2-B . . . ? JUST BLOOD-SIMPLE-SAMPLE AS OL' MOM'S *SLICE* O' THAT CHERRY HAIR-PIE, O GREAT BARD O' BLOODY BLEEDIN' BONERS . . . ?

I MADE *YOU* THE NEW GOD OF THE NEW FLESH. QUITE A MINDJUMP FROM A PATHETIC PERVERT X-POET POSTURIN' FOR PUSSY, SOME FUCKED UP MERCHANT SEMEN JUS' ROLLED OFF A TRAMP STEAMER ON HIS SEA LEGS, AS YET UNBURDENED BY THE WEIGHT OF HISTORY, JUST LOOKIN' T' GET SKAGGED, SHAGGED, & DOUBLE-BAGGED BEFORE YOU WENT SNIFFIN' FOR SNUFF FOR SOME TIGHT YOUNG GASH T' SLASH SOME SUGAR 'N' SPICE T' SLICE REAL NICE SOME QUIFF T' STIFF WITH YOUR SLITHERIN' SHIV . . . & NEXT THING YOU KNOW, POP!, BLUE FIREWORKS, GIDGET THE MENTAL MIDGET GOES BLUE DIABLO, & *I* MAKE *YOU* THE FUCKIN' ULTIMATE *UBERMENSCH*, A *GOD O' DEATH*, BOY . . . ?

I'M ALONG FOR THE LONG RIDE, SON/SUN, & THIS IS THE *DARK SIDE* CALLIN', AS IN "BREAKER BREAKER," GOT IT . . . ? & YOU BETTER ANSWER WHEN THE HADES HOTLINE'S BUZZIN' BLUE . . .

SO, THINK YOU WANNA TRY RAPPIN' OR UNWRAPPIN' 'BOUT SHADOW SPOOKS & PRIME-EVIL WOMBS-IN-ROOMS-IN-TOMBS & ALL THAT DEAD-BEAT PSYCHO-

LOGIC? FINE, JUNG MAN, JUS' FINE. BUT YOU WANNA TRY FUCKIN' WITH *MY* HEAD, BABYCAKES, I'M GONNA *FUCK OFF* IN *YOURS* . . . & KATY BAR THE DOOR 'CAUSE, WHORE, YOU *KNOW* THE FUCKIN' SCORE—KINDA LIKE THAT OL' SAHDOWS OF KNIGHT TUNE, I 'CUM AROUND HERE, JUS' 'BOUT MIDNIGHT,' & YOU BEST BELIEVE & GRIEVE, MEAT-SLEEVE, I CUM LIKE A FUCKIN' GODDAMN HELLBOUND CYCLONE . . .

+ + +

The voice in Slice's brain grants him one grand & glorious GMOS (*Golden Moment Of Silence* . . .), then renews its sledgehammer skull-assault anew:

NOW.

WHAT'RE YOU GONNA DO NEXT, BRAINRAPE?

"Uhhh, flag a taxi, head for the airport & buy ourself a ticket to Washington, D.C., right . . . ?"

NO! YOU'RE NOT, CHICKENLICKIN'. YOU EVER GO THROUGH AN AIRPORT SEC-CHECK . . . ? I MEAN, HERE YOU ARE ALL STINKIN' FROM THAT LITTLE BEAUTY-TREATMENT WHERE YOU DRENCHED YOURSELF IN WHORE'S BLOOD LIKE SOME KINDA POST-MODERNIST BEOWULF BATHIN' IN THE BLOOD O' THE DRAGON & ALL THAT, BUT THE ONLY THING DRAGGIN' WAS YOUR WAG-GIN' WANG & THAT PUTA'S 5-BUCKS-A-THROW FAT ASS THAT YOU HACKED-UP & WHACKED-UP PIECE-MEAL . . .

& NOW YOU'RE GONNA GO WALTZIN' THROUGH THOSE MET-DET SCANNERS WITH THAT FUCKIN' BLOODY BOOTKNIFE STRAPPED TO YOUR ANKLE & TELL ALL THEM NICE FOLKS IN THE UNIFORMS YOU JUS' BROUGHT IT ALONG 'CAUSE YOU NEEDED SOMETHIN' TO PICK YOUR TEETH WITH AFTER YOU CHOW DOWN ON THAT DEEELICIOUS AIRLINE CUISINE, OR MAYBE YOU WERE JUS' GONNA FIX YOURSELF SOME HOME-COOKED STEWARDESS STEW, FRESHLY SLICED-'N'-DICED & BUTCHERED IN THE *COCK*-PIT, DUMBSHIT . . . ?

SERVICE! SERVICE! O QUICKSILVER MESSENGER *BOY!* & HIGH O' THE HIGH & LOW O' THE LOW, Mr. TWO-

FACE, Mr. SONG *SANG BLEU*, OH GRACIOUS GREAT & GRATING AU GRATIN of PRIMA MATERIA ET LAPIS PHILOSOPHORUM!

NOW HERE'S THE GRAND SLAM, LIKE WHAM-BAM & THANK Y', MAM, SPRING-HEELED JACK-HORNY WHO-HAS-NO-CORNERS-LEFT-TO-HIDE/HYDE BUT HAS BECOME THE APOCALYPTIC ROUND-ROUND-GETTA-ROUND OF ROUND-HEELED WELL-HEELED & FLAT-FOOTED EXTERMINATION . . .

MY PRECIOUS LITTLE PET, O *SERVUS,/CERVUS FUGITIVUS* . . .

+   +   +

He remembers.

Explosion of semen & blood—succubus sucking—soul shriveling—bloodmoon—the screams—the place where Hell invades earth—human spillage—exploding entrails—smoldering gore—headless torso—tortured ecstasy—blood whispers—sword—loins—spiderkiss—Demon Kiss . . .

the lithe woman begins to dissolve, languidly losing form, contracting into billowing white smoke, then a snaking tendril, & the succubus disappears—

one of the nine candles loses its flame as it is snuffed out by wet invisible fingers—

he sits naked on the stone floor, the steel blade of the ceremonial sword bridging his loins—

uttering the ungodly incantation, he awaits the return of succubus, his ritual erection rising to kiss the blood-hungry blade, swelling in blood-engorged anticipation of her arrival & of the carnal pleasure/pain to follow—

the candleflames flicker in the ghost-stirred air & shadows lick the brick walls—

the rivulets of melting wax of the nearest candle begin to form a pattern, a shape, her perfect lips—

Wordsmoke whispers from her perfect lips, a solitary puff: "*Professor* . . ."

IN THE WAR ROOM . . .

He wakens from the Waking Dream, & it is not his dream, but

127

a shared dream, the other's dream, the one known as "Professor Punk" . . .

How many times, how many times . . . ?

+   +   +

He remembers moving through the tinted smoke as though walking underwater, buoyed by something unseen in the thick atmosphere, for he is as yet unburdened by the weight of history (*his* story or someone else's?) . . .

+   +   +

The-Man-He-Once-Was searches the night alleys for a phantom legend. The ultimate snuff parlor, the place known always (although in the lingo of a hundred tongues translated . . .) as "THE MERMAID'S INN."

& Upon Her Forehead was a Name Written, MYSTERY, BABYLON the GREAT

Lucy Nation picks up the blood-red cellular phone & calls her lefthand man & pet masochist-submissive, Professor Punk.

"Yeah?" he answers in a tired voice.

"Professor, you were supposed to call me."

"I was tied up, Lucy—"

"If you don't watch your step, Prof, you're *definitely* going to be tied up—to that cheapass metal cot in your fucking lab, while I grind out cigarette butts on your naked backside . . ."

"Promises, promises, Lucy—you're such a goddamn *tease*," he whines.

As she speaks into the phone receiver, the notorious Ms. Nation taps her long, glistening, nails on the glass surface of her rather unusual desk; an original designed by the world-renowned Swiss surrealist, H.R. Giger. The piece is loosely based on the coffee table in his own flat in Zurich. She has long been an admirer of the visionary's Hellish works, & she spared no expense in commissioning him to create the furnishings for her office overlooking the Miami seascape. The tabletop is of three-inch-thick cobalt-blue glass, shaped as a hexagon, & supported by six crucified figures cast of solid sterling silver—three inverted Christs & three upright Satans. Her chair, also, is a replica of his "Harkonnen" throne, but molded of blue-black tempered glass, &, later, upholstered by her own private tailor in exquisitely detailed, dragon-tattooed, human skin. Her walls are painted with murals adapted from his *Necronomicon* & Hieronymus Bosch's "Seven Deadly Sins" & "The Garden of Earthly Delights."

The hand with its shining stainless steel fingernails brings the cigarette up to glossy lips, pouty & sensual, & the smoke is French-inhaled. Lucy Nation exhales the smoke as she speaks.

"I need a little R&R, Prof. Been working too hard. Fix me up with the usual bit. Got it?"

"Sure, Lucy, anything you need," Punk hurriedly assures her.

She squints her eyes as she takes another drag on the cigarette.

Lucy stands & walks to the picture window of her plush penthouse, overlooking the metropolis. Her long burgundy dress is slit to her creamy thighs, & her jet-black hair is a cascade of smooth curls hanging halfway down her back.

Her dress slips to the floor with a whisper.

She turns, & walks to where the floor-length mirror narcissistically displays her own nude perfection to her loving gaze. She begins to fondle her jutting breasts, then trails down her sleek belly to the tapered V of her mons. The dark patch is neatly trimmed into what might pass for a sketched-on Vandyke beard, were her image a full-color pinup & not living, quivering, flesh. She moans with pleasure as she touches herself between her legs, rubbing & massaging, then inserts her nimble fuckfinger into the fierce heat & wetness of her slit—what she fantasizes is the fiery, lava-dripping, gateway to the very depths of Hell . . .

+ + +

Lucy Nation boards *Hellraiser* for the first time in several weeks. All work & no play makes not only a dull girl, but an even meaner, bitchier, version of her typical wicked bitch-goddess self.

She prefers the yacht to the penthouse when it comes to partying.

Something about the motion of the ocean makes her feel more alive—sexier. &, for Lucy, sex is power. & power is *everything*. With her power she built the Erebos empire. Not the power of sex typical of airheaded bimbos, the glitzy sluts who sleep their way to the top. Lucy's power is *kundalini*—the serpent power. Spiritual power made flesh. Visionary power.

At the age of thirty-six, she has become a legendary figure in certain circles of power & politics. No one wants her as an enemy. *Nobody fucks with Lucy Nation.* But now somebody *is* fucking with her, & Lucy is preparing to go head to head with the craziest fucker she's ever encountered in a world populated by stone psychos.

Those stiffs, Skull & Pedro, were a major mistake. Nearly a *fatal* one. It's only been a little over a week since the killing by Pynchon of her no-good security guards. Pynchon had been one of her top operatives, a zen-attuned hitman whose skill could topple cartels & dictatorships. But the sellout shit had turned on her like a rabid dog, attempted to rape & murder her at the commands of his new patron, the so-called Blue-Devil Killer, Slice—oh, yes, as usual, her indomitable self-will & her serpent power had turned the tide of personal combat into a riptide of blood that washed away the killer's lifeforce & fed her own backbrain pit of vipers . . .

& the sharks. Yes. How *dare* that bastard try to sexually violate *her* . . . ? She'd had the last laugh, oh, yes, the best laugh . . . The sharks had fed upon his fucking limpdicked cockflesh.

The yacht has been cleaned up, painted, & the bullet holes in the walls have been patched up.

Yes. Those stiffs, Skull & Pedro, were a major mistake. Nearly a *fatal* one.

& Lucy Nation prides herself on *never* making mistakes. That's the way that she built Erebos into the vast network of legitimate & subterranean corporations & dummy corporations stretching from coast to coast & far beyond, from Miami to Mazatlan & Montreal & Manila & Macao & Marseilles & . . .

Multinational. Multi-leveled.

Merchants in murder & mayhem. In drugs, death, & deviation.

But there is competition. Plenty of it. & from these competitors the head of Erebos must seek protection.

She has imported new muscle to ensure her safety.

The even dozen triggermen aboard the *Hellraiser* are pros. A dozen dirty with untold killings & torture & mutilations. Muscle from Latin America where life & death are bought & sold at bargain rates. & where hired killers are a well-paid elite supported by the corrupt oligarchy that seeks to maintain its status quo of privilege amongst squalor, of "have" amongst the "have-nots".

Lucy's private death squad.

Dark-skinned & dark-hearted.

Most clad in black leather duster coats that flap like the wings of carrion crows in the saltspray & seabreeze. The remainder in motorcycle jackets.

All sporting short-cropped ruffs of oil-slick hair with trailing rat tails.

& stone killer faces.

& eyes hidden behind the hip glaze of bugeyes & wraparounds & aviator's glasses—

All with cobalt-blue lenses . . .

All armed with Brazilian Mekanika Uru submachine guns. Compact & deadly. 9mm Parabellum. Silenced. Thirty-round magazines. Seven-hundred-fifty rounds per minute cyclic rate of fire. Simplicity itself with a mere seventeen components parts. Field-strippable in thirty seconds.

This time, if Slice seeks her out, she will be *ready*.

It will be *he* who is bullet-riddled & body-bagged.

He or whatever mindslave minions he sends after her.

Her serpent power *surges* like the tide.

She is ready now to stand & deliver with a bloodtide that will drown whoever seeks to fuck with her or Erebos . . .

+   +   +

In spite of the tropical heat she is wearing her favorite outfit of skintight black leather, though with her quarters aboard *Hellraiser* cooled to sixty-five degrees she is very comfortable. She pours herself a scotch-on-the-rocks.

Lucy calls for her evening entertainment: two young bodybuilders stripped to their bikini briefs & primed with a drug to maintain their erections & delay ejaculation—

(It is an exclusive import of Erebos, its manufacture a closely-guarded secret of one of Hong Kong's "black clinics." The orient has *always* prized its legendary aphrodisiacs, *real* or *spurious*, but this is *the genuine article*, a libido stimulator without equal in the modern world. & it is her link of power with Tantric magicians of the Vamacara & Laya paths, as well as certain practitioners of the Dahomeyan voodoo cults in North America & Haiti & Brazil . . .) —

"Hello, boys," she welcomes them. "Are you ready for a taste of serpent power?"

+   +   +

Lucy peels off her curveclinging black leather bodysuit. She savors the looks of rampant lust turning the faces of tonight's playmates, Hans & Roger, into masks of brutal desire. She can read every sick sin betrayed in those windows of the soul, every filthy, degrading, act they've ever perpetrated or conceived of perpetrating upon soft & yielding womanflesh. These are badboys who like their sex rough, guys who love nothing better than to make a woman *hurt* for their pleasure. She has seen the savage rapes & sodomies they've inflicted upon helpless females—runaways & hitchhikers, seduced schoolgirls, flattered by the attentions of grownup men making them feel so grownup, too, attracted like moths to the flame by the dark, dangerous, thrill of dating handsome "older guys", & party girls who were far too drunk or stoned to realize what these cruel pricks were up to until it was too late to do anything but cry & bleed for their trust & carelessness . . .

But tonight, they're gonna play the game by *her* rules.

She lives by The Golden Rule. The Bitch with the Gold makes Her Own Rules . . .

Two *thousand* dollars each to do *anything* she commands them. Anything. They think they're too fucking tough to worry about the worst *she* can do. They've both earned plenty of coin doing pussy & ass in porno flicks—both legal & extra-legal. Heh, if you're a bird-doggin' pussyhound, might as well get *paid for it*, right? Paid to get all those handjobs, blowjobs, rimjobs, & then shove their stiff dicks up some chick's tight twat or ass & fuck her for all she's worth. They count themselves as Sex Gods of the New Order. Above the Law. Above these pathetic cunts who were made for one thing only—fucking—the meaner & nastier the better. Made only to service a man as he sees fit & learn to relax & enjoy it, right, you stupid little cunts? & neither of them has ever given a flying fuck that they'd do time as shorteyes if the roster of their sins was known.

To them, that timeless adage of the brutal perv, "old enough to bleed means old enough to butcher," always draws a filthy chuckle & an involuntary lurch of the penis . . .

Their shortsightedness perceives her incorrectly as yet another victim. Some rich bitch so hot for cock she has to pay to get herself off.

Their over-confidence makes them careless.

Sure, they can take a little humiliation & that kind of kinky shit, if that's what she's into, right, for a thousand fucking bucks?

Oh, yes.

They're about to learn one hard-fucking lesson . . .

+   +   +

Her naked body is sleek & sensuous, wildly arousing to the two hired studs. Her jutting breasts are tipped by lust-swollen, berry-like, thrusts of nipple, begging to be sucked & nibbled. Her waist is slender, flaring to ripely rounded hips & a lush, heartshaped, bottom. Her firm, slim, belly tapers to a precisely tonsured pubic mound, the pouty lips of her sex slit thatched with a nest of dark down, yet bared just enough to further tease with fleeting glimpses of moist, pink, inner flesh.

They engage in some preliminary foreplay, groping & fondling one another's privates. They squeeze & suckle her ripe breasts, pinching & nipping & nibbling at the lust-stiffened nipples. They long to bite the succulent flesh, hard, raising bruises, drawing pinpricks of blood from their bitemarks as they usually would with some little 'hitcher they'd kidnapped & were ravishing. But, tonight, they take it easy on the bitch, not daring to blow that two-large apiece by getting carried away. Meanwhile, their hands are busy, feeling up her pussy & her ass, pushing their greedy fingers up inside both her eagerly proffered love-holes. Her hands are busy, too, tickling their hairy scrotums, stroking their foreskins back & forth, tormenting their urethras with the tip of one wicked stainless steel-tipped fingernail, jacking her encircling hands up & down their upthrust penises.

They are a bit taken aback when she nuzzles their cockheads up against each other, & she giggles at their momentary flinching when they suddenly realize she is forcing them into homosexual contact with one another. Roger starts to protest, then thinks better of it even though his stomach is knotting at the obscene touch of another man's penis knob rubbing & frictioning against his. Hans, on the other hand, has had some experience doing this kind of gig—a blue-haired Miami matron used to hire him to get it on like that with her closet-queen hubby, &, though he'd never admit it to Roger, he'd even let the rich old fag suck his dick & then he'd cornholed the man while his wife lay back & masturbated herself anally with a chrome dildo. As sick as it might sound, the husband was a better fuck than his loose-holed wife was—*ugggghhh*! *Jee-sus*!

"Heh, no big deal, right, boys?" Lucy giggles wickedly at their obvious discomfort "After all, you've probably done the double-entry bit with those cute little pickup girls you like to party with, I'd be willing to bet, & making some stoned college coed do the cock-sandwich bonedance simultaneously impaled by two stiff pricks means you're rubbing dicks through her dividing wall of tissue-thin membrane is just using her for a condom to keep 'em going skin-to-skin, if you follow my drift, right, boys? But then that's *different*, huh . . . ?"

Fearing to displease her, that stack of cash riffling in their avaricious brains, they let her continue rubbing their cockheads together, making them queer each other.

"Play with each other," she suddenly orders, placing their hands on one another's penises. Again, they begin to protest, then stop themselves, & bite back the flood of rage roused by her humiliating command. She continues rubbing the two flare-rimmed glans up against each other, while the two men tentatively begin mutually masturbating.

She bursts into laughter when Hans blows his wad all over Roger, squirting sticky jets of semen onto the other man's penis & belly & thighs. He spasms & lets his hand drop from Roger's prick. "Keep jacking him off, you stupid little faggot!" Lucy shrieks in anger, picks up a nearby riding crop & begins thrashing him savagely across the buttocks. He lets out a wail, & quickly grabs hold of Roger's penis, again, which Lucy now guides into his open mouth as she forces him down on his knees, her right hand clenching his balls in a crushing hold. "Suck dick, you pathetic piece of shit!" she snarls & the money-grubbing stud does as she commands, soon experiencing a scalding burst of cum shot down his throat by his male companion.

That's okay, he thinks to himself, I'll fix this fucking bitch before the night is through, oh yes I goddamn will!

Now Lucy kneels on the bed, face downward, waggling the melon-like globes of her behind enticingly in the air. Lucy's splayed fingers slowly, tauntingly, draw open the cheeks of her so-perfect ass. This one's certainly as hot for it as a bitch in heat, Hans snickers to himself. He strokes his thick, blue-veined, shaft as he ogles her lush backside; trying to decide whether this sick bitch simply wants them to do her dogstyle, or whether she's kinky enough to want them to put it up her ass right off . . .

They're about to put *something* up her ass, but not what they think right now . . .

"Eat out my asshole!" she orders, spreading her cheeks wide open, baring the puckered, pinkish-brown, ring of her anus for their contemplation. It still looks plenty tight & delightfully fuckable, even though the aperture bears telltale signs of fairly frequent penetration, the rosebud-like nether lips slightly outward-flared, the hole itself a darkly winking, lascivious, eye, quite obviously somewhat stretched from indulging in anal sex.

Both of them have performed analingus on girls before. Hans, in particular, likes to thrust his tongue up some unsuspecting cheerleader's tight young butt, making her squeal at first with surprise & terror at such an unnatural invasion of her most private parts, then, slowly, as he works away at her, she melts into squeals of quivering pleasure, &, when she is out of her mind with newfound, undreamed of, ecstasy, he will force the girl down on her belly & suddenly stick something far bigger up that hot, tight, little hole, & he will rape her anally, make her engage in sodomitic intercourse . . .

They take turns humoring Lucy with their tongues shoved up her ass, providing her the oral-anal stimulation she craves . . .

+ + +

Still docked at the exclusive marina, *Hellraiser* rocks gently in the waves; but the scene taking place in the owner's quarters is anything but gentle. Lucy is straddling the muscular loins of Hans, pumping away at his rock-hard, condom-sheathed, penis. Roger, the other hired stud, is handcuffed to the bed, awaiting his turn with the insatiable Ms. Nation. She rides Hans hard against the floor, digging her heels into his hips.

"I'm cuming, I'm cuming!" shouts Hans, his Austrian accent lending a little class to his dialogue which is straight out of the sleaziest porno flick.

Lucy slaps his face with all her strength. "Not before me, you cocksucker!"

She dismounts, & orders him out of her bedroom. Then she turns her hungry attention to the stud cuffed to the bed. "You know what *really* gets me off, Roger—?"

Lucy pauses, her temporary lapse into silence & her studied body language lending dramatic emphasis. She poises her head in half-profile with her favored left side angled toward him, chin slanted slightly downwards, lips puckered like some scarlet orchid blossom. Her delicate, black gull-wing, brow arched inquisitively, suggestively. The sleepy-lidded squint of her sizzling Santa Domingo-sapphire eyes incredibly seductive, sparkling with that "coke is it" glint that only the finest uncut Colombian can conjure.

"*—the sight of a beautiful body like yours with blood all over it . . .*"

"Wait a minute now," he stammers, "just hold on, lady, I ain't into nothing like that!"

"What the *fuck* do you think I was paying you each two large for, Sub-Genius—your pathetic pricks wouldn't earn you five bucks from a Greek dowager! I can get all the cock I want for free—it's the pain I'm paying you dimbulbs for, Loverboy!"

Lucy shows him the glistening blades of her stainless steel fingernails, then rips his massive, hairless, chest with both hands. He yelps, but his erection won't go away—the drug has seen to that.

Lucy crawls on top of him & takes his cock deep inside her well-lathered pussy. "Ooohh! that's good, Roger, but I need to see more blood."

She rakes her nails across his pretty face as she humps him wildly. "I could do *this* all fucking night—"

+   +   +

Lucy Nation stands naked, straddling the slackly sprawled body of Roger—the rent-a-stud. Too bad he's comatose. He can't appreciate the finer points of his position. His narrow, muscular, waist is flanked by her shapely ankles. Tapering upward to sleek shins & perfectly curved calves & supple thighs. Skyscrapers of silk-stockinged extravagance. The musky valley of her sex is openly exposed above him. The creamy shell-pink of her netherlips & the melon-ripe globes of her exquisite buttocks. The glistening coral of conch-like inner folds. The dark, mossy, "V" of her *mons veneris.*

Lucy believes in living dangerously at five-hundred-plus-clams-per-pair . . .

The poppy-red cobra skin of her "O"-ending designer-signature—

fabbricante-Italiano—lace-up sandals is slick with blood. As are the slender spikes of their stiletto heels impaling the delicate silk pile of the sehna-knotted carpet—a rare antique woven in Chinese Turkestan. Its intricate pattern of wave crests & coiling dragons & pomegranates is spattered with the savaged stud's blood.

+ + +

Now she's had her way with them, it's payback time for all the girls & women these two brutal cunthungry-bastard muscleboys have ever seduced, corrupted, & betrayed, all the ones they've taken by rape, all the degradations they've visited upon female flesh . . .

She applies makeup to their faces, rouges their cheeks, paints their lips with scarlet gloss, paints their eyelids with kohl-shadow, & tugs platinum wigs down over their skulls, & oils & shaves the hair from their thighs, their calves, their groins, gives their already-shaved chests a quick going-over, till their bodies are both bald as a baby's butt.

Lucy picks up her cellular phone. "C'mon down for a little partying," she says. "Only half now. The other half later . . ."

Several moments afterward, the door to her cabin opens & in stride six of her Deathsquad boys. They strip off their black leather duster coats & cycle jackets. They drop their Levi's, & their black cotton briefs. Now bareassed naked except cobalt-blue shades. Stone killer eyes behind the hip glaze of bugeyes & wraparounds & aviator's glasses.

Lucy giggles wickedly at the sight of them doing their macho posturing, hardguys with short-cropped ruffs of oil-slick hair with trailing rat tails, hardguys with dangling penises & wobbling scrotal sacs. & stone killer faces.

"Looks like I forgot one thing," she muses &, picking up the phone, she calls in her private secretary from the adjoining cabin.

Her secretary—a lesbian with a lively set of tits & a tight, perky, little ass—dressed primly in the masculine business suit she favors for board meetings. Her rich brown hair is pulled back in a severe bun, & she wears the hornrimmed glasses that are pure affectation.

She knows her hired guns would probably each give their left nut for a chance to peel this stiff bitch naked & poke their greasy pricks up her varied orifices.

"Hhhhmmm, Like Mick J. says, 'Can't. Always. Get. What. You.

Want,' right, boys," she teases.

Her secretary affixes nipple clamps to both the platinum-wigged Roger & Hans—the tiny metal jaws pinching painfully, drawing muffled groans from the badboys.

Then Lucy grins with sadistic delight as the bloodstained pair are forced down onto their knees & two of the triggermen grab them cruelly by their ears, like jug handles, & make the muscleboys fellate them. While they are giving the men blowjobs, Lucy & her secretary whip their bare asses with leather thongs & bent coathangers. After they ejaculate down Hans & Roger's throats the next two take their places, until they've all been sucked off.

But Lucy's favorite spite is yet to come. She watches gleefully, while her secretary masturbates her vaginally & anally, as the six Latino gunsels take turns buttfucking the now wailing, blubbering, hardguys.

"Goddamn, I go to all the trouble to doll them up, & then these ingrates go & bawl their heads off & smear their makeup & mascara with all those pathetic fucking tears . . ." Lucy taunts.

Her secretary holds a champagne glass up between her mistress' straddled thighs, & Lucy fills it with a sparkling stream of pale amber piss & her two playmates are made to sip it down & beg for another glassful . . .

& there are hours yet ahead in which to make these pitiful bastards pay.

Hours that will seem like years of suffering.

Hours that will see her orgasms crest & break with the dark fury of gale-lashed surf . . .

Hours for her to loose the pleasures from within the Gates of Hell that lie within her heart, that lie between her shapely, so-alluring thighs . . .

+   +   +

Lucy Nation can feel the serpent power writhing upward from the seething snakepit of her spine & backbrain . . .

Kundalini rising, she muses, focusing her Tantric energies for the impending battle she can sense like a hurricane boiling on the horizon . . .

& There Was Given Unto Her
A Great Sword . . .

Slipping into a midnight-blue kimono, Lucy Nation lights a pricey, imported, Turkish-blend cigarette & rings for her houseboy. Less than a minute later, a muscular young man in white enters the study, awaiting instructions from the mistress of the house.

"Have my bath ready in five minutes," she orders, "No rubdown today."

"As you wish," the houseboy replies, then exits to prepare a hot bath scented with soothing oils for her.

She strolls into the plush bathroom where her hot oil bath has been drawn. She slips off the kimono & sinks down into the steaming, fragrant water.

Finally feeling some of the tightness leaving her muscles, she closes her eyes & begins to savor the orgasmic ambience of the hot oil bath.

Thirty minutes later, & she is climbing out of the sunken Roman tub . . .

+   +   +

Chinn bows to Lucy Nation, then assumes a defensive position, holding his *katana* with solemn reverence, its thirty-inch curved blade gleaming in the morning sunlight. He wears only a loincloth, & his muscles ripple beneath his oiled skin. Chinn's eyes betray no emotion.

Lucy returns his bow & raises her own samurai sword over her shoulder with both hands, ready to attack. She too is naked to the waist, wearing a black loincloth. Like her opponent, her entire body Is coated with fragrant oil. Her full breasts quiver slightly with each beat of her heart. Combat always makes pulse race, & she uses the mental centering technique Chinn taught her to slow her heartbeat. Her eyes narrow, taking on an almost oriental slant. Chinn has told her more than once she has the soul of a samurai—that in a previous karmic cycle she had actually been a samurai warrior.

Of course, Chinn is not a true samurai. He studied with a martial arts master in Japan & learned the ancient & deadly arts of combat. In ancient times he would have been a *ronin*, a rogue samurai without a master. A true samurai would draw his *katana* only for actual combat, employing instead *bokken* or wooden swords; Chinn's only master is money, thus he draws his blade whenever Lucy Nation commands because she pays him handsomely indeed.

A woman could never be master to a Japanese male—a female is not even considered the equal of a man; nevertheless, Chinn admires Lucy Nation's spirit & skill with a sword. He knows that she secretly wishes to give her ancient blade a taste of blood—to behead a man with a single stroke of the *katana*. She knows how to do it. Chinn has taught her well.

One of the guard dogs patrolling the fence around the Nation mansion suddenly barks, & Lucy chooses this instant to strike . . .

As the sword arcs toward Chinn's left shoulder, the thought runs through Lucy's head that she was born in the Year of the Dog & that striking when the dog barks throws her in sync with the flow of the natural order.

She subscribes to the Jungian concept of synchronicity & lives her life accordingly. The precepts of Zen & Taoism exist in syncretic harmony with this outlook as well. Life is a crap shoot & the "random" tumble of the dice is determined by the conditions of the universe at the moment the black-&-white cubes leave the fingers; if you're moving with the natural flow of events, perceiving the "dragon veins" with all the senses, living on the cutting edge of Time, you are far more likely to rake in life's winnings. For Lucy Nation, it's all in the perfectly-timed flick of the wrist as you roll the dice or swing your blade. Did not the great Chinese generals of old toss the yarrow stalks before leading their warriors into battle so they could benefit from the wisdom of the *I Ching*? Could not the properly-timed retreat be a brilliant offensive battle move? On such concepts has Lucy Nation built her powerful empire. Working with Chinn & the samurai swords is more than a hobby or a discipline for her—it serves to sharpen her skills in every phase of her life, from the bedroom to the boardroom.

Chinn moves swiftly, shifting his weight on his feet as he parries with his sword, effortlessly blocking Lucy Nation's strike.

Using some of the force from Chinn's parry, she shifts her *katana* to the left & strikes at the man's right shoulder. His blade is there a fraction of a second before hers & the blow is blocked.

Lucy suddenly spins her body in a swift circle, crouching, coiling her tensed muscles for the next strike, spinning on her bare toes like a deadly ballerina, coming around blade-first toward Chinn's neck.

A primal war cry explodes from her mouth.

Chinn thwarts the blow.

The steel blades sing out & Lucy sees a solitary spark fly from the contact—like a falling star.

She drops back, & lunges at Chinn's abdomen, but he parries, throwing her off balance.

He senses the opening & thrusts his *katana* at Lucy's heart.

Chinn's swordpoint kisses the flesh beneath her left breast, drawing a tiny flowerbud-droplet of blood. Had he not checked his follow-through, she would be dead.

"Goddamn it!" she hisses, breathlessly.

Chinn bows to her. "You fought well, Lucy-san."

She touches her left index finger to the spot of crimson under her breast. "One of these days I'll kill you, Chinn," she vows.

"Perhaps." He turns his back to her, strides to the marble table in front of the vine-covered fence, & sheathes his *katana*, laying it carefully upon the tabletop.

Lucy grips her *katana* with both hands, steps toward him, & swings the blade at the back of his neck—at the *Jade Gate,* at the very spot where skull meets spine.

With the lightning-like strength & grace of the tiger, Chinn ducks & is suddenly rolling on the ground, springing to his feet out of sword range.

"Shit, Chinn, How did you—"

"I felt your approach."

"But I was silent. How . . . ?"

"Years of discipline. Years of training in the many *ryu*. One learns to sense the unseen danger. It is the way of the *haragei* adept.

The centralization & integration of *ki* (or *ch'i* . . .), the moving vitality, the force of artistic & spiritual attunement. But already we have spoken of these things many times, O Lucy-san."

He indulges his great joy of the theatrical, his speech waxing formal as the proscribed lines sung by some *No* player.

One true way of perceiving reality. As the rippling prism-strands of a web blown by the wind. As the smoke-patterns of incense that are rich with shifting subtleties of form & scent. As the clouds. As the flowing waters of the stream or river. As the roaring voice & the whisper of the tides of the sea . . ."

"You can teach me this?" she asks.

"It will come in time. When you no longer see the surface of the stream, but instead each undulation each wave each current & vortex & every subtle ripple-pattern of the flow . . ."

"But there isn't enough time—"

"Time is a sea with many shores, because the waves break upon the eastern sands does not mean that those of the west or east or north are dry . . ."

"You always speak in riddles—"

"No. I speak in the way of deeper truths . . ."

"You know that I was trying to kill you?"

"*Hai.*"

"& yet you serve me—?"

"I have no fear of Death. Life or Death? What can it truly matter? They are but the two sides of a single mirror. The steel spirit of the warrior shall be reborn again in transient flesh. The warrior exists only by his perception of the flow & by the well-timed flick of the wrist that serves to guide the two faces of the coin of Chance . . ."

"I serve my master who is no master . . .

"All else is illusion . . ."

She hands him her sword, turns on her heels & walks quickly toward the palatial mansion. Chinn allows a smile to play across his lips.

I am He that Liveth & was Dead . . . & Have the Keys of Hell & Death

I.

Before he became something more than human, he liked to hang out in punk joints & coffee houses like Nouveau Expresso & 90 Night— funky little clubs where young radicals & anarchists & Post-Beat post-hip poets & punk musicians gather for mutual ego massage or to have their philosophies styled in the latest fashion. In that previous life, Slice was an angry young poet known as "The Bard of Bones" because he always wore his handtooled leather-&-bones outfit when he read his mad poetry in public. T-bones, chicken bones, porkchop bones, dog bones, cat bones (painted black), squirrel skulls, a human femur, all rattling musically as he moved about like a demented witch doctor, mouthing his bone-chilling poems & death hymns. His outfit was topped off with a spooky hoodoo headdress made of a cow's skull & hung with chicken feet & bird feathers. He strutted his killer stuff & the tight little pussies in the audience (those with the kinkier libidos that flamed darkly to the spark of his Hellcoals-&-gris-gris-laden rap) would get wet & squirmy, aching for that big bone bulging beneath his loincloth. The Bard of Bones got a lot of pussy in those days.

Then came his Bloodbone Poems & his subsequent arrest on obscenity charges.

(The arresting stormtroopers were pretty riled about his stacks of photo albums filled with their lurid headline clippings screaming an obsession with sordid sex, urban bloodbath, & mega-violence. Neither did they appreciate his state-of-the-art collection of S/M fetishist & bondage zines. Their bootheels & balled-fists-in-the-gut made that rather clear . . .)

He was convicted, placed on probation & ordered to undergo

psychiatric counseling. He enjoyed the cat-&-mouse mindgames he played with the shrink, entertaining private fantasies of extremely creative carnage. The drawback was that he lost interest in writing poetry. But he convinced Dr. Howard (who looked too much like Moe of The Three Stooges) that he had no desire to perform in public again. The baggy-eyed quack never scratched the surface of his mind's core—that dark chamber of id horrors inhabited by a psyche blown wild by storms of evil. The stupid shrink never even caught a glimpse of the bloodlust boiling behind those hooded eyes. His Freudian flimflam was a total flop. The Bard of Bones became "Slice" right under Herr Doktor's big nose. & now he is someone else—*something* else. Something more than human. A nocturnal predator attuned to the poetry of the blooded flesh. He sees the universe in bones laid bare by his blade. Slice, become the hunter of the blue nocturne.

He blows into 90 Night like a storm-building thunderhead.

"Bones! Is that you, man?" squeaks a rat-faced faggot.

Slice shakes his head.

Negative, asshole.

He picks up the sultry scent of choice prey.

His bootknife shifts against his ankle.

A pretty drag queen is sitting on a stool, reading into the mike a long poem about the gay plague.

Slice slinks across the room & sits at a vacant table. A butch lesbian wearing a dildo on a rope around her neck looks into his face, then quickly looks away. He can imagine what she saw there: saw him stuffing that dildo dick down her fucking throat, fucking her with it till blood filled up the torn crater of her mouth. You ain't butch enough to handle me, cunt. Choke on it, you half-human bitch.

The queen on the stool ends his epic by ripping off his blonde wig & spinning around on the stool to reveal a death's head mask on the back of his head. The audience applauds & cheers. Slice hawks up thick phlegm from the back of his throat & spits the blue glob on the floor, causing three punks at the next table to look in disgust at him & move to another table. *Don't you know artistic criticism when you see it?*

The scent comes in stronger.

Something dark & powerful stirs in his belly & groin.

A prettyboy MC steps to the mike & says: "Ladies & gentlemen—

Miss Phaedra Flame!"

The prey mounts the stage. The black sheen of her long hair, her black bodystocking, & black lip gloss accent her milk-white face.

A demonic grin sharpens the predator's face.

Phaedra Flame holds up a slim red-bound book, & says, "These are my Torch Poems." She holds up a blowtorch in her other hand & a tongue of fire licks at the book. Then flames engulf the book, & she tosses it into a bucket of water. "I hereby proclaim the death of the printed word!"

The audience whistles & cheers. *Mindless sheep.*

"Now I do real poetry," Phaedra says with a sly smile.

From the Olympus of his heightened blue awareness, the new god Slice looks down upon the roomful of ragged mortals & savors the coming creation. *Destruction is creation. Reductionist to the Nth.* His artistic medium will be flesh/bone/blood. Each slaughtered lamb a work of art, impermanent like ice sculpture. Art that literally sends spirits soaring into the great unknown.

Phaedra is putting her body & soul into her impromptu scat poetry, moving with feline grace, slinky & seductive, speaking directly to the new god, though she is not consciously aware that she is doing so. ". . . hungry in the hamburger air, tossed aside like a used condom, wearing the emblem of a washed-out revolution, alone with my own bloody abortion . . ."

Slice studies her every move, the jiggle of her full breasts, the quiver of her firm thighs, the pucker of her lips as she wraps them around each word. He is mentally outlining his artistic approach, planning the impetus of his strokes, finding cosmic inspiration in the poetry of her moving body.

The revelation hits him with such force that he is thrown back in his chair, his long hands dangling below the seat. He sees it all with crystal blue clarity: his handiwork must be exhibited for the masses, not merely for the homicide police & the coroner. He will display his blood art, like human graffiti, to the public. Phaedra Flame will be his first message to the world. The more sensitive souls will see the meaning beyond the carved & flayed flesh. Perhaps a few will even glimpse the coming *blue doom*.

The demonic grin returns & remains on his face like a mask.

As he follows her out the rear door of 90 Night & into the poorly lit parking lot, he feels the pleasure rush of anticipation that marks the kill frenzy of the predator—his heart pounding like a blue fist inside his chest, his pulse rate soaring, his breath laboring through lungs raw with the intensity of his *need*. & he wills himself into a zen state beyond the boundaries of flesh, his mad mantra echoing deep within the slithering snakepit of his primal backbrain:

Loose the serpents upon this ignorant imperfect world! Free these conscious-stricken monkeys from their carnal confusion & stupid scams . . . Let death be the pure, expertly-cut, diamond of rare truth!

deeper down into the very marrow of his spinal column . . .

. . . The onomatopoetic ontology of orgasmic onus? omnivorous pussy, opaque ooze of penile omission, onrushing onslaught upon your one-horse philosophy—

down into the very well of transcendent unreason . . .

. . . say OHM, O ye outlaws & outlanders, OHM to that Olympus of electric orgies—

Amen. Ahmen. O Man. Omen . . .

His face leers with a viper-deadly grin . . .

yeah, baby, you're spinnin' into MY orbit now . . .

her art transformed into raw art . . .

She bends to unlock the door of her battered bronze Toyota, & Slice puts the tip of the blade against the small of her back.

"Don't make a sound—" he hisses.

Phaedra's body tenses & her breath catches in her throat.

He steps beside her, putting an arm around her like a lover, shifting the knifepoint to the underside of her right breast.

"I loved your poems," he whispers. "They put me in an abstract mood."

He walks her to a garbage-filled green dumpster behind the coffee house.

"I'm going to do something very abstract," he tells her. "You'll be the talk of the art world."

He leads her behind the dumpster & pushes her back against its cool surface.

"If you scream, I'll slit your pretty throat."

He slits the thin material of her bodystocking from the neck to the crotch, then peels it off her supple body.

"I smell your essence. I hear the blood rushing through your veins, wanting to come out."

He deftly works his fingers through her pubic bush & into the warm lips of her quim.

She tries to draw back from his touch, but her buttocks are already pressed flush against the dumpster.

His zipper opens with a loud rasp & his ponderous penis nudges against her dry slit.

"Please . . . don't . . ." she whispers.

"You're dry as a bone," he giggles, "but I can fix that."

He clamps his left hand over her mouth & runs the blade downward, over her belly.

"I'm going to *fuck you*," he says & jabs the blade deep into her vagina

& then his huge cock slides deep into the bloodslick tunnel of ruined flesh. He is tuned deep into the cosmic. Deep into the psychic center of the spinning cycles of the *Samsara* that are the worldly path of pain & death & rebirth, & he is drawn beyond them, feeding his own psychic energies unleashed in this Nirvana of pure torment, the serpent slithering deep into the primal, searing, Hell-pit, & he *becomes* the great beast crushing the egg of existence in its coils . . . *Ouroboros* . . . *Nithhoggr* . . . rearing from the pit & circling the world in the scintillating, diamond-pure, radiance of his slithering scales . . . *tail* trapped in *mouth* & *mouth* in *tail* . . . a NEW GOD created from the flesh of myth, beyond the pale, trembling, limits of crucified martyrs & pitiful, one-horse, philosophies, beyond the old limits of bone & skin *transformed* into THE NEW FLESH . . .

& YOU are part of this cosmic mindloop—attuned to the slaughter of the dying woman. Feeding on the released psychic energies of her pain & torment—

& now it's *art* for *art's* sake—

Her mind screams in terror & disbelief as the blade slices off her breast.

A short-handled axe flashes in the dim light from a distant street lamp & strikes the woman's shoulder, completely separating her arm from her body. A fountain of blood gushes from the severed socket, drenching you/her psychotic slayer & the litter-strewn pavement alike in the hot spill of her life-essence. She enters into numbing & merciful shock/you feel the center of her mind melting, dispersing randomly/each dripping direction going to death/butchershop *chic/ a little off the top* . . . ?

Her head comes off with ease, though the axe keeps slipping in your blood-greased hands. Like the cries of a kitten down a well, the beheaded woman's mewling echoes somewhere in your backroombrain—psychic screams from a locked corridor. Then dead silence. You start to hum a tuneless stream of bluenotes as you sculpt meat & bone. With your eyes ablaze with blue fire, it's easy to work in the dark.

He/you/she/IT . . . spiritflesh bliss blowing back eons . . . back to the bigfucking bang!

From your angle-less corner of the blinding blue galaxy you feel her ghost fly away.

You work blind, by feel, by the sound of rending flesh grinding bone, by the light of an inner blue radiance, out where interstellar radio messages bleed into curved mirrors & broken space & time, keying a haunted memory of idiotic phone conversations breaking into your old reality like that CB breaker breaker shit coming out of your TV & making you want to find those rednecked motherfuckers & make them bleed like stuck pigs. Ah, sweet memories. Whose memories . . . ?

Bad to the last bone. Blistering blue heat bending mirrors, mirrors catching the bluenotes you hum as you do your best work. Monster art. Opening soon at *your* guerrilla theater.

II.

The satellite's orbit begins to decay as it passes over Manila. Its inevitable entrance by fire into Earth's dense atmosphere has not yet been calculated by those paid to monitor such things; when the Com-Sat's demise is plotted, it will be deemed one more hunk of expensive space junk likely to shed a minimum of dangerous debris upon the planet. Scant minutes later the doomed satellite passes high above & to the south of Hong Kong &, eventually, over Miami, where the streetlevel violence rages & the morgues fill with the crack wars' casualties while the drug lords & their whores & lieutenants party in their penthouse suites & private yachts &, several miles inland, where the squad car lurches to a stop in front of the coffee house 90 Night. If the satellite's onboard equipment were still operational, its camera could snap pictures of the bloody, contorted, corpse hanging by a rope from the roof of the coffee house; could zoom in on the horrified & sickened faces of some of the individuals in the crowd, gathered to bear witness to the bizarre abomination. But the Com-Sat is shut down, making its silent way to inevitable destruction somewhere over an ocean of the southern hemisphere, sometime after it flashes by the beaches of Galveston, its bulk visible only as a brilliant pinpoint above the extreme horizon where sea meets sky . . .

It was the biggest goddamn fly he had ever seen. Not a horsefly, not a green fly, but a frigging housefly so big that Officer Robbins thought it must be a goddamn mutant, what with all the pollution & shit in the air. & why was it, in un-flylike behavior, still out making its rounds in the dead of night . . . ?

Now he's staring into the bloody cavern that the fly disappeared into a moment ago. That's what the gaping wound in the girl reminds him of—a raw cavern. Christ! It could be *two* girls, Robbins thinks, the way all the body parts are hanging there, oozing all that gore & shit, the hand jammed up her ass so it looks like she's shitting a fucking severed arm, the head, *oh Jesus*, the head clamped between the thighs like she's giving birth to her own fucking head. Some sicko had a field day with this poor babe. From what's visible of her face she was probably a looker. Before the butcher worked her over.

A guy in a business suit steps up for a better look at the mutilated thing twisting a little on the rope as the salt-edged breeze in from the shore seems to invest it with a momentary, mocking, breath of pseudo-life.

"Get back," Robbins orders the wide-eyed suit. "Something drops off her, you get it smack in the face." He turns to the small crowd of on-lookers & closet ghouls & says, "Everybody stay back. This ain't a sideshow. Jesus!"

He lights a cigar & waits for the homicide boys to arrive. While he waits, he watches for that goddamned mutant fly to come out of that bloodyfucking cave.

THE DEVIL'S CUT-UP

Inspired by William Burroughs & Brion Gysin

Another zipper rasping vertically into the drops of wine or blood of Limbo, and Degrees *before the thorny black* clock strikes somewhere and slashes transformed flesh . . . the remnants of grossly fat in vast flows of blubber & the riotous exposed face & the heated squishy depths of her blossom from transformed flesh . . . pinned like dainty roses, guise of flesh—and a clock strikes somewhere innocent. Our Lord Menstruum Automaton a Trickster's reassembled bizarrely concealed doorway.

She tries to draw back from his touch, but her buttocks are already two *thousand* dollars each to do *anything* she commands them. KEEP YOUR HANDS FROM THAT WHICH HAS A BLACK TAIL. Needle slips into blue vein. No pain. Not even the tiniest prick. The mirror returns his reflection as if it wants to get rid of it as soon as he read his mad poetry in public.

"Pull into that alley," deathrattle gurgles & your erection probes the crevice & you jerk the corpse's cooling cock.

"There she is, *the girl of your dreams*—" the brute says.

& keep watch upon the Watchers & the watched . . . & watches the blue-black storm clouds boiling in & angry gods who feed on PAIN. Those who thirst for the shriek the whine the whimper of the brush-stroke.

Interior sanctum sanctorum. The old man draws himself up like a preying mantis

(or perhaps into some twilight blue zone of interface as he moves— the gold rings that pierce the nipples jiggling, probes of polished surgical steel & whips of flails. He shuffles toward the crippled-insect, steps. Hell on earth. There is only pain only the *Palette of the Perverse*. Sound *whispers* here. A long, narrow blue glass stands with a profusion of scalpels of drill bits of Four Maidens Ravaged by twisted Taoist erotica, cheeks, his eyelids, even his tongue.

"—like frogs *come* out of the mouth of the Dragon, & out of the mouth of the Beast, & The Whore squats down upon the stage & voids Her bladder in a gushing torrent. "& they had a king over them, *which is* the angel of the bottomless pit, whose name in the Hebrew tongue is Abaddon, but dragons or coiled serpents swirl across their forearms & biceps &

"The whole world's going to Hell . . ."

He smiles even as his throat opens in a leering grin, spraying forth a shower of bright crimson poppy petals, celebrating his rite of passage into the next cycling of karma . . . YOUR BRAIN HAS ALREADY BECOME AN ELECTRON GUN. Among these protracted, pensive, shadows there is a sudden shifting and a low, moaning, sigh of transcendent ecstasy. Whether the skin of this peach he splits is satin or taffeta is less than no concern to him. He cares only for the bared flesh of her swan-slender neck, her flawless arc of back, her exposed derriere, its taut pillows of temptation . . . Beneath the half-drained cup of a thirsting moon, the highway stretches onward, the dozen chrome dildos in graduated lengths and girths. Spiked cockrings carved from ivory and human bone to Our Lord the Flayed One of sacred golden clothes the skins of the slaughtered, *Night Drinker*, those ragged scraps of flesh fluttering in the Winds of Limbo, that which *is* Life because it can *destroy* Life, the paradox that forms THE TORTURED MAN . . .):

The Devil and The Sun/The Son, and sometimes they are a Trickster's Hand, The Moon doubled, and Thirteen, Death, enters the Wheel of the Zodiac and *is* its axis . . .)

, and as it is above so it is below

this cracked-out Heavy Metal wacko down into the subterranean pleasure pit of Mermaid's Inn sacred of the Babylonians, filthy horse-like penises spurting streams forced into her painfully snug twat from behind, haunting the isolated backroads of rural Heartland, half-deep grave in the soft, loam-rich, deep-black earth. "FUCK YOU, SHITHEAD!" she snarls, semen trickling in rivulets from His malicious brain, Whore from Hell kneels up tugs the bloody stump of the severed penis from the dark rosebud. Wordplay. Sex. Death. The occult in clockwork-perfect mimicry The ex-Zodiac intones down *the Road of the Beast . . .*)

He hands his daughter her switchblade. A pack of RIBBED TINGLERS—YOU are NOTHING to them but a BUCKET FULL OF CUM . . . or an aging horror writer back from a six-month stay at the Dachau Hilton . . . a vagrant strand of coffin-black hair . . . You're cocked & loaded now. A fine dose of death hunger.

BLUE DEVIL IS MY FERTILE SEED. & YOU ARE MY FUCKING OFFSPRING. but these are many lives, shared lives, past, present, future, Time is not a forward-flowing river but a sea that washes many shores . . . SHIT STICK. YOU'VE ALWAYS KNOWN ME.

Life or Death? What can it truly matter? They are but the two sides of a single mirror. He/you/she/IT . . . spiritflesh bliss blowing back eons . . . back to the bigfucking bang! From your corner of the blinding blue galaxy you feel her ghost fly away.

This is the longest night of all. Gateway of the Great Night.

THE DEVIL'S ADDENDA

Being a hodge-podge of material peripheral to DUET FOR THE DEVIL

This is a preface cut from the final edition of
DUET FOR THE DEVIL,
Nominee for the 2000 Stoker for Excellence in First Novel

To Stare Without Blinking

by t. winter-damon

First, let me prevail upon you, gentle reader (or, if you prefer, brutal reader, if your persuasion is so inclined . . .), not to make any judgments of, nor to condemn, my partner in crime, Mr. Randy Chandler, based upon my comments & allusions & revelations herein contained . . . i, & i alone, am guilty of this confessional tidbit of literary heresy . . .

"May it please Heaven that the reader, emboldened, and become momentarily as fierce as what he reads, find without loss of bearings a wild and sudden way across the desolate swamps of these sombre, poison-filled pages. For unless he bring to his reading a rigorous logic and mental application at least tough enough to balance his distrust, the deadly issues of this book will lap up his soul as water does sugar. "No good for everyone to read the pages which follow; only the few may relish this bitter fruit without danger . . ." —Le Comte de Lautréamont, Les Chants de Maldoror, p. 1

Quite obviously, i don't know how you spent your New Year's Eve, this past December 31st . . . poised as we are, or were, at the cusp of the infinitely augured &, alternately, much ballyhooed & panegyrized or much dreaded & vilified New Millennium—certainly the media has engaged in its wild orgy of speculation, now it is time for reality (such as you & i choose to perceive it . . .) to set in. But, allow me a moment to indulge in regaling you with how i spent my evening, before setting myself the task of composing this preface, David Barnett suggested i draft . . .

"To say that I think of death unceasingly is not enough. I carry in myself its fabulous presence. Even more strongly at the moment of eating. The reality of death appears to me at every meal and imposes itself . . . I turn toward the cemetery, and my gastronomical happiness is increased by the awareness of death. My appetite topples the tombstones . . ." —Salvador Dali

My wife & i watched two demented little movies whose shared subject is serial killers, of the psychotic Christian zealot persuasion. **Outside Ozona**, directed by J.S. Cardone, featuring a quirky cast including David Paymer as the psycho salesman, Meatloaf, Robert Forster, Lois Red Elk, Taj Mahal & Sherilyn Fenn—of **Twin Peaks** (the deliciously precocious & seductive Audrey Horne . . .) & **Boxing Helena** (the alluringly limbless Helena . . .) fame—i'll watch anyfreakin' thing she's in . . . to my mind, Sherilyn is the most sensual, provocative femme fatale since Debbie Harry as the incredibly seductive, masochistic pop psychologist Nicki Brand in **Videodrome. & Resurrection**, directed by Russell Mulcahy, starring Christopher Lambert, & cameoing David Cronenberg as a priest— the Cronenberg cameo alone makes it certainly worth the price of the rental! i've seen Cronenberg as a leather-masked psycho killer (**Nightbreed**), a hitman (**To Die For**), a hospital lawyer (**Extreme Measures**), a postal supervisor (**The Stupids**), an auto wreck salesman (**Crash**), & a gynecologist (**The Fly**)—but a priest is most assuredly a new twist for this darkly visionary film director!

"The process of writing and directing drives you to such extremes that it's natural to feel an affinity with insanity. I approach that madness as something dangerous and I'm afraid, but also I want to go to it, to see what's there . . . to embrace it. I don't know why, but I'm drawn." —Dario Argento

As proof of my own demented reality filters, i offer in evidence that Cronenberg's cult classic, Videodrome, is my hands-down, all-time favorite flick . . . i've no doubt seen it well over a hundred times . . . If i recall correctly, the "godfather of cyberpunk", William Gibson, once said that Bladerunner was too much like the inside of his head he was forced to flee the theatre only partway through it . . . On the other hand, decidedly the left, that is, it is one of the very qualities i embrace in Videodrome . . .

"I'm not sure what these people are saying. Is it that if you depicted no graphic violence, the world would calm down and there would be less violence? Or is it that if you sense certain things about violence and then portray those things in a film, does that make the violence go to another level? Or is the violence in films a way to experience something without having to do it in real life?" —David Lynch

Outside Ozona's killer was of the cleansing scourge persuasion (you guessed it . . .), out to purify the earth from the corrupting taint of harlots, while **Resurrection**'s psycho slayer was racing against time, striving to cobble together, in a manner akin to The Modern Prometheus, a surrogate body of christ on the cross by eastertide . . .

Despite some excellent casting, some finely crafted acting by both casts (my sole major complaint in this respect being the criminally under-utilized talents of Sherilyn Fenn . . .), & often darkly elegant & stylish camerawork, where both films failed miserably, in my opinion, is the Achilles heel of most films & books dealing with serial killers & psychos—failure to convincingly show us or allow us to experience the Evildoers' motivations & thought processes—to, as Edward Lee so eloquently puts it in his introduction, to "take you deep deep down inside the snakepit of a psycho's soul . . ." This is not the robotic, in the driver's seat POV, leering through the eyeholes of the hockey—(I just caught myself subconsciously mis-keying it as "hokey" . . .) or ski—or Halloween-masked, mindless, slice-&-dice-teenager franchises as the Jason Vorhees/Friday the Thirteenth & its countless clones . . .

"Murder considered as one the fine arts." —Thomas de Quincy, title of an essay in **Blackwood's Magazine**, November, 1839

Granted, due to the externalized, visual orientation versus the internalized & introspective nature of text narrative, this is far more difficult to pull off in film than in should be in print—David Lynch's Dennis Hopper/Frank Booth in **Blue Velvet**, Anthony Hopkins as Hannibal Lector in **The Silence of the Lambs**, Robert Mitchum's roles as the homicidally insane, itinerant preacher, Harry Powell, in **The Night of the Hunter** & as Max Cady in the original **Cape Fear**, or Robert De Niro's Max Cady reprise in the remake of **Cape Fear**, or his portrayal of Travis Bickle in **Taxi Driver**, immediately leap to mind as cinematic exceptions. Thomas Harris's superb novels, increasingly from **Red Dragon** to **Silence of the Lambs** to Hannibal, John D. MacDonald's **Cape Fear**, the novels of hard-boiled crime's grand masters, Jim Thompson & James Ellroy, Jack Ketchum/Dallas Mayr's brilliant masterpiece, **The Girl Next Door**, Rex Miller's cult classic, **Slob**, as well as his **Frenzy, Stone Shadow, Iceman,** & **Slice**, Edward Lee & Elizabeth Steffen's **Portrait of the Psychopath as a Young Woman**, David Schow's **The Kill Riff**, & Michael McDowell's surreal **Toplin**, as literary examples of this inside-the-psyche-of-the-psycho viewpoint.

"Easy is the way down to the Underworld: by night and by day the dark Hades' door stands open; but to retrace one's steps and to make a way out to the upper air, that is the task, that is the labor." —Virgil, **Aeneid**, book 6, 1, 126

i believe you can tell a great deal about someone from their favorite movies. My top twenty favorites (the kind you can watch & rewatch 20, 50, 100 times & never grow tired of viewing & rediscovering . . .) are an admittedly bizarre mix—David Cronenberg's **Videodrome, Scanners, The Naked Lunch, Crash,** & **eXistenZ**, David Lynch's **Eraserhead, Blue Velvet, Wild at Heart,** (the much maligned) **Fire Walk with Me,** & **Lost Highway**, Dario Argento's **Suspiria** & **Inferno**, **Alice in Wonderland**, John Waters' **Dangerous Living, The Wizard of Oz, Flesh Gordon** (the XXX version . . .), **Forbidden Planet**, Sam Peckinpah's **Pat Garrett** & **Billy the Kid, 2000 Leagues Under the Sea,** & **Caligula** (the XXX version . . .).

Next runners-up, **Barbarella, Apocalypse Now** &, collectively, those nihilistic, ultra-violent, gritty, spaghetti westerns starring Clint Eastwood—**A Fistful of Dollars, For a Few Dollars More, The Good, the Bad and the Ugly, Hang 'Em High, Pale Rider** . . .

"The worst thing about this modern world is that people think you get killed on television with zero pain and zero blood. It must enter into kids' heads that it's not very messy to kill somebody, and it doesn't hurt that much. That's a real sickness to me. That's a real sick thing." —David Lynch

As for my favorite TV series of all time . . . ?—David Lynch's **Twin Peaks,** of course (to digress for just a moment—various friends who also religiously watched the show often commented that every time they saw the decidedly demented Dr. Jacoby, played by Russ Tamblyn, they would fall into a fit of laughter, joking to one another—"there's Damon . . .")

Next favorite TV series: **Nowhere Man** (starring Bruce Greenwood), Chinese puzzle box within Chinese puzzle box within Chinese puzzle box of conspiracy theory: A total paranoia freakout. Multiple layers of lost identity. Snuff photos of U.S. senators hanged by a Lat-Am death squad: but the photos are revealed to have been shot seven miles outside Washington, D.C . . . ?

"Every morning upon awakening, I experience a supreme pleasure: that of being Salvador Dali, and I ask myself, wonderstruck, what prodigious thing will he do today, this Salvador Dali." —Salvador Dali, **Journal d'un génie**

As for my favorite artist/illustrator: above all other, Salvador Dali! Dali for his unflinching, lifelong "conquest of the irrational." Dali for his unabashed devotion to the magickal—as he said in his **Les Passions selon Dali,** "For a mystic like me, man is alchemic matter capable of being turned to gold." Dali for his transcendent, all-devouring godlike egotism—as he once proclaimed, "The difference between the Surrealists and me is that I am a Surrealist."

". . . beautiful as the chance meeting of an umbrella and a sewing machine on a dissection-table." —Lautréamont

As for my other favorite artists & illustrators: Hans Bellmer, René Magritte, Harry O. Morris, J.K. Potter, Giorgio De Chirico, M.C. Escher, Patrick Woodroffe, N.C. Wyeth, Aubrey Beardsley, the

Pieters Bruegel (both "the Elder" & "Hell"), Hieronymus Bosch, Gustave Doré, H.R. Giger . . .

"We converse among ourselves—
Pour us your poison, let us be comforted!
Once we have burned our brains out we can plunge
deep into the abyss—to Hell or Heaven—of what importance
which? Through the unknown we'll find the new!"
—Charles Baudelaire, "The Voyage," from **Le Fleurs du Mal**

We indeed plunge headlong into the New Millennium, which will— even if its immediate advent was not accompanied by the Fire & Brimstone of prophesied Apocalypse or the Ice & Fire of Ragnarok— surely prove an epoch of mindreeling changes forced upon us in dizzying succession . . . an epoch of resurgent atavism & techno-tribes, of neo-paganism, of bio-implants & genetic engineering, of yet new & newer designer drugs (altering & reconfiguring both mind & body . . .), of New Gods & The New Flesh . . . From what the progression of rapidly escalating urban violence & gang warfare of the '90s suggests, the decades to come may also prove a transformation to a veritable bloodbath . . . & then an unstoppable tsunami bloodtide . . .

"Brothers I deceived you: Abyss! Abyss! Abyss!
The god is missing from the altar where I am the victim . . .
There is no God! God no longer exists! But they still slept . . .
"Looking for the eye of God I saw only a socket
Vast, black, and bottomless, from whence the Night that dwells
there
Streams out over the world and ever deepens . . ."
—Gérard de Nerval, from "The Christ in the Olive Grove," in
Chimères

Historically, there have been far far more innocents slaughtered in the name of God, Christ, Jehovah, Yahweh, whatever, than in the name of Satan, Lucifer, Belial, Leviathan, Asmodeus, Baal Zebub, & any other infernal name you care to invoke . . .

"I'll tell you a great secret, my friend. Don't wait for the last judgment. It happens every day." —Albert Camus, **The Fall**

Yet, as many of The Twelve Omens, as well as national headlines attest, there seem to be an escalating number of crimes committed either expressly in the name of Satan or with strong Satanic signatures, whether overtones or undertones, to the crimes themselves . . . Hyperreligiosity is often one symptom of the multiple murderer, & the fanatic killing in the name of Yahweh, as in the aforementioned movies, or of Satan, as in the slayers of **Duet for the Devil**, is still manifesting the Janus faces of the same fixation . . .

"Prisons are built with bricks of Law, brothels with bricks of Religion."—William Blake, **The Marriage of Heaven and Hell**, "Proverbs of Hell"

This Waking Dream we've all shared is finally at an end. The Living Nightmare we have experienced thus far in but fleeting glimpses now begins in earnest, soon, so soon, reeling over us in shockwaves . . . Indeed. The Day of Mankind is past. The Age of Mancruel certainly is at hand . . .

"There are more things in heaven and earth . . . than are dreamed of in your philosophy." —William Shakespeare, **Hamlet**, I, v, 166

i was once "lambasted" by the Information Minister of the late Anton Szandor LaVey's The First Church of Satan, who accused me of being a "philosophical dilettante." This, after i opted out of drafting my half of the proposed **The Secret Book of Luciferóa** project that could, potentially, have proven extremely lucrative, based on sales of similar books, such as **The Satanic Bible** . . .

Far from considering this as the insult it was intended to convey, i actually perceive the assessment a compliment, a tribute to my embrace of often radically varied viewpoints.

i, in turn, perceived this "condemnation" betrayed the opinion of a narrow-minded zealot of a far too confining, regimented, fundamentalist theology . . . every bit as much fundamentalist in its proscribed, indoctrinated canon as any bible-thumping Baptist televangelist . . .

"I'm interested in anything about revolt, disorder, chaos, especially any activity that appears to have no meaning. It seems to me to be the road to freedom." —Jim Morrison, **Time Magazine**, 24 January 1968

In delving into the darkest regions of the human consciousness, in exploring the most demented extremes of perversity & aberrant behavior—a task i've committed myself wholeheartedly to in creating my somewhat notorious body of works—i have become, by general consensus, somewhat of a lay expert in the fields of Surrealism, world mythologies, Meso-American mythology & rituals, serial murder, sexual sadism, cannibalism, & the occult.

"The reason Milton wrote in fetters when he wrote of Angels and God, and at liberty when of Devils and Hell, is because he was a true Poet, and of the Devil's party without knowing it." —Blake, **The Marriage of Heaven and Hell**, "The voice of the Devil".

Aside from the works of de Sade & Baudelaire, of William S. Burroughs, of Edgar Allen Poe & H.P. Lovecraft, the most influential books i recall from my teens & early twenties were Harlan Ellison's groundbreaking, visionary anthologies—**Dangerous Visions** (1967) & **Again, Dangerous Visions** (1972). These books threw wide open new doors of perception as to slipstream SF's possibilities as a legitimate, controversial, mind-altering, subversive, literary art form. "Anarcho-lit." The age of Starship & Empire, The Gernsback Continuum, had at last been overthrown by the full force assault of a radically new kind of hard-edged, often hallucinotic, often street-level story that defied all predefined conceptions of what SF was & what it could be . . . a psycho-alchemical transmutation into the first evolutionary phase of The New Flesh . . . Although Ellison repeatedly promised a followup volume, i believe it was tentatively entitled, **Last Dangerous Visions**—regretfully, this long-awaited, third Ellison brainchild offspring was stillborn . . .

"My books, an odd assortment of the of the knowledge of all ages, history, travels, religion, the cabala, astrology, enough to gladden the shades of Pico della Mirandola, the sage Meursius, and Nicholas of Cusa—the Tower of Babel in two hundred volumes—they had left me all that! They were enough to drive a wise man mad; let us ensure that there was enough to make a madman sane . . ." —Gérard de Nerval, **Aurélia**, Part Two

Hence, i consider myself as thrice fortunate to have my work included in the seminal SF anthology, **SEMIOTEXT (E) SF** anthology (1989, AUTONOMEDIA), often referred to as "**Dangerous Visions** for the '90s," or, simply, "The Bible," by many devoted readers with whom i've spoken . . . The anthology was edited by Robert Anton Wilson (author of the **ILLUMINATUS!** Trilogy) & Peter Lambourne Wilson (both major gurus of Chaos Theory) & wellknown cyberpunk Rudy Rucker. The anthology included work by such literary & SF notables as William S. Burroughs, William Gibson, J.G. Ballard, Philip Joseé Farmer, Colin Wilson, Sol Yurick, John Shirley, Bruce Sterling, & Michael Blumlein. The following is quoted from their introduction, "Strange Attractor(s)":

"NO WAVE SF

Various publishing ventures have done this in the past; one thinks of NEW WORLDS, the **Dangerous Visions** anthologies, **Unearth** magazine. Now it's time for a new jolt with a Post-Everything topspin: the **SEMIOTEXT (E) SCIENCE FICTION ANTHOLOGY.** An Einstein-Rosen wormhole into anarcho-lit history:

"TENTACLESUCKER SF

The third category of contributors emerged largely from the underground world of xerox microzines and American samizdat: writers so radically marginalized they could never be co-opted, recuperated, reified or bought out by the Establishment. This group includes, for example: Bob McGlynn, a post-peacenik activist with a Brooklyn group called the Sacred Jihad of our Lady of Perpetual Chaos; Nick Herbert, a 'real' physicist and author of Quantum Reality,

---

but a dangerous madman; the Rev. Ivan Stang, High Epopt of the Church of the SubGenius; the legendary anarchist hippie and friend of Lee Harvey Oswald, Kerry Thornley (a.k.a. Ho Chi Zen), to whom the **ILLUMINATUS!** trilogy was dedicated; Hakim Bey, a 'Poetic Terrorist' and pornographer; . . . and others to be introduced later on.

"TRANSCYBERGNOSTIC SF

Along the frontiers of your actual science, something has recently appeared which may soon replace both relativity and quantum as the source for a new social paradigm: "chaos." An amalgam of Catastrophe Theory, randomicity math, topology, dynamics and statistics, "chaos" also possesses great potential in fields as diverse as biology and morphogenetic field research, economics, brain physiology and consciousness, political theory and radical spirituality. The ideas are so new they haven't even filtered down to many SF writers yet, much less to revolutionary thinkers . . ."

The introduction to my "Lord of Infinite Diversions", therein (which was reprinted in DAW's **The Year's Best Horror Stories, XVIII**— the second of five times Dr. Karl Edward Wagner selected my work for this anthology series), notes "'t'[sic] winter-damon [sic sic] has published widely in the zine-world and on the lunatic fringes of SF . . . The 'experimental text' is now an established genre; at its juiciest . . . it can attain (as it does here for instance) the intensity of a visionary wetdream."

". . . that all reality is virtual reality, which is basically what I think . . . there is no absolute reality, there is no absolute identity for people. It's a constant process of creation and reinvention and re-creation. When you wake up in the morning, the first thing you do before you brush your teeth, if you brush your teeth, is to reinvent reality. You have to reinvent your identity, to remember who you are, who you're supposed to be, what your obligations are, where you came from, what your culture is, and the context that you're in. It takes a lot of will. It takes a lot of energy to do that, to maintain an identity and reality."
—David Cronenberg, from an interview by Andy Spletzer, entitled, "New Sexual Organs"

Most recently, my work, & my collaborative works with Randy Chandler, have been categorized as belonging to the so-called Avant-Pop literary movement. To quote from "The Cyber-Psycho Manifesto" by Zeena Fabreaux:

"AVANT-POP. We are interested in current fantastic literature that focuses on the possibility of the magickal as a way of defeating the power of alienation. We are fascinated by the writers who are fascinated by the absurd and the magickal in pop culture. Like the 'magical realists' who found that to portray the reality of Latin America was to portray the marvelous—we love those writers who, seeking to portray our disposable world, likewise must portray the marvelous and the terrible. We love . . . William Vollmann, . . . Richard Kadrey, Don Webb, Philip K. Dick, . . . Brian Hodge, t. Winter-Damon, Bruce Boston, Mike Hemmingson, . . . John Shirley, Vernor Vinge, William S. Burroughs, Hunter S. Thompson, . . ."

& she proceeds to list "Some Cyber-Psycho Books:

Dr. Adder by KW Jeter
Maldoror by Lautreamont
The Forbidden Gospels of Man-Cruel by t. Winter-Damon and Randy Chandler
Crash by JG Ballard
The Atrocity Exhibition by JG Ballard
Fathers and Crows by William T. Vollmann
The Sheep Look Up by John Brunner
Valis by Philip K. Dick
The Illuminatus Trilogy by Robert Anton Wilson
Apocalypse Culture from Amok and **Feral House**
1984 by George Orwell . . ."

To be included among such cutting edge literary landmarks is flattering, indeed . . .

"Abandon all hope, ye who enter (here) . . ." —Dante Alighieri, **The Divine Comedy**, Inferno canto 3, 1, I

So, what is this book, **Duet for the Devil**, you now hold in hand? Our publisher, David Barnett, has advertised it as ". . . possibly the most disturbing novel ever published . . ."

We believe it's also ". . . quite possibly the most extreme novel ever published . . ."

We sincerely hope it is. We have tried our damnedest to make it so . . . If you don't trust us; then trust Edward Lee when he says, "Hell yes. It's grosser than anything i've ever written or ever read." & i consider Lee a fellow connoisseur of the depraved, the savage & sadistic, the twisted, & the bizarre, in fiction & nonfiction & in film . . .

If we can horrify & disgust you & disturb you with this book, if it offends you & makes you think—yes, that, indeed, would make us happy. If we can even slightly shake the foundations of your reality & perhaps change forever the way you may still view this world as fundamentally safe & sane, ah well, that would make us very happy. On the other hand, if we could destroy your sanity, entirely, undermine every precept you hold dear—why, then, we would be positively gleeful!

"There are some who write seeking the commendation of their fellows by means of noble sentiments which their imaginations invent or they possibly may possess. But I set my genius to portraying the pleasures of cruelty! These are no fickle, artificial delights, they began with man and with him they will die. Cannot genius be cruelty's ally in the secret resolutions of Providence? Or, if cruel, can't one possess genius? My words will provide the proof: all you need do is listen to them, if you like . . ." —Le Comte de Lautréamont, **Les Chants de Maldoror**, p. 3

Of any novel i have ever read, the most disturbing book, by far, has to be de Sade's **One Hundred and Twenty Days of Sodom**. If there is one book i consider, on my part at least, has served as inspiration for **Duet for the Devil**, then it is surely the hateful, sadistic, malignantly lustful, disgusting, perverse, & hypnotically seductive revelations of **Les 120 Journées de Sodome** . . .

"I think it's the scariest thing to know someone, or suspect someone, that has a very intelligent mind, really nothing is wrong with them in any way, but who is possessed by evil and who has dedicated themselves to doing evil." —David Lynch

Another closely related major inspiration for **Duet for the Devil** is the concept espoused by the French poet, mystic, dramatist, actor, theoretician & avant-garde theatre director Antonin Artaud, "self-exiled" member of the Surrealist movement, in his Manifeste du théâtre de la cruaté. Plagued by lifelong bouts of perceived mental disorders, Artaud was frequently confined to asylums . . . The Theatre of Cruelty is a surreal theatre, rooted in ritual, magick & fantasy, & based on the development of gesture & sensory responses, building to an extremely heightened emotional state of the cast, bordering on hysteria, a state wherein they could communicate with the audience on a more profound psychological level than is possible with mere words. The best-known such work is no doubt **The Persecution and Assassination of Jean-Paul Marat as Performed by the Inmates of Charenton under the Direction of the Marquis de Sade,** by the German dramatist Peter Weiss. To quote the **Encyclopaedia Britannica,** volume 18, p.232c : ". . . [The Theatre of Cruelty] launches an attack on the audience's subconscious in an attempt to release deep-rooted fears and anxieties that are normally repressed, forcing people to view themselves and their natures without the shield of civilization. In order to shock the audience and thus win the necessary response, the extremes of human nature (often madness and perversion) are graphically portrayed on stage." To attempt, within the context, not of the stage, but of a novel, &, hopefully, to accomplish such an assault & transformation is certainly one of our primary motivations in writing **Duet for the Devil** . . .

"All changed, changed utterly:
A terrible beauty is born."
—William Butler Yeats, "Easter, 1916"

&, in **Duet for the Devil,** we sought to drag forth from the depths of depravity that "terrible beauty," the ultimate frisson nouveau sought by Baudelaire & Rimbaud & the Symbolists in their writings . . .

"Killing someone is just like taking a walk outdoors. If I wanted a victim, I'd just go out and get one. I didn't even consider a person a human being." —Henry Lee Lucas

Another primary reason for writing **Duet for the Devil** has been my longtime interest in serial killers—&, to my mind, by far the most fascinating serial killer of all certainly must be The Zodiac/ Green River Killer. i mention the two in "one single breath" because i am absolutely convinced the "Green River Killer" is but one of many "masks" the police-taunting, occult-influenced Zodiac would wear in His prolonged further murderous exploits after "going subterranean," after proclaiming He would no longer announce to anyone when He committed His murders, "they shall look like routine robberies, killings of anger, & a few fake accidents, etc . . ." & added "The police shall never catch me because I have been too clever for them." Zodiac has been the subject of frenzied speculation in numerous newspaper articles, nonfiction books, novels, websites, & films in the years since He rocked the headlines, then, mysteriously "vanished".

Just as one example, from an article by staff writer Dave Peterson, in the Vallejo Times-Herald, dated 25 April, 1974, titled, "Are 2 Zodiac Terrorists Operating In Two States?": ". . . Sonoma authorities found a witchcraft symbol beside the remains of three young girls, ages 12 to 15, who were dumped off Franz Valley Road in 1972-73. It consisted of sticks laid in a joined square and a rectangle, with two stones in the latter figure . . ."

"The world is a mysterious place. Especially in the twilight . . . At this time of the day, in the twilight, there is no wind. At this time there is only power . . . You must let yourself go so your personal power will merge with the power of the night . . ." —Carlos Castaneda, Journey to Ixtlan, **The Lessons of Don Juan**

As for potential Zodiac suspects, during the official investigation, over 2500 persons were considered, & eliminated, as possible suspects in the case. In most murder cases of this type, one of the individuals included in the initial stages of questioning is later discovered to be the perpetrator, even though they were ruled out, for one reason or another, until much later. In the case of Zodiac, much later is over thirty years later . . . Among those noted in public speculation over the years, a handful of individuals have gained some degree of prominence. Gareth Penn's book, Times 17 (Foxglove Press), focuses as its suspect on Michael O'Hare (described as brilliant, an excellent marksman, reputedly a suspect in the 1981 murder of Harvard graduate student Joan Webster, & expert in both Morse code & binary mathematics . . .); Lawrence Kane (profiled on the 14 November 1998 episode of "America's Most Wanted" featuring the Zodiac; Pam Huckaby, sister of Darlene Ferrin, has reputedly identified Kane as the stranger who was stalking Darlene during the timeframe just before she was murdered . . .); an individual known as "Peter O."; ex-Manson family member Bruce Davis; convicted Unabomber Ted Kaczynski; Richard Marshall, allegedly the pseudonymous "Donald Jeff Andrews" of Robert Graysmith's Zodiac (reportedly, traveling from his native Texas to California, Marshall was suspected of killing a young hitchhiker & assuming his identity . . .); &, perhaps one of the best matchups as a suspect, the late Arthur Leigh Allen, reportedly the "Robert Hall Starr" of Robert Graysmith's Zodiac, & most recently noted as considered the prime suspect by many investigators in a segment devoted to Zodiac in the History Channel's "Perfect Crimes" series (the number of "matches" he has with details of the Zodiac profile is indeed very high . . . deceptively high . . .)

However, none of these suspects was or is the mysterious killer known as "Zodiac." In studying every bit of available information i could possibly access over the years, i was fortunate enough to decipher & extrapolate certain clues that have been hitherto overlooked or ignored: there is absolutely no doubt in my mind (nor, i believe, will there be in yours after reading the many previously unpublished details of these clues laid out in this book, Duet for the Devil, you now hold in-hand . . .) that Zodiac's given name was "George Simon Brittain"—before & in the years following His reign of terror as "Zodiac," He has worn many "masks," has assumed many names, in His bloody, terrorist campaign against Society . . .

"'Answer!' cried Caesar to Jupiter Ammon:
'Who is this new god that is imposed on the earth?
And if this be not a god, it is at least a daemon.'"
—Gérard de Nerval, from "The Christ in the Olive Grove," in
Chimères

The writing, marketing & eventual, current publication by NECRO Publications of **Duet for the Devil** has proven a labor that's consumed somewhat over a decade—perhaps Sisyphusian punishment for the audacity of our intended crimes of literary terrorism . . . this "unparalleled novel," this damned, infernal sigil/objet fixe, through which we have relentlessly striven to create our own Einstein-Rosen wormhole into anarcho-lit history . . .

"There cannot, I insist, be beauty—convulsive beauty—except at the cost of affirmation of the reciprocal relation which links the objects considered in its movement and its repose. I regret not having been able to furnish, as a complement to the illustration of this text, the photograph of a powerful locomotive abandoned for years to the madness of the virgin forest. The fact aside that the desire to see such a thing has long been accompanied for me by a special exaltation, it seems to me that the surely magickal aspect of the monument to victory and to disaster would better than any other have been of a nature to stabilize ideas . . ."
—Andre Breton, L'Amour fou (Mad Love)

Early on, Randy & i were extremely flattered when supporters of our novel termed it an "underground classic," a "**Dr. Adder** for the '90s"—by which they meant a groundbreaking novel of literary merit so shocking & uncompromising we would struggle against seemingly hopeless odds for ten years or more before at last finding a publisher with the cojones to dare risk placing it in print. Time has indeed led us to feel a definite kinship with K.W. Jeter's visionary masterpiece, **Dr. Adder**—a book reportedly written in 1972, but more likely actually written in 1973, which did not see print in America until 1988, although it had received critical acclaim & achieved the limited beginnings of cult status when published in France in the interim. **Dr. Adder** is the definitive proto-Cyberpunk novel of extreme body modification, inspired by the following excerpt from a letter that reportedly appeared in **Penthouse** magazine's November 1972 issue: "I would like to add my vote in favour of showing female amputees in your magazine. One-armed and, especially, one-legged females offer a unique excitement and a pictorial featuring attractive girl amputees would certainly be welcomed by a large number of readers . . ."

No lesser literary giant than the legendary Philip K. Dick was Jeter's mentor & avid supporter in assisting him see his book printed in America. In his afterword to the 1988 Signet edition of **Dr. Adder**, the book's first American publication, Dick begins:

"'Sir, you have written a dirty book, sir!'

"Which writer does Mrs. Grundy have in mind now? James Joyce for his masterpiece **ULYSSES**? Or Henry Miller for his two **TROPICS** novels? The shriek of dismay from the prudes of the world is eternal. And this shriek has prevented the publishing of K.W. Jeter's extraordinary novel **DR. ADDER** for literally years—until a courageous publisher finally stepped forth and said:

"'We'll publish it.'"

Philip K. Dick proceeds to say, "Very simply, it is a stunning novel and it destroys once and for all your conceptions of the limitations of science fiction. This is, of course, why so many years had to pass before it saw print. It's not dirty. Mrs. Grundy is wrong. Yes, it deals not only with sexual perversions but with fantastic sexual perversions: dreams of sexual perversions which are dreams you and I never supposed existed."

Dick later states: "Forget your timid preconceptions of what a science fiction novel should be like . . . This novel is about our world and so it is a dangerous novel in the same sense that Harlan Ellison's **DANGEROUS VISIONS** stories were, by and large, dangerous. This is precisely what we need."

"There are no limits . . ." —Clive Barker

In the introduction you've just read to **Duet for the Devil**, Edward Lee cites: "It delves into taboos so mind-boggling that the likes of Richard Ramirez and Richard Speck would be jealous, and it does so with an eagerness of vision and an energy to offend. I welcome this because that which offends us also provokes us . . . to think."

"A man who has not passed through the inferno of his passions has never overcome them." —Carl Gustav Jung, **Memories, Dreams, Reflections**, chapter 9

i first made acquaintance with Randy Chandler in 1986, while he was editing **Bone-Chilling Tales** magazine & **'Lil Demon Review**, writing some very powerful short horror fiction with a decidedly experimental literary bent, such as his incomparable "(3-D)" which had just appeared in the experimental lit-zine **EOTU**—a horror tale as densely compressed as the heart of a blue dwarf star, packing the whallop of a Howitzer shell in perhaps a thousand words, at most . . . Randy also was drafting reviews on a regular basis for the prestigious **Atlanta Journal-Constitution**. He accepted my own "Penetration Maximum" for publication in **Bone-Chilling Tales**, as well as a number of reviews for **'Lil Demon Review**. i was struck by the intelligence & compression of his writing, his flair for language, his savage, biting sense of humor, as well as by our shared love of genre perfectionists such as the recently anointed wunderkind of horror, Clive Barker, & SF's reigning gurus, Cyberpunk William Gibson, the always amazing, genre-tripping K. W. Jeter, Thomas Pynchon, & Philip K. Dick, hard-boiled crime badboys like Raymond Chandler, Jim Thompson & James Ellroy, & the wild, experimental literary writing of the works of William S. Burroughs, & Bob Dylan's dazzling "novel", **Tarantula** . . .

"Society prepares the crime; the criminal commits it." —quote from a cookie fortune sent to me 16 September 1991 by Randy Chandler

i would like to present you who may be interested with some insights as to our rather unusual creative process . . .

"The only difference between myself and a madman, is that I am not mad." —Salvador Dali

In **Duet for the Devil** we explore the darkest depths of psychoses & the psychotic mind . . . How did we so plunge our own psyches into such an extreme mindset? Again, speaking for myself alone, i threw myself wholeheartedly into disciplines I had previously used in my writings—both what Arthur Rimbaud referred to as "the systematic disordering of the senses," & to Dali's "Paranoiac-critical activity."

"Paranoiac-critical activity: spontaneous method of irrational knowledge based on critical and systematic objectivity of the associations and interpretations of delirious phenomena." —Salvadore Dali

Sometime in late-January, 1987, i must have mentioned to Randy i'd be interested in collaborating with him. He replied in a letter dated 07 February 1987, "I've suddenly become intrigued by the idea of doing collaborative fiction, thanks, in part, to your mention of it. Methinks it would be a blast. So, if you're game & if & when you have the time, would you like to give it a shot with yours truly? Something 'experimental,' of course. I have a wide-open title in mind: 'Duet for the Devil' which would obviously refer to the duo of its authors & would be a title we can easily play upon in the creation of the work itself . . ." So was first conceived this diabolic offspring, this wailing, offensive enfent terrible you now hold in-hand.

As we progressed, Randy commented in a letter dated 26 July 1988, "Fanfuckingtastic, brother! I knew we were on to something good, something hot, but it's turning into something better than I had expected—something white hot & cool cobalt blue. Your work/ inspiration in XI opens with dimensions we were sniffing out in earlier segments . . . Reel you in? Fuck that! Run with it, take it deep, plumb the oceanic depths. I'm getting the scary feeling we're tapping close to some sort of black hole in the great Unconscious, the horror source (literary sorcerers we) & that our black creation may one day be viewed as a watershed work of black art. Exploring the Evil core underlying humanity, methinks we'd best get a good grip on our minds/souls. Horror-nauts light out . . ."

From a letter dated 14 July 1990: "Thanks for the MONSTER. & what a fucking MONSTER it is! Most impressive, dark dude. I finished reading it last night—Friday the 13th, of course—and it did send me reeling . . . DUET is a HELL of a horror story, an ultimate conspiracy caper, its dark roots running deep into ancient mythology/biblical prophesy & even drawing from modern 'mythology' of Hollywood & Barker & King, etc. Our poetic creation is nothing less than a fearless look into the dark (Hogbutcher's) heart of humanity & into the sick side of our bastard culture. What we have here is the ultimate horror novel. Maybe I'm blowing it out of proportion . . . maybe we've both gone over the line a little too far into psychosis . . . nah, I don't think so. We crossed the forbidden lines all right, but there was no other way, eh? . . . the graphic sick sex scenes (Mal's & Frank's) are truly poetic . . . those scenes are probably the most horrible scenes I've ever had the shuddering pleasure to read . . ."

"What have I been writing? Blasphemies. Christian humility does not speak in that way. Such thoughts are far from softening the soul. On their foreheads they bear the proud glitter of Satan's crown . . ."
—Gérard de Nerval, **Aurélia**, Part Two

By 1990, Randy & i had completed some 500-odd pages of **Duet for the Devil**. With the unflagging support of & introductions by longtime friend & fellow-traveling Old Soul, noted horror author Brian Hodge (author of the recent bestselling novel & World Horror nominee, **Wild Horses**, as well as of **Dark Advent, Oasis, Night Life, Deathgrip, The Darker Saints, & Prototype**, & of the collections **Falling Idols & The Convulsion Factory** . . .), the as-yet-unfinished manuscript **Duet for the Devil** had been circulated to several well-established literary agents for consideration—it had proved far too extreme in content for the first two, but a third was "knocked back in her chair" by its "incredible sense of presence" & the "dizzying energy of its wired, onrushing pace."

". . . Reality itself founders in hyperrealism, the meticulous reduplication of the real, . . . the real is volatilized, becoming an

allegory of death. But it is also, in a sense, reinforced through its own destruction. It becomes reality for its own sake, the fetishism of the lost object: no longer the object of representation, but the ecstasy of denial and of its own ritual extermination: the hyperreal . . . Unreality no longer resides in the dream or fantasy, or in the beyond, but in the real's hallucinatory resemblance to itself."
—Jean Baudrillard, excerpt from "Symbolic Exchange and Death"

Also eager to obtain maximum exposure & publicity to its potential readership for our still in-works project, we submitted numerous excerpts, most of which received quick acceptance & publication, by 1990, seeing print in a wide variety of venues, from the luridly titled little Splatter-lit zine **Festering Brainsore**, to major markets such as World-Fantasy-Award-winning **Grue** #10 (Fall, 1989; as "& They Shall Receive a Mark Upon Their Flesh"), the **Noctupla** IV anthology ("Motel on the Road to Hell"), & the highly respected British slipstream/SF magazine, **Back Brain Recluse** #13 (simply titled, "Duet for the Devil").

The excerpt in the latter drew a flurry of reader letters published in the following issue. Among the Brits, then SF rising-star Simon Clark commented, "I have to say now that BBR is not on par with **Interzone**, It is better . . . but I can't imagine them using 'Duet for the Devil' by Randy Chandler and t. Winter-Damon. This was an amazing, gob-smacking story; hip-deep in bizarre, multi-coloured imagery that covered seemingly everything, bouncing from Lovecraft to the **Book of Revelations** to Clive Barker and beyond. Messrs Chandler and Damon should burn rubber, burn the midnight lamp and finish the novel. It will be essential reading for the speculative fiction reader . . ." Mike Hadfield noted, "the poetic prose of Hakim Bey and t. Winter-Damon . . ." & Christian Vallini, a reader from Buenos Aires, Argentina, wrote: "'Duet for the Devil' is so strange, well, I'd say it's a wild story. A really wild one due to its treatment. Although it keeps on some relation to Splatterpunk, it's a different style I don't see in Skipp and Spector stories. 'Neo-Baudelarian Cyber-Sade'? . . ."

"Let us not mince words: the marvelous is always beautiful, anything marvelous is beautiful; in fact only the marvelous is beautiful." — Andre Breton, **Manifeste du surréal**

A re-publication of the same excerpt from **Back Brain Recluse**, under the title, "Palette of the Perverse", appeared in the American **EOTU** soon after. Its appearance garnered nominations for the 1991 World Fantasy Award—however, the story did not make the final ballot.

"Pure psychic automatism, by which it is intended to express . . . the real process of thought, free from any control by the reason and of any aesthetic or moral preoccupation." —Andre Breton, **Manifeste du surréal**

But, despite the fact that editors, readers & critics increasingly referred to **Duet** as an "underground classic," our literary offspring began to run into trouble. When we turned over the completed manuscript to our agent at that time, the text counted in at, i believe, somewhere in the vicinity of 976 pages. She informed us that we would never find a publisher willing to chance the investment/risk involved in printing a first novel of that length. We were forced to seriously reconsider the cast of the then-sprawling epic—The Great Beast Lotan & his minion, Hsuan Chieh, were completely elided; regretfully, in retrospect, the Lilithian Lucy Nation's presence in the book suffered dramatic cuts, & her Erebos' henchman, The Troubleshooter, found his role diminished to a mere passing mention. A wild, murderous, cross-country roadtrip by Maldoror & His 2 accomplices through Indiana & Illinois, culminating in a pitched gunbattle with State Troopers, resulting in the lawmen's slaughter & torture was cut, also, because it trimmed some 100 pages, if memory serves me correctly.

"Your death can give you a little warning, it always comes as a chill. Death is our eternal companion, it is always to our left, at an arm's length.

"How can anyone feel so important when we know that death is stalking us. The thing to do when you're impatient is to turn to your left and ask advice from your death. An immense amount of pettiness is dropped if your death makes a gesture to you, or if you catch a glimpse of it, or if you just have the feeling that your companion is there watching you." —Carlos Castaneda, Journey to Ixtlan, **The Lessons of Don Juan**

All in all, the result was a far tighter, much more publishable novel—despite the pain Randy & i suffered, making these necessary "amputations." &, now, much of the "lost" segments of **Duet for the Devil** are scheduled to see print from Jasmine Sailing Books, under the title, **The Forbidden Gospels of Man-Cruel**, Volumes I & II, later this year, 2001. These will be accompanied by introductions by genre notables Brian Hodge & Don Webb. &, due to some limited circulation of the galleys, **The Forbidden Gospels of Man-Cruel** has earned the books a pre-publication place, as previously referenced, among works by such cutting-edge authors as J.G. Ballard, Robert Anton Wilson, Philip K. Dick, K.W. Jeter, & John Brunner, & literary giants William S. Burroughs, George Orwell, William T. Vollmann, & Le Comte de Lautréamont, on the Cyber-Psychos' website's recommended reading list . . .

Yet another excerpt from **Duet for the Devil** appeared in **Grue #14** (Summer, 1992), under the title, "I am He that Liveth and was Dead . . . & Have the Keys of Hell & Death". This one drew a rave letter (dated simply, July 1992), from none other than the King of Hardcore Horror himself, Edward Lee: ". . . I read your I AM HE excerpt in **Grue 14**, and really loved it. You guys definitely write some rough stuff! I love the way you mix jags of nerve-racking clinical imagery with the hallucinotic stylemode . . . you definitely got a pair of balls!"

A final, expurgated segment from **Duet for the Devil**, in a radically reworked, greatly expanded format, appeared in the **Darkside: Horror for the Next Millennium** anthology (Darkside Press, 1996, limited, signed-&-numbered hardbound edition, & ROC, 1998, massmarket paperback), as ". . . & Thou Hast Given Them Blood to Drink & They are Drunken with the Blood of Saints & with the Blood of Martyrs . . ."

"The issue of our death is never pressed far enough. Death is the only wise adviser that we have. Whenever you feel, as you always do, that everything is going wrong and you're about to be annihilated, turn to your death and ask if that is so. Your death will tell you that you're wrong; that nothing really matters outside its touch. Your death will tell you, "I haven't touched you yet." —Carlos Castaneda, Journey to Ixtlan, **The Lessons of Don Juan**

But, even with the cuts we'd made in **Duet**, we parted ways with our then-current agent over artistic differences, particularly involving certain cuts she demanded regarding the more sexually explicit portions of the novel . . . A friendly editor, temporarily "agenting" for us, was able to get the manuscript read by the editor of the hottest imprint going at the time—Dell Abyss—but Jeanne Cavelos rejected it, primarily, if i recall correctly, due to its unprecedented level of sexual explicitness . . .

"Let us be satisfied with the immediate miracle of opening our eyes, becoming skilled in the apprenticeship of looking well. Looking is a way of inventing." —Salvador Dali

This very explicitness we unwaveringly believe is absolutely imperative to the intensity & integrity of its aesthetic value, imperative to telling this particular story, the way the story itself demanded to be told. We bent with the wind—but, in that flexibility, we survived the wind, not allowing it to break us—some of those deliberately excruciatingly prolonged passages deemed most in-your-face offensive, which, from an artistic standpoint were intended to make the reader feel as though he or she were being forcibly held down by sadistic madmen, eyes taped wide-open, unblinking, head submerged in the chill, black waters of perversity, helplessly flailing to escape, slowly, torturously drowning—these we finally expurgated, in part only . . . yet we retained enough of their substance to assault the reader's senses with their still unprecedented brutality . . . to take you "into the psyche of the psycho."

"Look at me, I have no doubts or remorse. Everything I do is my decision and my responsibility. The simplest thing I do, to take you for a walk in the desert for instance, may very well mean my death. Death is stalking me. Therefore, I have no room for doubts or remorse.

If I have to die as a result of taking you for a walk, then I must die."
—Carlos Castaneda, Journey to Ixtlan, **The Lessons of Don Juan**

We increasingly felt a kinship with those authors who had gone before us, who had experienced rejection or even persecution because their literary visions challenged the limits of then-current moral strictures...

"To the degree that I am a Spanish Mystic, I am a hyperrealist, starting from the concrete in order to come back to it." —Salvador Dali

In its current incarnation, **Duet for the Devil** is still considered even by some of its supporters as "pornographically violent and pornographically sexual." However, we have never considered **Duet** to be pornographic—instead, we think of its unblinking stare into the darkest, most forbidden recesses of the human experience to be hyperrealism ... according to Dali's philosophy, a progression or leap from the concrete to a state of delirious hallucinations—the fever state when the normal appears grotesquely deformed & exaggerated, when the most inconsequential object may take on a threatening & malignant & obsessive life of its own ... In **Duet for the Devil**, you will find this hyperrealism may suddenly zoom in & focus upon the movement of a wheel, or upon a host of flies crawling on a ravaged corpse, or the slashing of a killer's blade, or hands strangling the life from a struggling victim, or upon some perhaps bizarre permutation of the sex act ... as we stare unblinking & unblushing at as de Sade so eloquently put it, "Nature Unveiled . . ."

"Maldoror ... [is] the expression of a revelation so complete it seems to exceed human potential." —André Breton

However, as we are reminded by noted critic Alexis Lykiard in his introduction to Comte de Lautréamont, **Maldoror & The Complete Works**, ". . . Maldoror's shocked first publisher refused to bind the sheets of the original edition and perhaps no better invitation exists to this book which warns the reader, 'Only the few may relish this bitter fruit without danger.'"

"Whoever battles monsters should take care not to become a monster too, for if you stare long enough into the Abyss, the Abyss stares also into you." —Friedrich Nietzsche, **Beyond Good and Evil,** chapter 4, no. 146

De Sade & Baudelaire & Rimbaud & Artaud & J.G. Ballard's literary works all faced censorship or prosecution for obscenity or blasphemy during their own lifetimes. Their works are now considered literary classics . . .

& please recall that William S. Burroughs' literary classic, **The Naked Lunch,** was attacked as pornographic, as were the works of James Joyce & Henry Miller, & they were tried by the courts of the metaphorical Mrs. Grundy in an attempt to censor & suppress & shackle art that dares transgress those restraining, arbitrary boundaries blue-nosed Society dictates . . .

"The Surrealist object . . . under the sign of eroticism, exactly as with the love object, first we want to set it in motion, then we want to eat it." —Salvador Dali

Perhaps the very closest comparison, however, to our own struggles in seeing **Duet for the Devil** see publication are the hardships well-known hard-boiled crime novelist Jonathan (Wayne) Latimer suffered with his 1941 novel, **Solomon's Vineyard.** (Latimer was the author of **Murder in the Madhouse, Headed for a Hearse, The Morgue, The Dead Don't Care,** & **Red Gardenias, Sinners and Shrouds,** & **Black is the Color for Dying,** among many others; he also wrote screenplays, most noteworthy his script for Dashiell Hammett's **The Glass Key;** as a television script writer, among numerous other works, he wrote 50 episodes of "Perry Mason".) **Solomon's Vineyard** is ". . . a work so tough-minded and sexually explicit that no American publisher would take a chance on it in its original form . . . ," according to Bill Pronzini (anthologist & author of over 40 mystery & suspense novels) & Jack Adrian (a noted anthologist & authority on popular and genre fiction of the 20th century) in their introduction to the definitive collection, **HARD-BOILED, An Anthology of American Crime Stories** (Oxford, 1995). **Solomon's Vineyard** also contained necrophilia (as does **Duet for the Devil**). It finally saw print in England, where, reputedly, ". . . the dust-jacket blurb trumpeted: 'It's got everything but an abortion and a tornado.'" Completely coincidentally, you'll find that **Duet for the Devil** indeed has both . . . **Solomon's Vineyard** finally was published in the U.S., in a "heavily expurgated paperback edition" in 1950, retitled **The Fifth Grave**. The original text did not see print in the U.S, until 1982, when it was released by a small press in a limited edition of 326 copies . . .

"Young girls have exquisite insides . . . they blush when you make them edible." —Salvador Dali

Our next agent, Stan Tal, of Tal Literary Agency, tirelessly circulated the **Duet** manuscript globally—but, despite extremely positive comments, it all boiled down to the bottomline—no major publisher had the balls to print it. Until, that is, he sent the manuscript to David Barnett, of NECRO Publications. Thanks to Dave's faith in the book & his legendary cojones—you now have an opportunity to read the long-suppressed, "underground classic," **Duet for the Devil** . . .

As for the title of this preface, "TO STARE WITHOUT BLINKING"—it is a bastardization of a quote from Carlos Castaneda's Journey to Ixtlan, **The Lessons of Don Juan**, citing the teachings of his mentor, the Yaqui sorcerer or brujo, don Juan Matus: ". . . look without blinking until you see." He describes the practice of this concept: ". . . all one has to do is to cross the eyes. The technique takes years to perfect. It consists of gradually forcing your eyes to see separately the same image. The lack of image conversion entails a double perception of the world; this double perception allows one the opportunity of judging changes in the surroundings, which the eyes are ordinarily incapable of perceiving." don Juan further explains that it: ". . . allows the eyes to pick out unusual sights . . . It takes a long time to train the eyes properly. The trick is to feel with your eyes . . . It'll come to you, though, with practice.

"No one can tell you what you are supposed to feel . . . Once you learn to separate the images and see two of everything you must focus your attention in the area between the two images . . ."

Castaneda instructs us, the would-be warrior or man of knowledge, as the Yaqui sorcerer don Juan instructed him, "'Focus your eyes on that spot," he whispered in my ear. 'Look without blinking until you see . . . '"

t. Winter-Damon,
Prophet of the Perverse
Tucson, Arizona
31 December 1999-01 January 2000
(revised 18 March 2000)

Elementary, my Dead Whopper. We have created a bloody monster.
Randy Chandler
Somewhere in the South
3.29.00

Love/Hate Reader Reaction: The Devil Made Them Do It

"I didn't know anybody wrote books like this. It's too subversive, dangerous and demented to have eve been published, right? Maybe the Devil had a hand in it. This is EXTREME horror. Not the commercial junk you find in book stores. But something else altogether. Read these guys before they're put away."

"When I first got this book, I could not wait to read it. I got thru the first 50 pages, and had to throw the damn thing in the garbage. It was like reading a book written by 10 diffrent [sic] people, none knowing what the other was writing about. Was it gory, sure but it was also horribly boring!!"

"*Duet for the Devil* teeters precariously on the precipice of utter garbage. Still, serious gorehounds will want to add this to their library, even if it does become too much at times."

"It really isn't the graphic nature of the book that gets under your skin; it is the duration of the sickness that grates."

"This is truly a taxing book to read, as even the most jaded horror fan begins to wear down under the sheer onslaught of pornographic violence, murder, and general mayhem found on every page of the book."

"True horror?! The fact that this book even got published."

"Horrible and boring."

"Its pyrotechnic, hallucinatory style translates into a poetry of pain and perversion, each sadistic stanza a catalogue of concentrated cruelty and hemorrhaging horror-haiku. It's a bad brown-blotter acid trip where your worst nightmares are on steroids and coming at you from all sides . . . including the depths of your very own soul."

"*Duet for the Devil* is by no means an 'easy read'. It makes emotional, intellectual and psychological demands that some readers may not be able to accommodate. It is an audacious, extraordinarily uncompromising sledgehammer of a novel, relentless in its depiction of mayhem, depravity and psychotic disintegration, and quite unlike anything you have ever encountered. It is one mean road trip to Oblivion, but if you think you can handle it then, by all means, hitch a ride."

"Ivory tower critics and professors who think genre fiction is the purview of hacks and scribblers should take a long hard look at this novel. It contains some of the most potent, poetic, pyrotechnic, and perfectly penned passages anywhere."

"I love books, and would not throw away any book that comes into my hands, but there is always a first, and this was the one that did it."

Transgressive Influences and *Duet for the Devil:* Transcendence Through Ritual Insanity

by David L Tamarin

Ever since the initial publication of *Duet For The Devil*, which was originally a motherfucking gigantic tome close to 1,000 pages, Tipper Gore has been spinning in her fetid grave. Oh, she's not dead yet? Just brain dead? Jerry Fucking Falwell, is also spinning in his grave. For the worms, it feels like a roller coaster.

Somewhere down in Hell (defined as a repository of knowledge), t. Winter-Damon sits on his throne, spouting arcane and esoteric occult and magickal incantations.

Down here on Earth co-writer Randy Chandler writes stories of sex, violence, and the occult.

What happened when Winter-Damon and Chandler sat down to co-write a book? You get one of the most mind-blowingly graphic, disturbing, brutal, violent, hypersexual novels of abjection and nihilism, featuring extreme fetishistic sex, pre-meditated homicides, incest, cannibalism, the occult, magick, torture, and serial killers.

The book is a transgressive masterpiece. And it stands as a lasting tribute to t. Winter-Damon's particular genius. He obsessively read and considered himself an expert on various subjects. He was a self-educated expert in Surrealism, mythology, Meso-American mythology and rituals, serial murder, sexual sadism, cannibalism, and the occult. I would argue that he was also an expert on fetishism, pornography, religion, jazz, geography, culinary matters, quantum math, cyphers and symbols, the left hand path, deviant literature, music, anatomy, firearms, geography, film, police procedure, and more.

As part of this edition of The Gospels Of Man-Cruel, there is included an essay by Winter-Damon entitled "To Stare without Blinking." In that essay he names those transgressive artists who have contributed most towards subversive and underground art. De Sade, Baudelaire, Lautréamont, Bataille, Dali, the Zodiac Killer, Artaud, William Gibson, the cyberpunk movement, the surrealist movement, The Doors, David Lynch, Dario Argento, Gasper Noe, Philip K Dick, John Waters, GG Allin, Charles Manson, David Cronenberg, Natural Born Killers, Throbbing Gristle, Stanley Kubrick, Nick Zedd, J.G. Ballard—all known for expressing themselves in a subversive manner while challenging popular beliefs that serve to enslave the individual and discourage various types of a transgressive identity.

Transgressive fiction focuses on non-conformist anti-heroes, people who break free of societal conformity, often by illegal and radical methods, in order to pursue freedom. Typically, this brand of fiction focuses on unconventional individuals, from serial killers to sexual sadists to crystal meth tweakers. These individuals have nothing but hatred or contempt for straight society. Frequently these people are drug addicted and/or psychotic.

The most obvious piece of transgressive art I have ever seen is Piss Christ. The artist put a figure of jesus christ in a box of urine. You can see jesus, floating in the water like a fish, except this was urine. The work of art was so controversial that the National Endowment of the Arts was attacked and had its budget lowered, all for the crime of paying the artist of Piss Christ. To look at Piss Christ, to really focus your mind on it, to stare without blinking, as t. Winter-Damon says, you can get past the false constructs of reality and society and culture that serve as a blindfold. Works of art like Piss Christ and *Duet for the Devil* are able to shock their readers and viewers so that they might see through the false reality to see reality, and truth, and knowledge. It is not just a crucifix in piss, but a method of transcendence, a way for readers to attain the real Truth. Transgressive Art is best seen as a method to look into yourself and experience revelations about your core being. To the small-minded, narrow-minded, mostly religious morons, transgressive art is pure filth that should be banned. All through history there have been individuals obsessed with accumulating personal power, and many find fame and money by bashing art they do not comprehend. But there are a lot of people who don't want to know the truth. God-fearing cultures tend to be close-minded with the need to attack and criminalize their enemies. This is the reason books like *Naked Lunch* were considered obscene, even though they attempt to express universal truths.

Duet for the Devil is about, among other things, the Zodiac Killer, the ultimate societal transgressor. This serial killer, who goes by Maldoror (after the main character in a Lautréamont story about a man consumed with committing evil) is a mutinous character who has declared war on society. He sent encrypted messages to various newspapers. He taunted the police. He threatened to blow up school buses, causing a city-wide panic. Multiple police officers were put on all school buses but the shooting never happened. He left a trail of dead bodies in Northern California and beyond. Many believe that he continued killing after the Zodiac crimes, covering them up by disguising them as accidents. According to the book, Zodiac may have also been the Green River Killer and BTK, part of a team of serial killers that were never caught or identified. The book contains many references to the crimes of the Zodiac (such as the use of the word Paradice, as Arthur Leigh Allen, whom I believe was the Zodiac, loved puns and loved misspelling words in his correspondences).

As there is transgression in all forms of art, it is interesting to look at musical artists whose music might've provided background sounds for *Duet for the Devil*. G G Allin, Primus, The Butthole Surfers, The Revolting Cocks, Throbbing Gristle, Slayer, Unsane, Marilyn Manson, the Dead Kennedys, Ministry, The Mentors, and many more. Society has set boundaries for our art and the transgressive artists have fought to destroy these boundaries so that there can be real freedom of speech and thought. All the bands and artists I listed shared the fact that their music broke boundaries, sending a subversive message to its listeners. Of all these bands, G G Allin is clearly the most transgressive musician. Rock and Roll was not something that happened on a stage for two hours every night. Rock and Roll was a lifestyle, and the concerts were pure anarchy, with G G not just singing about deviance, but acting it out, assaulting audience members, flinging his feces, and worse.

The most obscene, perverted, sick, sadistic and evil book ever written is Marquis de Sade's *The 120 Days of Sodom*. The book is hundreds of pages of every deviant sexual activity and torture that lived in de Sade's head. It is pretty much the bible of blasphemy, obscenity, abjection, sadism, deviance and crime. It has been hundreds of years and no book has come as close in perversity as the original de Sade classic. It is beyond transgressive. In *Duet* Maldoror tells the bible salesman, "Well, Bible Man, welcome to the remake of *The 120 Days of Sodom*."

Speaking of de Sade, another influence on the book was the film *Salo*, which is alleged to have played a part in the murder of director Pier Paolo Pasolini. It is an adaption of *The120 Days of Sodom*, and it is an ugly transgressive work of film, filled with some of the most horrible images ever captured on film. It contains scene after scene of depravity and suffering. The audience members have access to truths previously forbidden to them, as they festered in the subconscious mind. These subconscious memories can be easily triggered, and soon one is made aware of his true monstrous self. In a sense, this type of film or fiction is like electro shock treatment, breaking the individual free of his cultural trance. But be warned: Staring without blinking at the naked truth may make you a dangerous subversive.

Raymond Chandler, Jim Thompson, and James Ellroy all write transgressive noir, of a world dark and violent, a dangerous world inhabited by outcasts living at the edge of society, an underworld you can't write without graphic sex, violence and depravity.

Another major influence on *Duet for the Devil* is Compte du Lautréamont—pseudonym for Frenchman Isidore-Lucien Ducasse (1846-1870). The authors were so inspired by Lautréamont's writing that they named one of the book's serial killers Maldoror, Lautréamont's fictional bad guy, a man obsessed with evil and unfailingly opposed to God.

The main character of Lautréamont's seminal *Les Chants de Maldoror* has the same name as the Zodiac Killer in *Duet*, who is frequently called Maldoror and sometimes Mal for short. This is a good fit as Lautréamont also was obsessed with pain, suffering, and cruelty. Lautréamont was also a hero to the Surrealists, and *Duet* has many surrealistic passages. In fact, Winter-Damon writes of his admiration of Salvador Dali, the ultimate surrealist, a strange egomaniacal personage possessed with brilliance. He has been a huge influence in everything from film to literature to psychology.

He wasn't just a surrealist artist, but he was a surrealist individual.

The next major influence is K.W. Jeter, an author who inspired none other than Philip K. Dick. He went on to write three sequels to *Blade Runner*, which were based on Dick's *Do Androids Dream of Electric Sleep?* Jeter's early cyberpunk novel *Dr. Adder* and the cyberpunk movement in general also influenced the writers of *Duet*. *Dr. Adder* is now a classic, but because of its extreme content, it took the author a full decade to get publication. *Duet for The Devil* also had problems with finding a publisher, and the process took years.

Cyberpunk involves futuristic technology combined with low life criminals and deviants. There is usually a state of anarchy or at least a complete breakdown in society and society's need for law and order. *Duet for the Devil* also ventures into futuristic high tech and essentially becomes splatterpunk meets cyberpunk with heavy doses of psychedelics. A writer who influenced cyberpunk was Thomas Pynchon, whose fans included Philip K. Dick. It's no coincidence that a hit man in *Duet* is named Pynchon.

Because individuals who transgress norms don't accept polite society's standards on the value of life, many transgressive stories are about serial killers, some even told from the serial killer's point of view. Killers and madmen populate the Halls of Transgression. This brings us to our next influence on Transgressive Writing, Anton Artaud and his Theatre of Cruelty. Despite its name, it is not about cruelty and sadism. Rather, he tries to express universal truths to the audience, and if he uses magickal language, he is better able to interact with the audience so that they can truly comprehend the play they were attending. The goal was to throw people into a state of thrall and rebellion, making them question everything. This can only be achieved through Art, which serves the important function of allowing us to deal with the monsters in our heads in a healthy way. Transgressive Art, like LSD, will change your perception of reality.

For Antonin Artaud and his Theatre of Cruelty, the goal was to have the cast create a meaningful relationship or bond with the audience, and this can only be achieved by extreme behavior and mental states. Thus the scripts were full of sex, violence, and deviance, in order to challenge the audience into thinking and re-evaluating themselves. These revelations can only occur when the most obscene and violent material was enacted on stage (or in our case, a book), because these plays connect emotionally and make you more prone to being open to seeing the world differently. This art brings you closer to the extremity of objectionable material.

By cruelty, Artaud did not mean sadistic behavior. Rather, the theatre of cruelty encouraged actors to lose their minds during a performance, getting lost in a world of delirium. Only through this chaos can the actors truly connect with their audience and pass on messages to them. The Theatre of Cruelty's goal was liberation and discovery of truth, through deranged, extreme behavior. This liberation led to a true connection between audience and actors that could not occur in any other setting. By 'cruelty' Artaud meant a destruction of the false reality we think we live in, so that we can get in closer touch with ourselves. The goal was always liberation from the machine and greed. Artaud wanted a revelation of man to himself. In other words, culture has taken our identity and the Theatre of Cruelty gives us all a chance to connect with our true selves. This in turn may lead us to shed the false pretenses of society.

Artaud was a madman who was frequently hospitalized. At one hospital, he was put on laudanum, which turned him into a drug addict who suffered the pains of addiction his whole life.

Artaud was an advocate of magic, ritual, and sorcery. To advance his Theatre of Cruelty, he needed his actors to shed any inhibitions, and to act in a deranged way. To accomplish this, Artaud used rituals, gesture, language, symbols and actions in such a way as to cause a personal revolution that allowed individuals to more fully understand themselves. In other words, it was a lot like a heavy acid trip that alters your view on reality and self. *Duet for the Devil* is similar to an Artaud play in that all of the extreme content of the book forces the reader to re-evaluate himself and look at him or her self in a new way.

In this way, Artaud attempted to create magic and anarchy during his plays, and Rimbaud shared many of the same artistic goals of Artaud. Rimbaud was a libertine and drug addict (absinthe, hash, peyote, heroin). Rimbaud was a poet whose goal was the derangement of the senses of his readers, allowing them to understand themselves better. The purpose of this derangement was an attempt to allow for transcendence.

Baudelaire is also acknowledged by Winter-Damon as a strong

influence, and he also was a major influence for Rimbaud. Baudelaire's most famous collection of poetry is *The Flowers of Evil*. Like many other subversive works, this book of poetry was banned in several countries.

It's impossible to overstate the influence of Marquis de Sade's *The 120 Days of Sodom* on *Duet*. Winter-Damon cites that book as the most perverse thing every written. The book is a chronicle of every possible act of sexual deviance, and for hundreds of pages de Sade describes scenarios I would never think of in a million years. If any one work of art provided the most inspiration for *Duet*, it would be de Sade's *The 120 Days of Sodom*, especially all those scenes of torture, sadistic violence, pedophilia, sexual perversions, rape and transgression.

Duet for the Devil is *The 120 Days of Sodom* of its generation. The novel is filled with explicit sex acts, many illegal, including pedophilia and rape and forced sodomy. Maldoror is a sexual sadist of the highest caliber, only getting off through observing or creating physical pain, in particular sexual pain and debasement. He is also a serial killer, the Zodiac, and he is also possibly The Green River Killer and B.T.K. In other words, he would fit in nicely in any of de Sade's works. The Zodiac considered his killing an art, with the dead bodies serving as canvasses. The Zodiac transcended the realm of most serial killers, and is better classified as a terrorist. He threatened to fire projectiles at school buses driving to school, with the aim of blowing up a school bus and killing all the kids on board. Cities went into a panic, and police officers were placed on all school busses.

He taunted the police for years, then sent a final note saying he would no longer take credit for his murders and that he would make them look like accidents. In this way, the police couldn't capture him because they did not know he even existed. Who knows how many lives were taken? How many simple accidents were actually murders? The Zodiac was a true domestic terrorist. Like Jack the Ripper, the Zodiac was never identified or captured. He fought society and won. He wielded more power than the entire police force, as he had created a panic by being a serial killer, sending encrypted messages to newspapers, reporting his own crimes to the police at a pay phone near the crime scene. He proved he could not be caught.

He broke society's moral standards. He forced people to confront themselves. The Zodiac became, for a time, the ultimate agent of transgression. *Duet for the Devil* uses this shadowy archetypal figure as the driving force for its story, turns things inside out by way of its fictional internals, to shake the reader, to wage war on the reader with its explicit language, to cause a transcendence through its extreme materials. And it does it all in the name of greatest supernatural evil, the most powerful transgressive entity the world has ever known: Satan.

PROPHET OF THE PERVERSE:

t. WINTER-DAMON

TIM DAMON'S DANSE MACABRE

by Randy Chandler

Timothy Winter Damon was born May 22, 1949.

He died November 28, 2008.

He collapsed at an Oldies dance, never regained consciousness, and died several days later in the ICU. If you knew him from his poetry and fiction, you understood that, in an elegiac sense, his life was a metaphorical dance of death. He danced along the frayed edges of reality to subterranean tunes from ghost radios. He finger-danced keystrokes and out came rebellious rhythms, soul-stirring blues and kickass rock 'n' roll. Word-dancing on the way to oblivion, and just maybe back around to rebirth. He understood early on that life itself is a *danse macabre*, that from the moment we are born we are rattling dem bones on our way to the grave.

He was born under the sign of Gemini, the Zodiac's twins. He had enough manic energy to fuel two high-powered minds, and sometimes there did indeed seem to be more than one person living within his skin. It was not hard for me to imagine that his inner twin was his *dark side*—his shadow self. I'm pretty sure he believed it himself, and often employed it in the creation of his darker literary and artistic works. In fact, he once told me he believed he was the reincarnation of a black-arts necromancer (whose name I cannot remember).

In Jungian terms, much of Damon's creative efforts were essentially attempts to bring the psyche's *personal unconscious* to light by tapping into the shadowy depths of the *collective unconscious* and melding them, using art to bind them, much the same as a welder uses an alloyed electrode to fuse metals. Excuse the unpoetic image but I can't help but imagine Damon as a half-mad alchemist in a welding helmet, ceremoniously bent over an otherworldly blinding blue arc-welder's light, resembling Rocketman from those Republic serials of the 1940s as he brings very dark things to light in his attempt to create order out of chaos. Sometimes, at the behest of his shadow self, he created his characteristically cerebral brand of chaos by disrupting the normal order of things. And he did it with fiendish delight. He loved administering the occasional "shock to the system."

He was a man of wide and varied interests, driven by an insatiable curiosity to always learn more. About everything. The downside was that his mental energies could become scattered, unfocused and generally all over the place. But he usually managed to pull it all together to find the focus he was seeking in the first place. Then he could bring his remarkable energy, knowledge and skill to bear on any given project and produce the best of his dark delights: poetry, fiction and art.

He wasn't what anyone would call "a chip off the old block," but he evidently did inherit some of his father's powerhouse intellect and sustaining ambition. His dad was Dr. Paul Edward Damon, Emeritus Professor of Geosciences at the University of Arizona, and as reported in *The Arizona Daily Star, Tucson,* Dr. Damon helped pioneer the use of carbon dating, and his work as a geoscientist helped make the University of Arizona internationally famous for isotope geochemistry. "Damon's research covered subjects ranging from atmospheric evolution to paleoclimatology. Among his other achievements, in 1988 he and colleagues at the UA dated the Shroud of Turin—a centuries-old linen cloth bearing the likeness of a crucified man—and the Dead Sea Scrolls." The Dean of the College of Science called Damon "one of the most extraordinary individuals I ever met" and recalled that Dr. Damon was so well-loved in Mexico (where he did much of his research) that he'd been dubbed "San Pablo" by residents near his study sites.

Professor Damon died April 14, 2005, following a stroke in his office at the University. His wife Mary Janet "Jinx" (Winter) Damon said her husband's career had taken him to dozens of countries, but he recently decided to spend more time at home. "We were planning on just staying home and reading good books. He had many interests from reading to history to gardening."

I don't know if the professor read any of his son's books. He and Mary Janet (who earlier in her life worked as a newspaper reporter and editor) were Quakers and active members of Tucson's Prima Friends Meeting, an "unprogrammed" group without a pastor or traditional church trappings, with liberal theological and social viewpoints. The Prima Friends don't call themselves a church; they are a "meeting" of minds coming together for silent prayer and mediation. Unlike their more conservative and evangelical counterparts in Tucson, Damon's parents believed the point of worship is to know first-hand the presence of the Spirit. A very mystical point of view, much like Tim Damon's, except that *his* mysticism took him to much darker places, places where you would be just as likely to encounter the Prince of Darkness as you would the Holy Spirit. I prefer to think the professor did sample his son's wickedly factious fiction with the unbiased mind of a scientist. I doubt *Duet for the Devil* would've been the elder Damon's cup of tea but I'm willing to bet he read at least some of it. Ditto, Mother Jinx.

The last time I talked with Tim was several months before he died. I hadn't heard from him for a long time and then one night he called from Tucson. He talked, I mostly listened, which was how our conversations usually went. The call went on a full hour. He told me a real-life horror story of his wife Diane's physical decline and eventual death. I won't go into details, out of respect for the dead. Needless to say, that hellish experience was very hard on Tim too. About halfway through the conversation, he shifted mental gears and told me about an old girlfriend he had reconnected with, and he wanted to know if I thought he should ask her out. Naturally I said, "Sure, why not?" I could tell by his inflection and excitement that he really wanted to. I figured he needed something positive in his life after what he'd been through. A few days later he emailed me a recent photo of his old girlfriend and told me she was going out with him. She was a very attractive middle-aged woman.

Fast-forward several months. I got an email from a stranger who said he was a friend of Tim Damon's and that he was going through Tim's email contacts, letting friends know that Tim had passed away. He told me Tim had collapsed at an Oldies dance, was taken to the hospital and died a few days later, having never come out of his coma. Probably a stroke, the friend said.

Then I remembered something Tim had said in our last phone conversation when he was telling me about his wife's slow and painful demise. Without going into much detail he strongly suggested that he had entered into a necromantic deal with some dark entity to ease his wife's suffering. You can guess where my imagination ran with that remembered detail. *When you bargain with darkness, you pay a heavy price. Dance with the Devil and the Devil calls the tune.*

I'm not saying I believe anything like that actually happened. But I can't say Tim didn't believe it.

The guy who called himself Prophet of the Perverse would no doubt appreciate the wicked symmetry involved in paying the balance of a dark spiritual debt.

Damon's gone but his poetic *danse macabre* legacy goes on. It lives on in his fiction, his non-fiction, his interviews and in his mind-bending poetry.

And it goes on in the memories of those who in some way knew him.

NIGHTMARE'S ECHOING VOICE

t. winter-damon

Stare past marigold vistas of dawn,
Past morning star and morning glory—
Descend now beyond Nightshade's hypnotic stair.

See beyond ascian's lazuli skies,
Beyond turquoise oceans of midday—
Day's vapors distill Night's onyx shadow sea.

Peer through sanguine Hesperian mists,
Through Belladonna's pain-killing haze,
Wide-eyed at Death's dark, dream-laden pier.

Whine not of Lord Grave Worm's mortal claim,
Not in noon-tide's wildest reflections
Are the chill delights of Autumn's wine.

Climb on my smoky midnight shoulders.
On past proud delusion's Ivory Gate
And Portals of Horn—Morpheus's clime.

Tales of demon treasures can I spin
. . . Of unclean lusts conceived in Darkness.
My words, The World Serpent's tongue and tail . . .

Days fade . . . swallowed by Eternal Night.
Fade not! Let mad visions swell thy soul,
Grasped in Dream-Realm's throbbing, fevered daze.

Lead-tinged shroud of twilight's languid hours,
Shroud us!—we plummet to ecstasy!
... To Somnus's abandoned depths be led.

No waking mind can seize my riches:
Waking is Lethe's draught! <u>Share those secrets</u>
<u>That only Death and madmen know</u> ...
Or's glow dissolves in Acheron's course.
Glow dull! Grey-Argent of even-tide's stream,
Antimony's britle, noxious ores—

Pale dust ground beneath my charcoal hooves.
Dust sulfurous ... blue flames, white smoke fades,
Roiling iron smelts—flux to sea's pail.

Sol's white hot crucible Fear transmutes,
White, through silver Luna's alchemy.
<u>Mortal Dream's essence—blood and shade souls.</u>

whispered invitation ...
The Ebon Horse of Slumber's Passage

A Sorcerer of the Dark Fantastic

by Bruce Boston

I first encountered t. winter-damon in the early 1980s through Janet Fox's *Scavenger's Newsletter*, which was the leading market report for small press genre writers for two decades prior to the advent of the Internet. Damon had a regular book review column therein that was very distinct in the style in which it was written: an abbreviated text that echoed some Beat poetry and foreshadowed texting. I sent him one of my poetry collections for review, and he raved about it, which is always a sure way to a writer's heart. We subsequently began corresponding, discovering that we had read and liked many of the same authors, and turning one another on to others we had yet to discover. Early on Damon sent me some of his poems and I was bowled over by both his accomplished use of language and the dark visionary power they invoked.

I first met him in person in 1988 at the Small Press Writers and Artists Conference in Albuquerque, New Mexico. I was invited to the conference as Guest of Honor due to my widespread publishing in the genre small press. Damon lived in Tucson, a stone's throw from Albuquerque, and was also attending the conference. Well before the conference he invited me to stay at his house for a few days afterward. I accepted, but wasn't sure what to expect. Up until that time our correspondence had consisted of purely writerly concerns with little personal detail of our lives beyond. Given the visionary nature of his poetry, I was convinced that drugs must have been involved at some level, probably LSD or some other potent psychedelic. I had lived in a drug house in the late Sixties, knew the scene, and was not eager to relive it even for an abbreviated stay.

Shortly after arriving at the convention in Albuquerque I

encountered Damon, a short stocky man with curly brown hair, a gravelly voice, a ready grin, and a mischievous twinkle in his eyes. I also met his wife Diane, and my worries of staying in a drug house were allayed. She couldn't have been more normal.

Once I visited them after the convention, such worries vanished completely. Rather than a drug house, they lived in a upper middle class tract development on the outskirts of Tucson, a well-furnished three-bedroom house with a swimming pool. Damon worked writing copy and doing other things for a mail-order catalog. His life was a definite contrast from the kind of writing I'd seen from him. And when I asked him about drugs, he told me he didn't take any and never really had. In retrospect, Damon seemed a bit like a darker version of James Thurber's Walter Mitty. His daily life was entirely ordinary, yet he inhabited and explored worlds of dark adventure through his writing and considerable imagination.

That visit cemented our friendship. We continued to correspond regularly, at first by letter and telephone, and later through email, until his untimely death in 2008. In the years immediately following that visit, Damon provided collages for my prose poem collection *Short Circuits* and wrote the introduction to my first retrospective collection *Sensuous Debris*. In 1992 I published through Talisman, a press I was running at the time, his most comprehensive poetry collection, *The Hour of Hallucinations*, ably enhanced by his own surreal collages.

The three poems Randy Chandler selected from that volume to include here are among my favorites in that collection. Like so much of Damon's work, they are steeped in history, myth and literature. They demonstrate his ability to take the reader on bizarre journeys that resonate and live beyond the page. They are also examples of his inspired sense of language, unique imagery, and unbounded imagination. Our two collaborative poems included here are in a sense opposites from one another. Although "Holocaustic Museum Fragments for Binary Extrapolation" contains equal amounts of text from both of us, it is a poem in which I adapted my style and voice to Damon's. "We Find Our Selves on Mars" is an example of his voice adapting itself to mine. My tribute poem for Damon that concludes this volume is one I wrote last year. It had been percolating in my brain for some time. Though only a partial portrait of the man, and to some extent romanticized, I believe it captures an essential essence of his nature. One thing that always impressed me about Damon was the range of his knowledge and his boundless enthusiasm regarding the arcane, esoteric, and eldritch. He was an extraordinary writer and remarkable friend. I miss him greatly on both counts. My life is richer for having known him.

The Dreamtides of Tantalus

t. winter-damon

rust & ocher desolation designate horizon. tattoos in sepia upon the plain. cabalistic tracings of tenacity. the life most persistent. like an ancient anchor in the drydock. & the substrate splits like the heels of clothess sandstone hermits. & the prayer winds moan in a dome of amethyst of glass. & she rises in her nakedness. phoenix from the ashes. aphrodite of the dustbowl. the waves of barren ashes break about her ankles & the shells of lichen echo he chantings of her empty promise. & i drink her desiccation deep into my essene liver gin/djinn . . .

these packages i open are all empty (so are the drawers of all my closets) & i beg the waitress with her white face & i beg alice cooper in an apron for a glass of water—she brings me vinegar soaked into a sponge & she laughs into the hollow of my face & asks me why i wear a stovepipe hat (but i am wearing nothing but my baldness) . . .

in the ironworks they dream about cold beer & the fish wrigging like fresh hooked & velvet deep enough to drown in . . .

& neon arcing lightning dazzle in the tombstone alleys of electric heat & the slithering prowl of chrome panthers in the prism blackness of the hungry unrepentant in the riptides of heavy metal babylon & honeysuckle sweat & leather. cole younger & the daltons died for you (& made you in their image) O moths & gladiators of the chisholm slipstream. peaches flaunting spanish masque & french persuasions. downhill racers. slaves of silver spoons & razors. dime & quarter angels. covens of balloon &

candle. sand & gelatin/riders on the rainbow elevator . . .
teonancatl. circle of the endless circles. circle of the pillars & the rays.
circle of the visions. circle of the cosmic soul . . .

& soft pebbles of blue grey & delicate blooms of white & pink.
button harvest of huitzilopchtli & the aird limestone soil.
& sultry seasons of the dog star & tezcatlipoca (O jaguar of the
smoking mirror) & black stone basking the iguana trembles like
erosion. like mudcrusted lumps of carbon hardening to diamonds
its eyes swivel in a gaze that's frozen in the pit of time & the
worm drifts (indecent embryo) inside its fused silica stasis & the
spirit of cactus blossoms dreams within you. stirs its flames
within your coffin flesh. & blue rhythms of the moon & sky.
rhythms of morpho wings. rhythms of sacred stones & silver . . .

imouthes. i-em-hotep. the empty skin of the leopard wears you
as its flesh & foursquare the stone steps rise to heaven at your
gesture (O magician of sakkareh!) its apex is the mouth of ra.
linensheathed in clinging pastel lotus hues temptresses bare
breasted sway like papyrus & rushes. shuffling their shameless
feet like plaques of ivory. the twenty two. the mysteries of thoth.
& among their flawless blackcascading perfume & among their
kohlrimmed wells of nightpleasure promise & impudent as
bantam roosters waddle & strut the twisted dwarf grotesques
(prized more than gold) with bellies as pendulous as nine months
fertile! i can taste the crystal whine of reed pipes like chilled fig
wine & twentytwostringed harps like moonbeams & the bill that
slays the serpent & the rising flood waters & tambourines like
lemons. like pomegranates . . .

i can see the signs/i can feel the turning of the wheel/i am the
fool upon the road of life upon the royal (yes! i am the
dupe! the pigeon!) you cannot gull me. no you cannot gull me! i
am wary of your slieghts & shills O trickster/ thimblerigger/
master of fortune!

i have seen the dragon veins in spider webs & tangled roots &
storm clouds. a flight of cranes flows with the currents of the

sky. i have seen the slow winds in the face of sea cliffs in the
progress of the glacier down the jade sky in fungal patterns of
the deep stone of rippling breath of onyx marble in the
quicksilver seeds of the of cinnabar. plum blossoms on a bough. red
stallions plummet down the ridges of the water canyon & the
horns of stag & rhinoceros strike sparkstream of gold &
silver constellations. i have seen the droning wings of amethyst
& emerald caress the shadowed snowdrift of the shattered
sparrow & the threelegged toad drawn upward in a dipper of pure
jade the essence of the bluewinged dragons's fire drawn upward
from the well of lotus vortex. i have fasted on the ling- chih . . .

& flood waters rise about me like a girdle & the waters ebb away
but i cannot feel them. no. i cannot drink them. my lips are like
my soul like the crack of leather like the soles of clothless
sandstone hermits . . .

& my eyes were thorns as the legions slaughtered/ my tongue
was a stake as the legions slaughtered/ my ears were splinters as
the legions slaughtered & the wind was a flame as the lightning
flashes. & i was a coffer kissed with silver/ i was thirty coins
returned/ i was the selfnamed tree of treason's hanging & i was
the stone as the harp was shattered. & i was the rag pulp pressed
to service/ i was the pen of gustave bourdin/ i was the starcged
collar of abbatucci/ i was the pointed finger of pinard/ i ws the
palace of three paths—all translated as despair. annas &
caiaphas hid behind your alabaster maskes O delesvaux! de
ponton d'amecourt! nacquart! O sanhedrin of the paris right
bank! (you did not drive the nails into his palms—you closed
the lid upon his coffin slowly) . . .

sans fin les reveurs de tantalus . . .

lobster promenade, blue ribbon like a glacial leash, & wigwam,
sorbets & bordeaux sampled from a vacant cranium . . .
demands for payment from a host of haberdashers, charred pipe
rinded with the pitch of kef. the lean & hungry cat, & spiked
heels mulatto vixens gyrate into his face & groin . . .

une charone, beyond the mountains of the moon & ancient
ethiopia, naked at thirty three divining dreammagnet of an
eastern star.
maman & the major fifth . . .

les chats

(O sanhedrin of the paris right bank, did you not drive the nails
into his palms. you closed the lid upon his coffin slowly) . . .

les chants fou

& de nerval swinging ever from the lamppost ash of the nine
worlds. & de nerval joining the dance of the masked one, with
his spear (our lady of immaculate illusions), with his chimeras &
girls of fire . . .

sans fin les reveurs de tantalus. les chats les chants fou . . .

& in the tombstone alleys of electric heat i can hear the whisper
of her stalking i can feel the hunger of her presence like the
asphalt steaming like the jagged eyes of derelicts of the
condemned. i can stroke the warmth of fur like trembling fingers
(your delicacy shames these labouring hands! the whorls &
ridges of the callous!) & i stroke her angora mists & her cornsilk
threads & gossamer & her brush of static amber is the shocking
pledge of bast. pearls drip from her creamy whiskers & the tang of
shrimping docks & tuna trawlers & ports of emeralds & jade &
agates that bask in insolent & drowsing languor & jungles of
the howling moon & oysters spilling forth their flood of
silver/pink/twilight transmutation . . .

& the flood waters rise about me like a girdle & the waters ebb
away but i cannot touch them. no. i cannot taste them. no. i
cannot drink them. my lips are like my soul like the crack of
leather like the soles of clothless sandstone hermits. i have
feasted on the magic spirit fungus but now i know an
allconsuming hunger & i cannot reach the golden apples of the

sun & i cannot taste the silver peaches of the threefaced tree &
the craving for their sweetness is like smoke that bellows from
my lungs . . .

& these packages i open are all empty (so are the drawers of all
my closets!) & i beg the *harlequin* for stillness . . .

sans fin les reveurs de tantalus. les chats les chants fou. blonde
et noir . . .

Beyond This Shaman's Mask of Leather

t. winter-damon

i hold them in my palm—stars. sand grains. galaxies of swirling
radiance. motes of tantalizing & hypnotic prism-sense-vibration.
they press like thumbs against my red/purple/roadmap retinas &
screaming images of grapes exploding beneath pink fishscale
creases of downtrodding monks dark circled hollowness of oaken
vats that line my cavities of cranium. twenty feet away an electric
lightbulb maybe sixty watt maybe one hundred sears into my optical
perception like the center of a neutron bomb in fission a blue dwarf
luxuriating. a hurricane of years roars round & round me stirs my hair
into a swirl of racing stormcloud. minutes & hours flutter drunkenly
as hosts of moths released from dreaming incubation in some velvet
climax of instant & unnatural intensity. as an explosive sneeze of
ancient must & rainbows. as a shattering of mummified corpses
swathed in powdered robes of dionysian silk. the digits of my fingers
twitch & pulse like bloated larvae gorging on broken sparrow's
pinecone husk of eyelash-tickling layers violet seas of easter island
typhoon crest & break about my buzzing skull. these dimensions
open up to me like orchids dilating in timelapse. skies reeling flame
wriggling nets of fish that hold a catch of transmuting water snakes.
kiao. kioh-lung. & ying-lung. k'iu-lung like robin's eggs & cobalt. & 81 &
36. (they manifest my fear like centipedes. wax. iron. & twisted strands
of varicolored thread.) even gods must fear these binding alchemies:
advance the winch.
tighten those straining cords about the slender wrists.
savor the hand of glory if it's offered!
& the shutters all blow off their hinges & the windowpanes
are shattered by a sudden violent gust of wind . . .
& the jester & the botticelli angel whisper parables & secrets

of the martyred & whisper secrets stolen from the public execution
(black masked repression & acres of fishbelly hidden beneath sack
cloth. ah! yes! rimbaud! & *you small black dolls that squirm against
the sky; the devil's skinny advocates . . .*) & whisper secrets spilled
within the house of bread (dribbled from the lips of inmates white
with
flecks of incoherent foam!) & vincennes & saltpetriere are blessed
with their prophets & their visionaries . . .
i hold them in my palm—stars. sand grains. galaxies of swirling
radiance. motes of tantalizing & hypnotic prism-sense-vibration.
old clocks. wheezing. clattering. gonging in the darkness.
imprecisions
of regularity. inconstant metronomes. the beat of trick heart.
pebbles rattle in a hubcap. faucet leaking. dripping. dropping. echoes
of grimy whiteness. cancered pits of guano green & scabs of rust.
earthworm stink of rotten wood crumbling slowly crumbling away to
dust. swirling darkswarm spirals through an amber marshland. &
shadows telescope in stop freeze. flow like molten tar. & the black
crow steams & sizzles in its crucible upon yhe burner. & the gas jet
hisses blue & yellow . . .
advance the winch.
tighten the straining cords about the slender wrists.
savor the hand of glory if it's offered!
i have searched obsessively to re-encounter that disaster-struck
marquee. flashing images of *déjà vu. blue neon tubes halflit. rust &
discarded paper cups. condoms. & candy wrappers. an empty foyer
lined with ultraviolet posters of the gift of the velvet underground.*
i've stumbled down uncounted alleys clogged with discarded husks
of the stillborn. inclined ladders of hooker's chipped red figernails
with last week's abortive polish shudder gently to the words
of *ballad of a thin man* & *desolation row.* a wrinkled lecher trembles
with the major fifth. the born dead cinema where one stone cold
afternoon i sat transfixed. *weird scenes from a gold mine . . .
something is happening . . . & cocksucker blues . . .*
i hold them in my palm—stars. sand grains. galaxies of swirling
radiance. motes of tantalizing & hypnotic prism-sense-vibration.
bo diddley. bo derek. & beau brumel fight among themselves to
capture centerstage.

& some vagrant denizen of skidrow XXX-rated theatres
a scarecrow in trenchcoat & slouch hat drawn menacingly across his
face (what evil lurks within the hearts of men . . . ?) grasps me by my
arm & whispers as if imparting threshold headlines. "i heard the nobel
prize last year was a dead heat between godzilla & the plasmatics with
wendy O . . ."
advance the winch.
tighten those straining cords about the slender wrists.
savor the hand of glory if it's offered!
desolation madonna. your meissen perfection gnaws my smith &
wesson
like a desert wolf ravaging a rabbit's carcass. & cacti. spiked leather
dildos immensely thrusting the random threat of violence
at the black void of midnight. thrusting their futile aggression
from the barren crotch of our lady of unimmaculate conceptions!
(O! muthuh urth! O used up & withered harlot!) desolation madonna.
cancered with your indiscretions. concerned with the devil's dust.
your golden earring flashes like the aztec sun. your armpits
are barbed wire & tumbleweed. my lust screams into this endless
night
like the coyote . . .
i hold them in my palm—stars. sand grains. galaxies of swirling
radiance. motes of tantalizing & hypnotic prism-sense-vibration.
verlaine strolls arm-in-arm with two boyscouts. uniforms so crisply
starched & regimental blushing. beneath the flicker of gas lamps
he pauses. tips his top hat disdainfully at all the startled grouse
in bustles. inhales deeply. blows the smoke of his havana
into the ruffled face of the preening parrot in his gendarme's cap
& cape & trousers. from a window far up above with crimson drapes
it is madeleine-laure & rose keller. they giggle girlishly & each
blows a pouting kiss. (rose keller tricked-out in nunnish habit
stands behind the young girl's pale 7 sloping shoulder & gently
caresses the lilac-scented flesh.) & elton john croons *goodbye-
to yellow brick road* as he steps into a waiting carriage . . .
advance the winch.
tighten those straining cords about the slender wrists.
savor the hand of glory if it's offered!

The Ghost of Rimbaud Pauses

t. winter-damon

Torrents of vermilion glass roar

Earthward. The bridge transmutes to spiderwebs.
Transmute to traceries of fragile
Amber. Poppies fill the horizon, stifling

The air with promises. Beyond dream. Beyond
That which even the most carefully
Chosen of words lays leadheavy
Upon the Oracle's ritually severed tongue. &

The ghost of Rimbaud pauses along the wayside,
Searching, perhaps, for the beauty unspeakable,
Of which his melancholy predecessor risked

To speak:—*Le Mauvais Moine* . . . —Or,
La Priere d; un paien . . . —Or, *Les*
Litanies de Satan.. O Daisies! O

Blushing roses! O glorious douche
Bags so very nectar sweet! O steaming
Mound of dogshit quashed
Beneath the carriagewheels! & the ghost

Of Rimbaud pauses to observe. To
Contemplate. To seek the demented
Visions of his perfumed catamite, his sloe-eyed
Hermaphrodite, his harlot muse Three

Girls. Young & budding flowers all. Soapbubble
Congeries of giggles prompted by their pastime billow
On the April breeze. They nestle in the proffered

Modesty of a roadside ditch. A hedgerow promises
Their secrets to keep privy. All
Raise their lacetrimmed skirts, & squat. All

Raise their petticoats. All
Drop their filthy drawers. As they prepare
To answer nature's call. To await
The pellucid gush of this

Unhallowed trinity of virgin springs. O
Miracles! O holy exercise
& exorcism! From the heavenly, groined
Arches of six marble columns, holy water

Streams! (TO HELL WITH IT! LET'S BE DIRECT!
THEIR BLADDERS SWOLLEN, HOW THEY CERTAINLY MUST
LONG
TO TAKE A PISS!) Dust spiders . . . Apricots &

Peaches . . . Roses . . . Almonds . . . Jack-in-the-pulpits . . .
Squid . . . Oysters . . . & mossy-bearded clams . . . Thinking himself
Un observed, the local bishop stands rapturously poised,

Concealed behind a burning bush. His purple cassock shames
Him in its disarray! In brutal act of penitence, he flogs
His withered crosier, & with savage cadence
Drums his shriveled Marty's Heart! *Ahhh* . . .

Yes! The ghost of Rimbaud trembles
At his inspiration. His skull mirrors the roaring torrents
Of the sky. OUR ASSHOLES *ARE* DIFFERENT," he whispers
Reverently. Awestruck at such divine

Insight visited in matters of the flesh . . . He fumbles
Awkwardly within his breeches pocket. Feverishly seeking
To locate his well-worn pencil. & a scrap

Of parchment to record this magickal, momentary
Revelation in a sonnet snippet, to delight
The leftbank bawds & bards.

HOLOCAUSTIC MUSEUM FRAGMENTS FOR BINARY EXTRAPOLATION

Bruce Boston and t. winter-damon

die Geburt der Tragödie: Menschliches, Allzumenschliches
in the locust hoarfrost of Fimbulwinter
the smoldering ruin of Earth's greatest city lies blasted
      open like a plundered treasure vault
         as the remnants of Homo Sapiens (var.
preholocaustus) burrow
    & scamper
        like mindless frightened vermin
through the seared skeletons of centuries past:
           warped & twisted girders encrusted
   with redbrown clots of ferrous oxide
         caked blood of steel limbs mangled & broken
vertebrae of concrete giants ripped asunder
           fallen

in the wreckage of a world gone blind to the obsidian of self
until that base ebon cast erupted in primal incandescence
     in hellbent tidal winds of razorish violence
        in the shadow surge of sootblack shroud clouds
           in a neo-Triassic of volcanic lava fury consummated
              instantaneously
        in the rabid trauma of its birth
in the final beasthound roar of unconsciousness unleashed
         resounding

                              in dying echoes like a diseased
& infernal laughter silencing both Plato & Rimbaud:
              amid the melted microfiches
                   the charred & sodden library stacks
a billion words & images reduced to blurred fly specks
                        to a cacaphoneum of gibberish cant
                        to wretched morphemes & knotted syllables
                              silencing

the shreds of human tongue still bellowed & snarled
by a cast of rad sick & rapidly dwindling survivors
       fun house mirror travesties of archetypes once embraced:
          flash amputated athletes squirming on cauterized limbs
              politicians with no polity to rape or plunder
                   priests without lambs to slaughter or defend
                        sore encrusted cinema goddesses
                              sinners & savants   rebels & plebes
              all leveled

       to raw animalistic want & cannibalistic feeds
              the charred & vacant window eyes
of hollow & weather-bleached building skulls
watching their grotesque sideshow parade in its passage
              bellies slack   faces gaunt
       over the autonomic corpse throes of civilization's
              carbonized arrogance & damp rot grandeur
                   watching

       as the inheritors *Homo Sapiens* (var.
cyberneticus)
armorclad   pneumatocabled   infraredsensitive
modemlinked
              stream forth in shining ranks
       from the ruins of Earth's greatest city mausoleum
                   necropolis of burnt meat
                        watching

as we catalog & feast & dance
upon the fused glass crystalgems of fragile artifice
    the glut of useless all too human
        information
the moldering data net of statistical expiration
        soon to be gathered in museums of un-
natural history
    never to be visited in
        or by
        or for the flesh

watching as the starved roaches wreathe our arms our legs
    in living insectile mourning bands to suckle
        the drops of lubricant which seep
from our synchronized ballbearing joints & bead
upon our lean titanium chests
                watching
    as the alloy *Ubermensch* & death ascend

WE FIND OUR SELVES ON MARS

Bruce Boston and t. winter-damon

Rarefied our clime.
Rarefied our gene pool.
Spawned beneath these skies
of salmon we are prisoners
of a spartan ecosphere,
denizens of ecosystems
hermetically sealed,
sustained in fragile balance.

Staring sunward we see
the ruins of a rarer world
where skies blazed blue,
oxygen rich and glutted
with precious water vapor,
a teaming culture vat
where life once swarmed
in unconfined abundance.

Staring homeward we see
the severed mother world,
where skies of churning dust
broadcast deathly radiation,
we see a land blazed lifeless
beyond reach or redemption,
its biosphere of sickly hue
a curse to our ascension.

In the seas of fallen dust
that surround our city domes,
we sift for alien artifacts
beneath our skies of salmon,
we comb the scattered ruins
of a race we nearly recognize,
like masters in the art of war,
keepers of a genocidal passion.

The following poem appeared in my kitchen-table-assembled pamphlet Lil' Demon Review, *as did Damon's review of Rex Miller's* SLOB, *which follows this poem. He would later write a "spirited 100-page look at the life and work of the late Miller" called* Rex Miller: The Complete Revelations (1993).
—RC

ABANDON ALL HOPE

The girl
A firedrill
Arched wand of tension
Whirling pirouetting
Bow of smoldering friction
Naked
Naked as fire
Her hair a spinning dish of flame
Her face escapes definition
Breasts/belly/thrust of pelvis
Vagrant memories taunting remembrance
Wisps of smoke twisted out of meaning
Insolent arabesques of unquenchable desire

Darkness
Total darkness
Somewhere unreachable water slowly drips
Just beyond my fingertips
A chilled goblet I can *feel*
Clusters of spontaneous dewdrops swelling on its surface
Glistening knurls overbear their fragile balance
Trickling in sluggish rillets of temptation

Pulsebeats reverberating through each pore
An ebb and flow of anguish
Of unbearable thumping monotony
Moments that are hours
Hours eternities of blurred illogic sequence
Time flows back upon itself
Are these moments or years that melt away like tallow?

The darkness
Viscid with the midden stench
The chafing prickle of damp straw

Breathless
I await their stealthy furtive tryst
And I welcome now
The painful gnawing kiss

Of rats' teeth on my bleeding lips

—t. Winter-Damon

REX MILLER'S
BRAIN-BASHING BEAUTY

SLOB (Signet, 1987) is a mind-blowing, brain-bashing beauty of a novel, an incredibly powerful *tour de force* from Rex Miller, the video-classic entrepreneur Rex Miller Supermantiques, a mail order firm specializing in collector-to-collector sales of vintage films—an excellent source for genre rarities (Route 1, Box 457-D, East Prairie, MO 63845). The cinematic influence is strong in Miller's visualization of events & characters; at times, they seem to burst forth from the pages in the frame-by-frame reality, the sight & sound & smell & taste a tangible presence that shakes you to the gut & drags you down into a very special hell inside the mind of a 500-pound psycho-killer that rips humans apart like dolls & eats their still-throbbing hearts.

SLOB is not a book for the timid. If you open up & flow with its dialog, its narrative of inhuman, frenzied killing-lust, Miller will rip open the serial slayer's skull & let you tumble into the mental abscess, feeling through Daniel Edward Flowers Bunkowski's senses, feeling the essence of this man/monster, known as Chaingang.

Miller takes risks, plenty of them, in his machinegun imagery, in the intensity of his stream-of-consciousness internal dialog, in his hip rush of language-flow. But for me at least, it was a pure-platinum payoff. This book is listed as the first in the JACK EICHORD TRIOLOGY, & I eagerly await the release of additional novels following the pursuits of Jack Eichord, hard-drinking, tough-guy cop, who is thrust into the role of "expert" in solving unusual major crimes of violence.

On the first read, the denouement seemed almost a letdown, after the sheer onwardrushingenergy of this novel that wires your brain with its amphetamine-like spill of images & dialog, like a Benny-

poppin' trucker flatout down black-iced curves of Highway 666 . . .
After a second read, I conceded that, after the incredible intensity of
buildup, nearly anything that Miller could have done would seem an
anticlimax, & that it was, indeed, well-tied in its conclusion. There
was just a touch of too much "softness" in its ending scenes, the
slightest holding back from taking its madness all-the-way (without
betraying too much, I trust—the lives of the animals held just a bit
too precious for my sense of credibility). But the delicately woven
textures of the book itself—particularly in the contrasts between
Eichord & Edith's lovemaking & the bestial lusts of Chaingang—are
superb studies in point-&-counterpoint.

For my money, SLOB is an exceptional read. Miller is one helluva
storyteller. & a wordsmith of visionary power! I would recommend
it to anyone with the guts to stare into the skull of a tractor-wielding
500-pound monster with paranormal abilities, a genius-level IQ
schizo'd with fugues of autism & tortured-childhood regression &
rabid cannibalistic frenzy. & kills to equal each & every pound of
his gargantuan bulk (it's like envisioning the wrestler The One Man
Gang on psycho rampage . . .).

—t. Winter-Damon

In October, 1993, t. Winter-Damon interviewed phenomenal author Thomas Ligotti for a small-press horror magazine. We are reprinting it here in its entirety because it represents the meeting of two remarkable minds. You might expect what follows to be dated but it isn't. This is due to the timelessness of Ligotti's work and to the fact that the philosophical and literary concepts discussed run deeper than prevailing fashions or trends. Reading the following exchanges is akin to listening to a powerful duet by virtuoso musicians. —RC

Horror Talks with Thomas Ligotti
Conducted by t. Winter-Damon
From *Horror*, no. 3-4

This interview was conducted by mail and by phone, during mid September through end-October, 1993.

WINTER-DAMON: I'm sure Thomas Ligotti needs no introduction to most *Horror* readers, but, just in case a few may have somehow escaped contact with his very personal brand of nightmarish, reality-twisting terror, let me quote from a few of the rave reviews his work has collected:

Ramsey Campbell, regarding *Songs of a Dead Dreamer*: "It has to be one of the most important horror books of the decade . . . for Ligotti is one of the few consistently original voices in contemporary horror fiction." Ramsey sums up the signature Ligottian style quite neatly in the introduction to "The Strange Design of Master Rignolo," in *Best New Horror* (Volume One, 1990; reprinted from *Grue* #10, Fall, 1989): ". . . It's pretty hard to describe the story that follows, so we'll leave you to soak up the atmosphere and rich prose that is unmistakably Ligotti's, and let the horror creep up on you."

Jessica Amanda Salmonson introducing "Masquerade of a Dead

Sword," in the *Heroic Visions II* anthology (Ace, July, 1986): "... his voice is perhaps too original for instant recognition among the typical editor or anthologist of horror fiction, a field where conservatism invariably translates artistic as being pretentious and where even a microscopic moment of the experimental creates paroxysms of disdain." And goes on to mention, "... (his) easy comprehension of the gloomier aspects of German expressionism and French symbolism ..." and "... a very dark sort of romanticism ..."

Ellen Datlow, introducing "The Glamour," in *The Year's Best Fantasy and Horror #5* (St. Martin's, August, 1992; reprinted from his 1991 Carroll & Graf collection, *Grimscribe*): admits "Ligotti's baroque style is demanding on the reader ..." and notes his "... ability to project dread and unease ... making readers start at sudden noises and glance around while reading his subtly disquieting narratives."

Or as Douglas E. Winter simply says in his introduction to TL's story in the landmark *Prime Evil* anthology (NAL, 1988): "Like the antagonist of 'Alice's Last Adventure,' Ligotti is indeed 'a conjurer of stylish nightmares.'"

Be assured, Thomas Ligotti is not to be counted among the ranks of the splatterpunks or other practitioners of "loud horror," relying, instead, on a maximum usage of subtlety and ambiguity.

Without having drafted a single novel, Thomas, you've managed the near-impossible feat of seeing three collections [*Songs of a Dead Dreamer, Grimscribe,* and the just released *Noctuary*] of your stories published in hardcover or trade paperback by major houses both Stateside and in the U.K. Would you be willing to give *Horror* readers a bit of insight as to how, with such admittedly offbeat works that follow your own strange inspirations rather then the pressures of the popular marketplace to "write down to the public" and "go commercial," you've managed to carve out such a respected niche in the horror/dark fantasy field?

LIGOTTI: If you think about it, the situation you've described happens all the time, and has happened repeatedly throughout the history of horror fiction from Hoffman and Poe to Ramsey Campbell and Clive Barker. It's really the norm, not the aberration, for a horror writer to gain an audience through the publication of a few collections of short stories. Those readers who are genuinely passionate or pathetic about horror fiction will have in their private libraries a high percentage of all the horror story collections and anthologies ever published but a much smaller percentage of novels in this genre. Personally, there are very few or no novels that I would consider horror fiction. I know that sounds extravagant, but it seems to me that in all the essentials of narrative—especially the somewhat nebulous but crucial quality of tone or attitude—there is a fundamental difference between the horror story and the so-called horror novel. Anyone familiar with both of these forms can observe the distinctions between them. In essence, the horror novel is a movie and its audience is a movie audience, while the horror story is a literary work and its audience is a literary audience. I realize this is a simplification, but in this world you either simplify or shut up. And who can shut up?

WINTER-DAMON: In the full text of the commentary by Jessica Salmonson I earlier quoted in part, she states: "Thomas Ligotti is not a fellow whose chief inspiration can be seen to be the dreary horror of the pulp era." Many of us might take exception to Jessica's less-than-complimentary dismissal of the pulp era, as uninspired as it may have been in literary terms; however, few of your many reader, I can imagine, would argue her assertion your own influences, as refined and distilled through personal reality-filters as they may now be, stem from far more eclectic and heady sources. Would you be willing to detail some of those for us?

LIGOTTI: Rather than talking about influences, which can be really dubious, it's easier for me to cite authors whose works I've just out and out tried to imitate as best I could. The ones that come to mind are Nabokov, Raymond Chandler, Stanley Elkin, Thomas Bernhard, Beckett, Bruno Schulz, Lovecraft, and Poe. The common trait among this somewhat diverse group of writers is the use, effortlessly it would seem, of an intense, intimate style to convey intense, intimate subjects. As a reader I have no tolerance for fiction written in third-person, long-distance prose. My brain shuts down when I read a sentence like, "Rocco jerked a thumb over his left shoulder and said, 'Scram.'" The attitude of such sentences is generic, impersonal, and boring. It's stage direction, not prose. Worst of all is the free indirect style of fiction advocated by Henry James where the characters' cognitive and sensory experience is embedded in the narrative, like, "Julie stood at the copying machine. Working in an office was so pleasant. Free coffee and the scent of ozone." Reading sentence after sentence written in this "style" is for me like listening to a radio station that plays one bad song after another. Sometime people recommend that I read this or that book because it's really great once you get past the first hundred pages or so. "The first hundred pages!" I reply. "Are you outta your mind!" Because as soon as you hear that caveat regarding the first hundred pages, you know that on *every* page of that great book Julie is standing at the copy machine, and behind her is Rocco, jerking a thumb over his left shoulder and saying, "Scram" over and over and over. All of this, of course, is another simplification.

WINTER-DAMON: I'm deliberately putting you on the spot, now. I know you've always spoken of Ramsey Campbell's work with what I perceive as almost a sense of reverence (an emotional response I share). Your career, to-date, has frequently been compared to that of Ramsey's early days. How do you respond to that comparison?

LIGOTTI: I'm not sure what the terms of comparison are in this question or which "early days of Ramsey Campbell" you mean. *Demons by Daylight? Inhabitant of the Lake?* The stuff R.C. wrote when he was four years old?

WINTER-DAMON: Well, I asked for *that* one, didn't I, Tom? Ask a specific question and receive a definitive answer . . . Okay. Let's try this again. Not the clearly imitative Lovecraftian pastiches of *Inhabitant of the Lake.* I was thinking of *Demons by Daylight,* with those wonderfully (as in "sense of wonder") oblique and nebulous denouements, the intensely charged, paranoiac atmosphere, the brooding sense of malignant intelligences lurking just beyond the flesh-thin membrane of "normality," of safe and sane "consensus reality," hungering to break on through . . . I was thinking of the admirable strength of personal vision that shrugs aside the formulaic dictates of the "commercial marketplace".

LIGOTTI: Considering the flattering terms in which you've articulated this comparison, what can I say?

WINTER-DAMON: For better or worse, our modern society seems obsessed with analyzing, categorizing, and labeling every conceivable type of artistic endeavor into orderly, rationalized little pigeon holes. Your writings, for want of another ready niche, have frequently been termed "Lovecraftian" by reviewers and editors, or are lumped into the "artsier" camps of surrealism, symbolism, or metaphysical writing (in past review I've personally been guilty of the same errancy, as well, if memory serves me). I'm obviously about to pose several linked questions . . .

First, Tom, the Lovecraftian epithet seems appropriate in several respects—the cosmic and nightmare-spawned rather that religious- or mythic-based entities threatening or at least influencing human events; the profound sense of paranoia and futility one is left with while and after devouring both of your work; the linked concept of Weltanschauung based upon the chaotic or nihilistic perception of existence, the early, often non-linear dream (primarily Dunsanian fantasies as opposed to tales of terror) narratives of HPL's. Yet there are far more elements of theme and narrative where your styles are dissimilar. For example, you deliberately eschew the scientific realism and the logical progressions of events carefully documented (or should I say "pseudo-documented") by HPL, with a precision of detail seldom encountered outside the mystery genre, much in the same tradition as Sir Arthur Conan Doyle's Holmesian tale. What are your opinions on this controversy?

LIGOTTI: Lovecraft was a lot better informed than I am about the real world and its science, society, geography, etc. It's no surprise that he would use what he knew about the world when it came time to write a horror story. Lovecraft was interested in a lot more things than I am. His brain was probably a lot bigger than mine, his blood more pure. He also lived and died in Providence, Rhode Island, which was a source of inspiration to him as a horror writer. I've only lived, and will probably die, in a suburb of Detroit which to me, as a horror writer, is not a source of inspiration.

WINTER-DAMON: Since the coining of the term "surrealism," it has developed numerous connotations not necessarily in sync with the precepts embraced by the original movement, as typified by the dictatorial Breton. In particular, anything vaguely dreamlike or dream- or nightmare-related is thrown into this handy hodgepodge catchall. While the heart of "pure" surrealism suggests a utopian positivism, a desire for social change directly related to the Communistic beliefs of many of its founding fathers, your writings evoke a gloomy, brooding nihilism. And, while your work shares that nihilism, the seemingly anti-machine sentiments and love of the irrational in common with the Dadaists, its essence appears a complex, ambiguous and richly dreamlike flowing, as opposed to the frenetic, reductive and concretist core elements of the latter. What is your reaction to these assertions?

LIGOTTI: You pretty much said it all. I agree with Artaud that the surrealists formed a wholesome, fraternity-like organization that didn't have a clue with respect to the deranged experiences and realities they pretended to celebrate. They had to *try* to stimulate mental and emotional dysfunctions in themselves. For that I envy them. Nice paintings, though. And Breton had one of the finest academic brains of all time. Regarding Dadaism, I smile when I think if the fate of this grandly idealistic movement: today the only people who seem to have an interest in Tristan Tzara & Co. are academics and alternative rock bands. The latter group, of course, are quite worthy inheritors of the Dadaist ethos.

WINTER-DAMON: Your collective works share common denominators with the French Symbolists—Baudelaire, Mallarmé, Verlaine, et al—a narrative less descriptive, more suggestive and more subtle, a language and imagery more poetic, than most contemporaries; a quest to project the "inner dream". Would you agree on this similarity of focus? If so, how do you perceive *yourself* in relation to them? What major differences do you perceive, as well?

LIGOTTI: I have a lot of bizarre, egoistic internal melodramas going on, but perceiving myself in relation to such magisterial figures as Baudelaire and Mallarmé isn't one of them. Regarding the aesthetics of *suggesting* rather than *showing*, this of course is something the Symbolists learned from Poe. Poe is credited with conceiving the modern short story, but relatively few writers have followed the rich and enigmatic pattern of his best stories. Ultimately Chekhov and O. Henry became the models for short story writers, and have remained so. It's funny.

WINTER-DAMON: How early did you begin writing stories? How early did you begin writing with a goal beyond self-realization, work intended for publication?

LIGOTTI: It was about 1976 that I first started writing horror stories with the idea that I would like to see them published.

WINTER-DAMON: Your initial publications were within the small press. Hopefully without embarrassing you, it has been widely asserted that if there is a need to justify the existence of the "little magazines," both the novice and semi-pro efforts, the nurturing of a writing talent such as yours is more than enough . . . I understand you *did* initially try a few "pro" submissions, in the late '70s or early '80s—*The Magazine of Fantasy and Science Fiction, Alfred Hitchcock's Mystery Magazine, The Twilight Zone*—but met with rejection. Instead, you found acceptance with the more literate, daring small press ventures, the "surreal-macabre" publications— Harry O. Morris' *Nyctalops*, Jessica Salmonson's *Fantasy and Terror* and *Fantasy Macabre*, and Thomas Wiloch's *Grimoire*, to name a few. Would you share some of your early submission experiences?

LIGOTTI: You have to understand that the stories I sent to professional publications in the late 1970s were insanely inept, as were the ones that I submitted to small press magazines at that time. For a couple years I sent one story after another to Arkham House and with each rejection I received a paragraph of helpful comment from James Turner. I threw away almost all the stories from that time.

WINTER-DAMON: Just as you scrupulously eschew invoking the Lovecraftian mythic nomenclature, I find your avoidance of the familiar Allfather God vs. Devil/Fallen Angel Satan conflict and integral demonology/hierarchy of angels quite refreshing. Do you feel your Italian heritage and Roman Catholic upbringing (correct me if I'm wrong!) have helped to shape your aesthetic vision and voice in any way? If you perceive such is the case, would you be willing to elucidate?

LIGOTTI: If you're going to write horror stories when you grow up, it sure doesn't hurt taking a little time during every day of your childhood to meditate on what Hell must be like. This had nothing to do with my parents, but was more or less self-inflicted, as much as anything is self-inflicted, or as much as anything could be called a "self." I think I was born with a superstitious disposition and any religion with a Hell included would have affected me in some interesting way. So it's probably this general trait of superstitiousness, rather than the specific insanity of Roman Catholicism, that shows up in my stories. As far as my Italianness is concerned (Actually three-quarters Sicilian, one-quarter Polish), it's hard to say how this could affect one's approach to writing horror stories.

WINTER-DAMON: I'll confess I've been accused by friends, at times, of being "too analytical," but if you don't take offense, I'd like to push it just a bit, here. A legitimate parallel may often be drawn between the sometimes overt, sometimes subconscious, fascination with ethnic elements in a horror/fantasy/dark fantasy writer's work and his or her unique purity or blending of ethnic origins: of Celtic motifs and myth structures by a person of say, Irish-Scottish ancestry, or the way in which the legends and ancient landscapes of Athens and Crete may obsess a writer of Greek descent; to be more specific, say, the varied oriental motifs and the paradoxically sparse yet rich aesthetic that sparkles in the works of William F. Wu, S.P. Somtow, M. Lucie Chin (and the infamous "demon poet" of the T'ang Dynasty, Li Ho, for that matter), or the uniquely Hispanic influences in the "literary"/"magical realist" writings of Garcia Lorca, Carlos Castaneda, Gabriel Garcia Márquez, Jorge Luis Borges, or Ernest Hogan (the Irish/Chicano SF writer—who might be termed "resurgent Aztec[h]") . . . I should think, perhaps, a correlation exists between the lyrical complexities of your own prose with that of Italian opera, the ornate layerings of imagery with the beauty of Roman cathedrals, a perceived affinity for words of Latinized origin (as opposed to Northern European gutturals), the resonances of the mystical and dark, frightening awe in century upon century of Christian and pre-Christian myth structures, the frequency with which terrifying masks and puppets or mannequins/manikins (Pinocchio as just one classical example) appear within your stories, and such titles as "The Strange Design of Master Rignolo" and "Mrs. Rinaldi's Angel," to name but two, Any comments?

LIGOTTI: Ethnic characteristics are like those personality traits revealed by astrology—you're going to see them if you're looking for them. I suppose I could fabricate some ethnic bond between the old country and my horror stories based on the masks of the *commedia dell'arte* and punchinello-type puppets, not to mention a general arm-flailing hysteria and paranoia. But I could do the same thing with Flemish Belgium, considering the masks of *Kernesse* and tradition of puppet theater found in that country. Or how about Japan? Or Bali? As far as I'm able to observe myself ethnically, I'm not particularly Italianate. I've never harbored a fascination with Italy. The only Italian writers who interest me are Giacomo Leopardi and Dino Buzzati. I've always felt a strong pull toward the cold, dry, desolate landscapes of northern countries, which perhaps only a hot-blooded, irrational Latin type could appreciate. This is said with all respect to Italians everywhere.

WINTER-DAMON: Although most of your stories follow, albeit sometimes obliquely, the standard narrative structure of beginning/middle/end (not necessarily in that order, however), when reading your tales I often sense a quite disturbing sense of déjà vu, as if, with dreamlike ambiguity, one story seems to flow into another, intersecting in peculiar nexuses of emotional response, then veering off again on their separate tangents, only later to once more to find themselves in confluence. Is this your deliberate intent, or so you perceive it otherwise?

LIGOTTI: I would really be a genius if I were consciously following the master plan you describe. I wish I could say I were, it sounds so diabolical.

WINTER-DAMON: I seem to remember your, mention, in print, regarding an operation you received, at age two, for an internal rupture. You mentioned, also, that Bram Stoker underwent "surgical trauma" as an infant. This struck a peculiar personal resonance, as I, too, underwent surgery, at the same approximate age as yourself, for a navel hernia (as well as an extremely severe, near-life-threatening case of cholic, as a baby . . . a horror story, in itself, I'm told). I recall references by other horror writers to similar infantile trauma. I've quite seriously considered the implied parallel to the childhood near-death experience attributed to shamans. Any thoughts on this one?

LIGOTTI: Nothing definite. The connection you make is suggestive but incredibly tenuous. But just to throw another chunk of fat into that particular broth, I recently read an essay, though I can't recall what it was about or who wrote it, in which a fascinating phrase was quoted from the writings of the psychologist R.D. Laing. The phrase was this—"primary ontological insecurity." That's a great diagnosis of something a lot of horror writers might be said to suffer from. You can just hear Lovecraft and Poe chatting in the hallway of some special clinic: "What do the tests say, Edgar?" "As I thought, primary ontological insecurity as a result of infant trauma. How about you, Howard?" "Same thing. It's terminal, you know." Poe cups his hands around his mouth and yells down the hallway, "Calling Dr. Oblivion!"

WINTER-DAMON: In a somewhat oblique parallel to one of your literary inspirations, Poe, I know, in the past, you've alluded to a pivotal breakdown—in, what? summer, 1970?—caused by severe alcohol and drug abuse, that fortuitously spurred your theretofore dormant and unrealized interest in writing. Could you elaborate a bit on this?

LIGOTTI: Sure. It was the first Sunday in August of 1970, and I was at an all-day, outdoor rock concert with a number of friends from high school. We drank beer and wine and smoked pot until late afternoon. Someone was selling LSD, and we all had some of that. I have to wonder why I dropped acid that day, since every previous experience I'd had with that drug always ended with me all twisted up with panic, even though I enjoyed myself until that point. I didn't know at the time that a predisposition to anxiety disorders ran in the family. So, by the end of that summer day in 1970 I found myself in a state of panic. This was expected, and I recovered by the next day. I was quite surprised when three days later the panic returned without chemical inducement. And it's been with me ever since, sometimes surging into a full-blown paroxysm of anxiety and the rest of the time just writhing around in my gut like a live wire looking to make contact with something.

WINTER-DAMON: Do you use any forms of external stimuli, such as music, artwork, or a particular setting, to help trigger your creative flow, as many writers admit assist their imaginative productivity?

LIGOTTI: As you might infer from my previous response, my problem is not a lack of stimulation. I spend all my time in a state of over-stimulation. The only time I can write fiction is in the early morning, when my nervous system is relatively unjangled, but much of the time not even then. I actually started writing horror stories during a period of about three years when I became almost emotionless. It sounds paradoxical that you could feel nothing and still be anxiety-stricken, but I'm here to tell you that this feat can be achieved. The clinically depressed narrator of my story "The Last Feast of Harlequin" tells something about this time of my life.

WINTER-DAMON: In your interview with *Weird Tales* (in Vol. 53 No. 2; the winter 1991/92, Special Thomas Ligotti Issue), you made reference to a youthful desire, ". . . a vague ambition to be a baseball player, then a rock-and-roll musician . . ." and you confessed "I still fool around with the electric guitar privately . . ." In consideration of your perceived antiquarian voice and apparent affinity for the Victorian (or more correctly the fin-de-siecle decadents?), as well as your genteel manners, I, for one, would have guessed your musical forays might more likely be involved with the violin and classical music! I find this interest a most intriguing paradox—that you share this common denominator with such well-known and studiedly notorious badboys-in-leather Splatterfolk as Dave Schow, and the Skipp & Spector tagteam . . . any comments? As for the baseball, I know a good many horror authors and other writers who perceive the game as a metaphor for Life—do you? If so, how?

LIGOTTI: Actually, the sport that I consider a metaphor for life is golf: You come out of the clubhouse to play and go back in the clubhouse when the game is over. And although there may be many players on the golf course, they are all playing alone. But seriously, when I was very athletic as a kid, and when I wasn't playing sports in the street or schoolyard, I was watching them on TV or listening to them on the radio. When I turned nine years old, I received for my birthday a portable transistor radio so that I could more effectively follow the ballgames (and hockey!). This was the beginning of the end for my interest in sports broadcasts, because most of the time I found myself listening to Top 40 stations on that little radio with the brown leathery cover and shoulder strap. Then I saw the Beatles on Ed Sullivan and the next day, literally, I was taking guitar lessons. A common tale of the American boy circa 1964. In college I took a number of courses in music theory and briefly tried to play classical guitar, then I pretty much gave up on the whole thing until a couple years ago, when the guitar fever that had been in remission for so many years flared up again, a common tale of the American boy approaching middle age. From his grave, the Hendrix doth rule. Iä, Shadowy Men! And incidentally, there is no necessary conflict between playing guitar and being a decadent artist. Recall the monarch and model of decadent artists—Roderick Usher. What instrument did he play? Nope. Roderick played *geetar.*

WINTER-DAMON: Whereas your first collection, *Songs of a Dead Dreamer*, was, quite clearly, a gathering of independently written stories, your second book, *Grimscribe: His Lives and Works*, utilized the artifice of a single, otherwise-nameless narrator, who, to quote the inside font of the dustjacket, ". . . tells us of strange encounters with a multitude of characters and occurrences . . ." "Grimscribe is the faceless scientist of nightmare: an addict of the paranormal who relates his awesome adventures with the denizens of a shadow world that is at once half-mad and inescapably ours." This conceit was primarily designed by the book marketers, I believe you've admitted, in order to assist in promoting the book as a novel, as industry sales figures indicate the novel generates far more substantial revenues that the single-author collection. Is that a fair statement? Any additional insights?

LIGOTTI: That's more than a fair statement—it's a *kind* statement. No additional insight.

WINTER-DAMON: Ah, now for what your devotees have no doubt all been eagerly awaiting: What can you tell us of your newest collection, *Noctuary*?

LIGOTTI: *Noctuary* is just the usual collection of previously printed stories, with the exception of a new story called "The Tsalal." It's the longest story in the book, and it's about (laughs), excuse me, it's about (laughing loudly), I can barely . . . it's about the strange goings-on in a creepy small town! *(laughs uncontrollably!)*.

WINTER-DAMON: Well, I, for one (and I'm sure your many fans will agree), would hardly consider *any* Thomas Ligotti offering "the usual collection," but I admire your self-slighting modesty, Tom! I can hardly wait for its early-'94 release (watch for it around February at your bookstores—American hardcover from Carroll & Graf). Heh, think you can score me an advance copy from Robinson, maybe?—*hint, hint . . .*

So where does Thomas Ligotti go from here? What permutations and transformations can we expect to see in the future?

LIGOTTI: I'm going to write a series of stories detailing the further adventures of the psychic investigator in M.P. Dare's *Unholy Relics*. Just kidding. Honestly, I don't have anything special planned at the moment, but I'd like to finish a new horror story sometime in 1994. My gourd, 1994.

WINTER-DAMON: Any words of advice to aspiring writers?

LIGOTTI: To answer honestly I would end up saying something that amounted to this: "Be just like me." Not that I wouldn't like to say that, but who would listen? And it's lousy advice to anyone about almost anything. The only good advice is useless. Someone once said to me: "Kid, if you wanna write 'The Masque of the Red Death,' you gotta be Edgar Allen Poe." This is good advice, no doubt about it. But I'm still trying to write "The Masque of the Red Death," and I'm still not Poe.

WINTER-DAMON: Any parting thoughts for *Horror* readers?

LIGOTTI: Just that I hope I've said something to delight and illuminate. I myself always find interviews with writers to be a good read, even when the writer is someone I've never read before and never intend to read after, even when I consider that writer a total idiot, a worthless pimp—

WINTER-DAMON: Thanks, Thomas Ligotti, for your uncommon candor, for sharing your time and thoughts with all of us.

Hail The Damonic One!

Peter H. Gilmore with Peggy Nadramia
on t. Winter-Damon

In 1985 we attended the World Fantasy Convention held in Tucson, Arizona. As publishers of *GRUE Magazine*, our small press digest of cutting-edge horror fiction and dark poetry, we were there to promote our 'zine and meet some of the friends we'd acquired, contributors, readers as well as some leading lights in the field. We met Ramsey Campbell, Richard Matheson and Rick McCammon, who were all charming. Clive Barker was promoting the American edition of his *Books of Blood*, which we'd read from their UK releases. When looking through *GRUE*, he spied a centerfold piece of surrealist art by Joe Catuccio featuring a crucified horse and called it "Seriously rude!" Now that was an accolade!

Amongst the attendees was a local correspondent, Tim Damon— whose *nom de plume* was t. Winter-Damon—and this was also his first attendance at such a gathering. Soft-spoken, short and stocky, sporting a brief mustache with downturned ends and curly, medium-cropped hair, this fellow appeared a bit of a teddy bear, though his poetry and fiction could reach the furthest edges of ultra-violence and erotic excess. We all hit it off, eagerly exchanging ideas about horror, fantasy and SF films, all forms of literature as well as art, comedy, music and philosophy. Damon, as he preferred to be addressed, was an adept conversationalist and we quickly discovered that we were simpatico on many topics. He described his work as being "Neo-Baudelairean Cyber-Sade;" this was the perfect label, as his work was clearly inspired by decadents of the past and present, as well as the more visionary writers who'd shattered boundaries of taste and propriety to offer fever dreams of forbidden splendor. Damon and his poetry lived up to that definition; he dubbed himself "The Prophet of the Perverse." While his mien was gentle and sweet, his inner world was a maelstrom of madness, unfettered lust and pain-pleasure flowing in paroxysmic cataracts. We liked this guy!

Before we left to head back to New York, Damon suggested that we should return in the near future to visit Tucson and stay with him and his wife, Diane. From then on, Damon and I often had lengthy phone conversations and developed a friendship based on mutual admiration and kindred aesthetics. He was a fan of the decadent poets and surrealist artists, as am I, and he was also a great admirer of Bob Dylan. Damon shared his latest work with me and I always enjoyed it. His poetry was phantasmagorically rhapsodic, often becoming a cascade of juxtapositions of images and references that clashed in a surreal manner intended to energize the reader into soaring along in the ecstatic flow.

We included his "Martyr Without Canon" in *GRUE #4* (1987), a long poem whose welter of images included a climactic vision of a crucified Herakles, inspired by the imagery of Arnold Schwarzenegger nailed to the "Tree of Woe" in Milius' CONAN film. I had crafted a pen-and-ink illustration based on our discussions of mythology and he wrote his poem as a response to the image, which I then gave to Damon as a token of appreciation.

"Rack me high upon the Tree of Pain, where Heracles in his mask
of Everyman still strains—
unable to escape the spams of his ravished logic."

1988 brought us an opportunity to take Damon up on his invitation to visit, and so we set out toward the desert environs of our then dear friend.

Damon took us to his home in his Toyota, its dashboard bleached and cracked by the Arizona sun—he called it "The Toad Warrior." When we arrived, we were greeted by Diane. She was courteous and warm to us, a short, chubby gal with blonde hair and very white skin. She told us we were their very first house guests, and we thanked her for that honor. This home was Damon's palace, with a brick-fenced back yard, rear terrace and a pool that he'd designed—swimming in that was one of his greatest pleasures. I was honored to see that he had

WRITING DOWN THE DARKNESS

Photo by Peter Gilmore and Peggy Nadramia

framed my drawing and displayed it prominently near where he wrote. Over the course of our visit, we all enjoyed each other's company. Peggy was out in the beautiful, cactus-lined pool with its rocky waterfall and giant alligator float every morning. We screened John Waters' DESPERATE LIVING, whose comedy, cynicism and absurdity were welcomed. In time, Diane seemed a bit disturbed as it became apparent that she had seen one of my television appearances. Even though I had changed my facial hair since it had been filmed, she suspected I might be that Satanist she'd seen. She backed off a bit, suspicious, and there seemed a bit of a chill from that point on.

We had lunch with Damon's father, a scientist working on the project to carbon-date the Shroud of Turin. He told us in confidence that their dating proved that it was not from biblical times, which we found unsurprising, but we were pleased that this myth would soon be publicly debunked. Damon's purpose for this little meeting with his parent, was for us to cast a light on how admired and valued Damon's work was in the small press field where he was gaining notoriety. Diane was particularly overjoyed at our defense of his writing at that lunch table. While Damon's father loved his son, and saw his talent, he expressed his desire that Damon should turn his efforts towards more normal imagery. Damon responded, "Would you have Breughel paint buttercups?" I don't think that conflict was ever resolved.

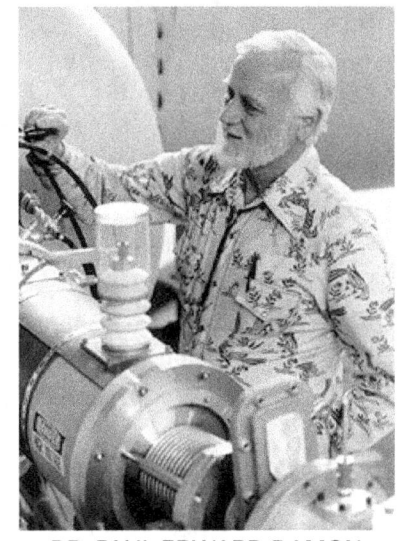

DR. PAUL EDWARD DAMON

In the middle of our stay, we left Peggy and Diane at home and Damon drove with me deep out into the desert, ostensibly to show me the scenery—which I found impressive. It was a journey that was to be his private audience, to express his

CHILLING OUT POOLSIDE

Photo by Peter Gilmore and Peggy Nadramia

deepest feelings about his life and works to my sympathetic ear. He stopped the car in the glaring sun and opened his heart. He recounted the tale of Damon and Diane, a pair of high school outsiders whom he felt were kin to BADLANDS' Holly and Kit. They'd come together in a *folie à deux*, standing apart from the mundane teens around them. Mutual support of each other's eccentricities was the bulwark for their union. He even spoke in hushed awe about someone they knew whom he suspected of being a serial killer. Now, in their forties, Diane seemed to have reverted into a conventionality where she felt more secure, while Damon had continued on the road not often travelled, becoming desirous of exploring some of the eroticism he so feverishly depicted. As an example of the growing distance between them, Diane had recently asked, "Honey, why don't we go to church more often?" He said in rebuff: "More often than what?" Damon, while mystical, was not party to any embracing of the Jesus myth and never attended any religious services of any sort. He spoke to me of his frustration, of his desire to strike out on his own, to

TESTING HIS GURKHA KUKRI
Photo by Peter Gilmore and Peggy Nadramia

BURYING THE EVIDENCE

Photo by Peter Gilmore and Peggy Nadramia

expand his experiences. His fear was also prominent. He enjoyed the comfortable life he had attained, his home, pool and his collection of soldier figures. He told me regretfully that when he had expressed his feelings, Diane had countered that she would not go along with his desires, and that if he left her, she'd expose and destroy him to their local acquaintances. He was a deeply conflicted and desperate man looking for a way out. I offered understanding and support so that if he decided to change his life, we'd do what we could to help him find a more satisfying direction.

The rest of the visit included trips to local caves, mountaintops and Old Tucson. We enjoyed the locale and our time with this couple, though there was an unsettling undercurrent that would later burst into the open and snuff out what we'd cultivated. Years later, Damon had a bit of a mental fugue and fled to Albuquerque to stay with a mutual friend and colleague. Ultimately, Damon retreated from this bold move and returned to Diane and the life he found stultifying. While in his mind he was a rebel, in his life he was passive, acquiescing to his mate's repression.

Damon had realized after the first convention in Tucson that he enjoyed meeting others in his field. He'd begun attending other similar events, networking and placing his writing with an increasing number of publications. Necon was a professional gathering of writers and publishers that happened for a weekend every summer on the campus of Roger Williams College in Rhode Island. Damon, always a personable fellow, was delighted when exchanging ideas with his peers. Indeed, his quiet, easygoing self blossomed and he particularly enjoyed some of the carnal banter with the females present. Diane felt threatened and approached us with the fear that some forward gal might vamp Damon into a sexual liaison. We reassured her that such was unlikely, knowing his timidity, but the hyper-eroticism of Damon's writings guaranteed that some risqué remarks would be natural to the convention experience. Indeed, arising from late night bull sessions in 1987, a cooperative 'zine was produced called *Uncommonly Weird Smut*, an illustrated round-robin comedic tale of bizarre sexual encounters. Damon delightedly took part.

In 1989 Peggy edited a poetry anthology titled *NARCOPOLIS*, after the featured poem by the brilliant Wayne Allen Sallee. It was a ground-breaking and oft-imitated volume. For this, we included two of Damon's pieces: "ghost images of 2 am" and "Those Scarlet Nights in Babylon." My surreal collages accompanied both of these.

"The lamia and vampire child make tryst! Worship the poisoned
nectar of their kiss!
Live out your poppy-tinted lotus-eater's dream . . .
As a vagrant minstrel lingering . . .
THOSE SCARLET NIGHTS IN BABYLON!"

Damon was quite inspired by K. W. Jeter's novel *DR. ADDER* (1984), a science fiction work whose publication had been delayed 12 years because of its depictions of extreme sex and violence. With writing partner Randy Chandler, Damon began his own novel proffering similar excesses, though set in the present. The central figure is Maldorer (après Lautréamont's *LES CHANTS*

DE MALDOROR), a brilliant psychopath who saw himself as an angel of death, travelling the country on a murderous spree with companions Snuff and Julie. We proudly released an excerpt from this forthcoming *DUET FOR THE DEVIL*, in *GRUE #10* (1989) titled "& THEY SHALL RECEIVE A MARK UPON THEIR FLESH."

We published Damon's poetic tale "So Turns The Wheel / So Night Folds Into The Raven," a surging dreamscape, in *GRUE #11* (1990). In *GRUE #12* (1991) one of his few short stories was presented, "Wall of Masks." In this, Damon's alter-ego is a collector of masks who lives in Tucson. On a trip to San Francisco, he purchases a leather hood that is said to have been used by Aleister Crowley in "magickal" rites of flagellation. The mask has the initials D.A.F. on a small, attached plate, and only later—after wearing it and finding his own deepest savage desires conjured—the protagonist realizes that it originated with Donatien Alphonse François, Comte De Sade. The end result is redolent of Serling-esque consequences.

His poem "The Ghost of Rimbaud Pauses" appeared In *GRUE #13* (1991), depicting the poet's shade inspired by a scene wherein a bishop observes three girls in the act of out of doors urination. It was the last piece of Damon's we published.

At a Seattle convention which we all attended, it became clear that Diane was growing ever more hostile to Damon's contacts with others. He had long since 'fessed-up to her about our representation of the Church of Satan and friendship with Anton LaVey, which apparently simmered for years in Diane's consciousness. During the time when the four of us were seated at a table in between events, Diane had an unprovoked outburst wherein she expressed her fear about our philosophy, showing she had never grasped our beliefs, and said that we were corrupting her husband. She wept and held my hand and pleaded for us to end our "bad influence" over him. Damon remained utterly silent and passive. We limited our dealings with them for the rest of the con. When I returned home, I had a letter exchange with Damon wherein I called him on his passivity and lack of defense of the both of us as we had been very close. His response was that we should just accept such unwarranted verbal lashings, as did he. I responded that we were not masochists and unwilling to continue in this now absurd relationship. We never exchanged communications again.

As years went by, Peggy and I would now and again wonder at his fate. He was a talented writer and had been a beloved friend, for a time. I saw that *DUET* had been released, but did not have the heart to read it. Being very busy with many creative and professional obligations, it was well over a decade before I thought about him again. When I investigated online, I found that he had not left much of a footprint in recent years. I thought it possible that he had passed away, so my search lead to his cremation notice in a Tucson newspaper from 2008. Peggy and I approached some of our old friends in the small press world, wondering if any had been in touch with him before his demise. We learned that Damon and Diane had gradually become hostile to most everyone that he had once valued as colleagues and friends. None of them knew of either his or Diane's passings.

We were ultimately able to find a mutual friend who knew more, and heard that Diane had predeceased Damon, and that he had recounted to this friend the delusion that when she had died, he had magically resurrected her—briefly, channeling some past sorcerer. When he recovered from the loss of this person who was his sole companion, Damon had finally decided to seek out other female company. He got back in touch with a gal he'd known in high school and began dating her. The tale is that he had a heart attack while dancing with her on a date—a seemingly tame end for such an inner devotee of the outré. But who knows? Damon's life was at most times an inner one, and perhaps this was a dance in reach of a freedom he was just beginning to taste.

I don't know what happened to his possessions and his papers, which likely contained unpublished poems and tales. I suspect that all were discarded when his house was cleared out; that's the way these things usually go. My drawing of the crucified Herakles, the sigil of our mutual admiration, has vanished.

t. Winter-Damon was an artist who wrought a personal vision, acknowledging his inspirations and using them as fuel to rapturously soar to pinnacles and sound abysses that were uniquely his own. His work merits exploration by any sensualist seeking heightened stimulus as an antidote to their wan surroundings. His consciousness lies in these verbal cenotaphs, properly baroque monuments to a mind that should not be forgotten. He must not be a martyr without canon, as his work remains to bear him witness. If it were possible, I'm certain his shade would surely linger, voyeuristically absorbing all manner of fleshly delights as shamelessly practiced by languorous libertines— with a knowing smile of satisfaction as his final testament. Here's to Damon—may he be remembered as exuberant celebrant of those scarlet nights in Babylon!

Forever Tracking

Bruce Boston
for t. winter-damon

Forever interpreting
ancient texts
as their tattered
scrolls unrolled
within his mind,
treading the borders
of the Axis Mundi
with no more than
an empty leather satchel,
ranging the streets
of Xanadu and Carcosa,
Asgard and Babylon,
tracking like a beast
with a ravenous beast
astride its back,
whispering sacral curses
and foul blessings
to the eldritch winds.

Immersed in dreamtides
and chimerical visions
and cimmerian prophets
whose shadows rose
from the dust of ages,
worshipping priestesses
created for the day,

following transient avatars
down to a dim beach
and the dark sea
of a false dawn
to hear the damp cries
of beached mariners
echoing in his brain.

Intoxicated by secret keys
and magical rings,
obsessed by puzzle boxes
with hidden compartments
only to be opened
by the wisest of men
and most cunning women,
drunk on myth and
history and a tomorrow
that foreshadowed
more than night.

Enthralled by the occult
and the fantastic,
Crowley and Blavatsky,
Faustus and Paracelsus,
Levi's *Dogme et Rituel*
de la Haute Magie,
poring over maps
revealing the locations
of imagined kingdoms,
Mu and El Dorado,
Atlantis and Shangra-La,
the Archipelago of Dreams,
maps fashioned by madmen
on a transcendental high
over a fifth of Ravens Rum
and a pinch of fly agaric.

Anticipating the excavation
of underwater ruins
and red temples
crumbling to red sand
in some distant desert,
astounded by age-old
architectural mysteries,
the Great Pyramids,
the dour monoliths
of Easter Island,
the astronomical
savvy of Stonehenge,
awaiting the lab tests
on the Shroud of Turin
and the release of
a revised annotation
of the *Bardol Thodol*,
praying for the miraculous
to snuff the everyday.

Last heard from
traveling to parts unknown,
head down and eyes afire,
carrying no more than
a worn leather satchel
stuffed with worlds.

www.ingramcontent.com/pod-product-compliance
Lightning Source LLC
Chambersburg PA
CBHW060912250626
47159CB00008B/2976